WE MEANT WELL

WE MEANT WELL

A NOVEL

ERUM SHAZIA HASAN

Published by ECW Press
665 Gerrard Street East
Toronto, Ontario, Canada M4M 1Y2
416-694-3348 / info@ecwpress.com

Editor for the Press: Pia Singhal
Copy editor: Crissy Calhoun
Cover design: Zoe Norvell
Cover artwork: © Adam Segal
Author photo: Geneviève Caron

This is a work of fiction. Names, characters,
places, and incidents either are the product of the
author's imagination or are used fictitiously, and
any resemblance to actual persons, living or dead,
business establishments, events, or locales is entirely
coincidental.

LIBRARY AND ARCHIVES CANADA CATALOGUING
IN PUBLICATION

Title: We meant well : a novel / Erum Shazia Hasan.

Names: Hasan, Erum Shazia, author.

Identifiers: Canadiana (print) 20220428557 |
Canadiana (ebook) 20220428581

ISBN 978-1-77041-665-9 (softcover)
ISBN 978-1-77852-087-7 (ePub)
ISBN 978-1-77852-094-5 (PDF)
ISBN 978-1-77852-095-2 (Kindle)

Subjects: LCGFT: Novels.

Classification: LCC PS8615.A775 W4 2023 | DDC
C813/.6—dc23

This book is funded in part by the Government of Canada. *Ce livre est financé en partie par le gouvernement du Canada.* We
acknowledge the support of the Canada Council for the Arts. *Nous remercions le Conseil des arts du Canada de son soutien.*
We acknowledge the funding support of the Ontario Arts Council (OAC), an agency of the Government of Ontario.
We also acknowledge the support of the Government of Ontario through the Ontario Book Publishing Tax Credit, and
through Ontario Creates.

PRINTED AND BOUND IN CANADA   PRINTING: MARQUIS   5 4 3 2 1

For Safwan

1

"I have no idea how long I'll be gone," I say, stuffing clothes into a suitcase.

Steven yawns. He pulls his silk eye mask from the bedside drawer. He fumbles for the remote, pressing buttons. Spa-like music swells; noise from my frantic packing muted under sounds of raindrops, sitar, and birdsong. This is part of Steven's self-care ritual. To erase.

"I'm only going because it's an emergency, I'm worried about leaving Chloe," I babble.

"Don't. She can stay with your mother and I can take over on the weekends. Besides," he says, "she's used to your departures."

I look at the man wearing the eye mask. He looks content in that artificial darkness of his, in simulated sounds of forests that don't exist. A smile rests on his lips, though it shouldn't.

"Someone's gotta go save the poor, so go. Don't worry, our kid will be just fine," he says.

Is it sarcasm? Sincerity? With his eyes masked, his voice sedated, I can't tell.

Whatever it is, I hate every part of that lie.

2

There's a rap on the windshield. It's a couple of children. They raise their T-shirts, show me their ribs. They want something. Food, money, anything. I look straight ahead, my sunglasses on. We're not allowed to give money to beggars. And I can't look them in the eyes while ignoring their pleas. I'd have to be a sociopath to do that. Instead, I continue my conversation with Philippe, the driver, trying to evoke an intimacy between us that doesn't quite exist.

These are children—like my Chloe—begging, showing their underfed bellies; I should be more appalled by this, but I'm not. If you see enough of anything, it becomes ignorable. Even hungry children.

I once used to hold scrawny children like these. I used to nuzzle their hair under my chin, feel their small palms slide in my underarms for warmth.

The 4x4 laces up the dusty broken road. It's beautiful here. The sun sears through the window. I hear the staccato yells, the buoyant laughs of the market adjacent to the road. I smell the sea over the sweet scent of rotting garbage. Bougainvillea spills over every broken wall. There are bodies all around us, walking alongside, hips brushing my car door, people crisscrossing in front of our vehicle. Loud conversation, misshapen words from mouths of chipped teeth. It's familiar—all these strangers holding us in. I've stopped feeling most things, but this feels good.

A woman carries twins in her arms and balances a ten-liter plastic container on her head. I wonder which she picked up first. Did someone else place the container on her head? These are miracles of the poor. How they carry so much and don't break. How they walk in kilometers, while we walk in steps. They have a strength my body can never know. The strength of birthing nine children in a hut or plowing fields by hand. Even their breasts are more potent than mine, producing milk on cue, babies latching as they should. No pumps or lactation consultants here.

———

Seventy-two hours ago, my phone rang in the middle of the night. It was Burton telling me to fly out as soon as possible. Tickets had been reserved; I needed to confirm. I tried to focus on what he was saying, but was half-asleep, nervous that my daughter would wake up. I tried to sound professional, my mouth dry, annoyed that he hadn't taken the time difference into account when calling. But then I heard his words and sat upright in bed: Marc is in the worst kind of trouble. The fallout could be dire, for all of us. So, I have to be here, one last time, to clean up his mess. Even though I'd secretly been planning my extrication from this job, from this place, from its people.

On sterile days back home, I miss this country's noise. I miss how free I am here despite the mosquitos and violence. I even sound different here. An accent takes birth on my tongue. It's inadvertent; languorous *s*'s, long *o*'s emerge. I long for them in a bizarre homesickness that spreads while I'm buttering toast or driving my daughter to Montessori in Los Angeles. A homesickness that doesn't make sense. Why yearn for war and hardship when you have the Hollywood Hills—the holy gifts of the first world?

Besides, here can never be home. These people, they're familiar but I don't really know them. I'm driven among them. I have polite conversations. What am I really doing here? For years, I was convinced I was saving lives.

Philippe and I have a polite relationship. I see him a few times a year when I visit to check up on things. He drives me places; I ask about his family. I crack a few jokes to appear relatable. It's forced, but he smiles. I can't help it; the words teem, wanting attachment, even a temporary one. But Philippe will disappear, from my mind and vicinity, as soon as I step out of this Land Cruiser, like all the others.

Despite this, Philippe, in his crisp blue-collared shirt, with his shiny forehead, is the one I trust with my life. If hoodlums show up, tapping their guns on the windshield, he'll intervene, standing tall between his countrymen and me, the foreigner. Perhaps even giving up his own life.

The locals, they know a first-worlder when they see one. They see me. Sunglasses on, in the tinted vehicle with my charity's fancy blue logo painted on the door, ignoring emaciated children. They walk by without ever hurting me. That guy sauntering with the rooster, holding it by the neck, he peers through my car window, then walks away. That old man, sitting in the dirt, dusty laminated pictures of 1980s porn stars dangling from the ribs of the umbrella he holds over his head, barely looks up, as though I'm a landmark, a building he's used to seeing.

5

If someone ever did attack me, I'd end up in the hospital the UN diplomats use. I'd be hooked to beeping machines charged by generators that will run to the end of time, bypassing power outages that plague the rest of the country. The media would be there in an instant. My smiling face blitzed across TV and phone screens, and magically I'd be repatriated to my land, where I'd appear on talk shows to recount how I survived brutality in a war-torn country.

But nothing like that ever happened, even though other things did. Things that did not warrant a talk show segment.

3

Philippe stops the Cruiser in front of the hotel where I like to lunch. Le Paradis, its unironic name. The last stop before we take real dirt roads to the countryside, leaving the capital city, its comfortable hotels, its shantytowns.

Philippe turns off the ignition. He's not allowed to wait with the air-conditioning running, to save on gas and to prolong the life of the vehicle.

"I'll only be an hour or so," I say, opening the car door.

Philippe nods and smiles.

"What would you like to eat? I'll have a lunch packed for you," I ask.

"It's okay, Miss Maya." He shakes his head.

"No, please, tell me what you'd like. It's a long drive," I say.

Philippe says nothing.

"I'll grab something anyway, might as well be something you like."

He smiles.

"Chicken? Fish?"

"Yes."

"Which one?"

Philippe continues smiling. I wait, trying not to feel exasperated.

"I'll get a chicken sandwich," I say, stepping out of the vehicle.

This place. I can't help but pause and inhale. I hold my breath until far-off scents are expunged, until I'm spinning with fragrance. The terra-cotta building sits on a lush hillock overlooking the valley. I'm surrounded by palms, shrubs, jasmine, bougainvillea, and hundreds of fat flowers whose names don't exist in my language. A gravel path leads to large wooden doors. It's so green up here it almost feels cool.

Le Paradis is owned by a French couple who had the place built in the seventies. They were the heart of the expat social scene. The parties they had. Bankers, investors, diplomats, UN staff, politicians, military men, and, from time to time, humanitarians and aid workers such as myself, intermingling with the most influential.

Now the owners are old. They sit in the restaurant, smoking and drinking, gazing at the valley below. They wave at people like me from afar, bored of engaging the unending flow of foreigners, content to look at the vista, content with all they have created. The rest of us still find our way to their hotel restaurant, seeking oasis in the madness.

I walk into the lobby. My shoes tap against the stone tile, just so, making a sound I don't hear in California. The manager, Veronique, recognizes me and rushes over. Veronique—that's her French name, her actual clan name is something she gave up explaining decades ago—is a local. She wears a black dress with a starched white collar, the one she always wears, reminiscent of some colonial cleaning lady's uniform. She may be the manager, but the owners' dress code never lets her forget where she sits on the food chain.

Veronique is effusive with her attention. She holds me by the elbows. She gives me wide, straight smiles. She asks about my daughter that she's never met. But ballet classes and waitlists to get into the right school don't seem right to talk about; I give her a version of a child that doesn't exist. She's so sincere, I don't want to wreck it. As I make things up, I wonder whether anything about me is real anymore. The me in California, she pretends too. She tucks these places in her pocket, acts like she's thinking about the same things everyone else is. She mimics the gestures, the expressions, until she becomes them. Just another American wife and mother.

I escape the conversation and head to the back terrace. I'm not spending the night here. Just lunching and bracing myself for the grueling drive to the project site in Likanni.

There are places in the world that transcend war, poverty, human mayhem. This is one of them. I stand on the stone terrace and the valley falls before me in dramatic swoops. Green drips in all of its splendor—trees, grasses, ferns, palms, ivy, it all dangles, hanging off thick carpets dotted with red and yellow blooms. I can't tell what's air and what's light. A wet film appears on my shoulders. I'm not thinking of my husband's betrayals, or of Marc and the possible violence at the project site. I'm here. Light as air, untethered.

I didn't really believe in nature, only in people. But years ago, this place made me change my mind. When I first visited this terrace in my twenties, I was overcome. I pointed and babbled. I took photographs from every angle, lying on my belly, large and small lenses in hand. Nothing caught its essence. I described this grandeur to my friends back in the States, pointing to inadequate snapshots, using colorful language. It was futile. I couldn't convey that places like this existed.

That's the beginning of the chasm for all of us out here.

At first, our people back home are mildly interested in far-away stories of the poor, of child marriages, of the hungry. If we throw terrorism or genital mutilation in there, we're a real hit, satisfying curiosities, flaunting heroism. But if we delve into the nuances of the pain we see, or our role in fostering it, or if we go on too long about a valley on the outskirts of the capital, they lose interest, and we enter the ranks of the verbose. My own husband doesn't care for these haunts of mine. To him, I disappear into a continent he built out of movie scenes and tragic books, with no sights to behold.

I drag a heavy chair to sit on the far corner of the terrace away from lunching Canadian and American diplomats. There is a pool in which a couple of Belgian women lap around. There are men in white shirts, navy blazers, leather loafers. It looks like a damn ad campaign. You would hardly believe we're in a war zone.

Two young ones, likely interns, walk in with cargo shorts, baseball caps and matching T-shirts from an evangelical Louisiana church. Their eyes pop open like cartoon characters. They couldn't have imagined a poor country to be such an Eden. What fun it must be to proselytize here. Biblical metaphors alive and well. Droughts, floods, the gospel everywhere in full glory. At first, this place is like that—a miracle. And we believe we are the miracle workers.

Thierry walks over with the menu. I've known him for years, but he always looks at me like we've never met. He's one of the rare few I've come across in this country who never asks questions, other than those pertaining to food or drink. First-worlders always assume he's new because people here are so hospitable, so eager to establish relationships, curious to know our backstories. But not Thierry.

"Bonjour," I say.

He nods.

"I'll have the usual." He shrugs. It's the slightest of movements, barely perceptible. As though he can't afford to give me something more significant, like a raised eyebrow or, god forbid, a smile.

"I'd like the filet mignon with truffle sauce and a bottle of water. Could you also pack a chicken sandwich and a bottle of fruit juice for takeaway, please?" I ask. He barely nods and takes his lazy walk to the kitchen.

I eat better in this city, where most of the population is hungry, than I do back home. I eat steak and lobster for lunch. I drown myself in exquisite sauces emerging from colonial and local hybrids, feasting on the creativity of people who cook with shortages of spices, eager to produce the best for the first-worlders. My belly grows, my body changes; it's liberating to expand, to occupy more space even though I'm in the land of the emaciated. It's an uneasy bargain, to balloon as others shrink, but somehow one gets used to it. One gets used to anything.

I lean back in my chair and put my sunglasses back on. I feel the sun darkening my face, darker than the other expats but not as dark as the people here. I recognize some voices from across the terrace but close my eyes. I don't want pleasantries or to make conversation about the dreaded Marc affair, which, according to Burton, is garnering some attention in international circles in the country. I just want to rest awhile, invisibly, and listen to the rustle of the valley. There are enough difficult conversations to be had in Likanni.

One of the staff turns on the music. An old Charles Aznavour song, "Emmenez-moi," swells. The Americans and Canadians smile, sway their heads uncertainly, misjudging the cadence of the song. How romantic, sitting in the colonial aftermath, listening to French standards, drinking dry wine.

I wonder if Charles Aznavour has been here. Whether he's heard his song echoing off the stone terrace into the valley. The melody floating up then landing into depths unseen. The song is not from here but fits. Any song would. It's that kind of place.

The vines, the trees, the greens soak up the notes, transforming them into chlorophyll. That's the thing with this place, it takes all of us in.

———

I finish my food and ever so slowly wipe my mouth with a polyester napkin, the last bit of luxury. I unzip my carry-on suitcase, sitting by me like an obedient dog, and pull out my hiking shoes, caked with mud. These boots make my husband think I'm going on a hiking holiday, but they are my dog tags. They take me through thick swamps, protect me from snakes. They crunch branches, trespass farmlands. It saddens me that he can't imagine the settings they've plowed me through.

I tie crusty shoelaces. The uniform is complete: linen shirt, khaki pants, dirty hiking boots. The visiting first-worlder's uniform. Most of us are in some shade of khaki or some shade of linen. I don't know why. A Hawaiian shirt would be just as appropriate; it would billow colorfully in the breeze. Instead, we subscribe to the unspoken code, that of the weaponless army, conveying our expertise in formal compassion. The first world has arrived, our savoir faire bound in neutral cargo pants. Stay a few years though, and colorful skirts appear on women. Every year spent in the field spawns a daring color in the wardrobe. Perhaps in a scarf, in dangly earrings. It's harder to tell the passage of time on first world men here. They live in khaki, at most donning leather bracelets. Newbie or veteran, difficult to say until they drop their stories.

I look at my valley. Everything in soft movement. I don't want to leave. I know I won't be the same when I return from the field. I put local currency on the table, grab Philippe's lunch, which I hadn't noticed Thierry place on the table, and head to the toilets. The last clean lavatory and flushable toilet I'll be able to use for the next few hours.

I swing the door open: there's urine all over the floor. Screw you, diplomats, for it's one of them who's done this—staff aren't allowed to use these bathrooms. I come out leaving a trail of pee boot prints on the tile. I don't know whose urine I carry on my feet. As I obsess over this thought, someone calls out to me.

"Maya," he says again. It's Claus from the Danish ministry. He's in a white shirt, khaki pants, and black Converse shoes. He smiles at me, his blond hair patted flat against his head.

I lean forward and kiss him on both cheeks.

Claus smiles. "I can't say I'm surprised to see you. I heard what's going on in Likanni and knew you—"

"It's so nice to see you," I interrupt.

He nods, about to open his mouth but I speak before he can. "It's been ages. I've missed our debates."

"Ah yes, our famous debates. Too bad your arguments were never as rational as mine," he says with a smirk.

"You're not going to get me started," I warn, smiling.

"Don't worry, you don't need another defeat. You have enough to worry about. Everyone's talking about what's happened in Likanni. I've heard the Swiss might pull out their funds?"

I try to conceal my alarm. The Swiss are our biggest donor; losing them would shutter our offices. I say nothing.

"You'll be fine," Claus says, noting my discomfort. "They've clearly pulled in their finest PR expert—you'll manage the team out of this."

The board of my charity was clear: don't acknowledge any wrongdoing. And I can't, even if I wanted to. I know so little.

"How are you?" I pose the safe question.

"Very well, especially now that we're leaving," Claus says.

"Really?" I'm surprised. He's an old-timer, a dozen years under his belt. I thought he would be a lifer.

"We're moving back to Copenhagen in two weeks. Erika and I bought an apartment close to her family. I'm moving into a senior post at the Ministry of Foreign Affairs. We're finally getting out of this shit place—just like you," he says. I wince at "shit place."

Claus looks self-satisfied. I imagine him adapting seamlessly to life in Copenhagen, riding a bike in a suit, ranting over long dinners. He has his diplomatesque war stories; now he can get back to real life and live the kind of hygge I thought I would have after moving back to California.

"That's great. I should give Erika a call to catch up." I have no intention of calling her but can't help feeling nostalgic. Is everyone leaving this country? Is it going to be a flock of newbies that arrive, as curious and idealistic as we once were, who'll try the same things we did on the locals? Who will screw up in the same ways?

"Are you getting sentimental?" taunts Claus. "Don't. This place is much worse than when you lived here. I don't know what kind of trouble Marc has gotten into, but I don't blame him. The militias aren't making empty threats anymore—they've attacked UN staffers. The locals are completely terrorized. It's very difficult to accomplish even the smallest task these days." He looks serious. "Is your driver armed?"

"I have no idea," I answer blankly. We've never needed weapons before. There's been a tacit understanding that white people don't get hit with whatever warfare is going on between other groups. I'm not white, which complicates things, but I'm clearly an outsider.

"Check. Be vigilant. Don't stop and talk to villagers you don't know. Make the necessary arrangements with headquarters; keep people posted on your whereabouts beyond your security protocols. And stay on good terms with the military contingents, especially the Americans."

"I can't believe you of all people are telling me to deal with the marines." I groan.

We first-worlders have our roles, and the soldiers here are in a class all their own, lower on the foreign social scale than diplomats,

UN personnel, and NGO workers, but with far more ammunition. The marines are the lowest on the soldier rung, scoffed at by other peacekeepers. They mosey around like cowboys, hands on their weapons, even in the smallest and most peaceful of villages. Back home, they're sung as heroes, champions for freedom, thanked at football games for service. Here, they shove steaks and beers down their throats, grind with local women in bars, taking selfies in front of tanks. Because along with their heavy weaponry, they're somehow always armed with selfie sticks. It embarrasses us Americans who try to shake the warmongering stereotype.

Claus nods. "I'm serious. I know you visit every few months, but it's not the same. You need backup, more than from your piddly organization."

"Thanks for the tip. I'd better hit the road; I'm heading to Likanni today. Maybe I can catch up with you on the way back?"

"We won't have time for social engagements. We're very busy with the move." Claus's bluntness makes me smile. Scandinavians are always so damn honest.

"Besides, if you still believe in God and fairy tales, I don't know if there's much for us to discuss," he goads. Claus is so progressive that he's looped around the spectrum and become close-minded. He doesn't understand how people can believe in anything they can't see.

"Screw you, Claus," I say.

"There she is, the Maya I know and . . . tolerate." He laughs.

I swipe at his arm. For an instant we are in our twenties again, fresh out of university. Two excited loudmouths in a foreign land arguing about the existence of God, local rituals, politics—anything, really.

"Take care, okay?" Claus says seriously.

"I will, thanks. Good luck with your move."

He kisses my cheek and I go out to the parking lot to find Philippe.

He's got the seat drawn back and is fast asleep, the car under the shade of a leafy tree. It's so intimate to wake someone. I open the trunk and pop my carry-on in with a thud. He wakens with a start and immediately turns the key in the ignition, like a natural reflex. I hand him his sandwich and climb onto the backseat to catch up on sleep.

I stretch out, eyes closed, lulled by the vibrations of the vehicle.

Claus and I came to this country in our early twenties. We were part of the same circle of foreigners who drank on the weekends, threw house parties in little rooms, and united over novel adventures and frustrations. We were part of charities and diplomatic corps, PhD students and interns, we were childless and adventurous. We came from rich countries and marveled at where we had landed—this place that was wholly unfamiliar, except on those Friday nights when we would meet after work, gripe about our bosses, the heat, the traffic, or the corruption, and blast our own music. We thought we would be pulling people out of misery, feeding the poor, but most of us were tethered to administrative tasks in those early years. We would see each other with dark notebooks under our arms, following senior staffers, at meetings in embassies, UN offices, and charities—we were like an English country dance, switching partners then coming face-to-face in one boardroom after another, recording and organizing minutiae.

Claus didn't notice me for a few months. Most of the Scandinavians didn't. I wasn't white like them and wasn't Black like the locals. I was that Brown of immigrants to their countries, a Brown that prevented them from seeing me as a first world peer. But my insistence on hosting as many get-togethers as possible gave me a face. I invited them, fed them, forced my way in. I twirled around that first-worlder circle, I learned my friends' histories in the U.K. and France, Norway and the Netherlands, until all our stories melded into one big first world reality. I took trips to my friends' countries. That faraway thing that was Europe when I'd lived in America became intimate. The whole first world began to feel like home despite the fact that I was living in a developing country on a developing continent. I lived through the Europeans surrounding me, visiting their continent and cities on every break. I picked up their manners, their accents, their ways of being. I became whiter through kinship, through the foreigner status given to me by the locals.

I close my eyes. I see Claus, young, dancing stiffly at one of the parties in my apartment. There's Aurélie and Sebastian, and Kate and Filippo, and Hervé. We're happy, not yet thirty. We dance like we're going to change the world the next morning. Aurélie, with her dirty light-brown curls, is what my husband would call a "spirit dancer." She throws herself around, eyes closed, arms writhing as if in a painful trance at Burning Man.

My husband. My eyes open.

All I see is the swimsuit tucked in my drawer. Not my swimsuit. She leaves clues all over the place: trashy romance novels in my bedside table, small tank tops in my closet, straw-blond hair all over my house—in my drain. Slight enough things that only I would notice. Steven would never notice what book I read, or whether a tank top is a size small or medium. Slight enough things to make me feel crazy. She wants me to find her things, erupt, take my daughter away, leave her my husband, my home.

She's become more brazen over time. She used to cover her tracks; she was good at it. She would make only the smallest of errors, like leaving contact solution in a house where no one wears lenses. But in the last year, every time I've returned from a work trip, her presence has grown. Things sit differently; her things poke mine. She must be feeling the urgency, to get me out of there, to formalize her own dubious status before she gets too old. Being the secret other woman must be losing its luster.

She shouldn't underestimate the weary generosity of a woman who has seen children die at her work. Play your sick little game while I gather myself and figure out what's next. I've seen things. I can handle petty gestures. I've held weak little hands, I've seen hungry bodies. Swimsuits don't scare me.

I've got to hand it to her. Most women would hide—this one, she's audacious, primed to take a shortcut to my life. So, I've said nothing. Even after I've crouched behind my bed with Scotch tape to capture blond hairs left behind. Even when my husband insists that it'll be nice for Chloe to stay with my parents while I am away, freeing the house for him and his tramp, I say nothing. Once words are spoken, they will become, they will have consequences, and I'm too tired for that weight right now. I can't make any lasting changes, not when I'm slippery myself.

Why spur consequences when nothing is proven? Everything is in the realm of the hypothetical. Maybe blond hair flew in through the window, settling in the deepest corners of my home. Maybe the housekeeper has an odd fetish of leaving other people's clothes in my closet. Maybe working here has deranged my mind to the extent that I see things where there aren't any. There are a million stories I can dress into explanations. I cannot lock Steven into the role of a villain, not when there could be so many truths. When it could just be someone else trying to sabotage us, trying to edge me out of my life.

There's a romantic portrait that people like to draw of a woman scorned: she's feisty, vengeful, she burns things, takes money, gets a makeover, leaves a man impotent. The reality is a lot less satisfying.

A woman scorned feels empty, concave. Like someone took her most meaningful insides and threw them out for people to trample. She can't stand straight. Her gait becomes a limp. She hates her partner, because he forgot her. She was negligible, as transient as a good meal. He ate, digested, and shit her out.

But I'm not scorned yet. I don't even know the truth. I'm probably making things up. I can't misjudge, not when the consequences could devastate. I need to give credence to "till death do us part," believe that he would never take it so lightly.

"Two-one-four-four-seven-thirteen," I hear Philippe say into his cellphone. It's the security code we have to give at various checkpoints so our office in the capital is aware of where we are.

I focus on the back of Philippe's neck—the width of it, the straight edge of his hairline—pushing out thoughts of blond hair from my mind. Black curls. That's what I need to look at. Likanni. That's what needs to be dealt with first.

4

It's getting dark. We're not allowed to drive after sundown because of bandits, so I ask Philippe to stop in Somoko, the only place where there is a decent hotel, if you can call it that. It's really just six corrugated metal shipping containers sitting side by side, sunken into the earth. Cockroaches flit about the floors. The owners are a lovely, shriveled old couple who live in one of the rooms.

I think of the passionate nights I've spent here. How even the fluorescent lighting that makes one look a jaundiced yellow, the smell of mothballs felt like a romantic experience. Then, of course, I lose myself in the memory of Anders. My beautiful Anders. My hands in his dirty hair.

Philippe swivels around and asks if I'm alright. Did I moan out loud? I fake a cough. I'm embarrassed. Not just of the sound slipping my lips, but that thirteen years later the memory of that man can make my body do things I cannot govern.

I wonder if other wives feel like this. If they hunger over old loves. If they ache to occupy a time that has passed them by. There's such futility in yearning for something you've already lived.

Anders came to this country because he believed it was the right thing to do. He didn't come to flee demons or climb a savior's pedestal. When he realized there were places where people were sick without access to healthcare, his vocation was clear—at twenty-six he joined Médecins sans frontières (MSF) and left his wholesome life in Sweden.

I first met Anders in a bar where foreigners hung out. The MSF crowd was usually relegated to their compound. But there they were that night, the lot of them, charming, sharing laughs. Some of the staff were returning to Europe and they were in a bitter-sweet mood—celebratory that they had survived another mission, but sentimental about going home.

Anders didn't notice me at first, but I couldn't take my eyes off him. He had dark curly hair, looking more a Spaniard than a Swede, his neck tan against his white shirt, his hands moving elegantly through the air as he spoke. He was slender but strong-looking. Not a single excessive muscle or roll of skin. All I wanted to do was touch him. I wanted to touch that skin, feel the precision of his gestures. His eyes flitted away from me when we were introduced.

The more boisterous among us told outrageous stories. I needed something to command this man's attention for a moment. He had such a polite laugh. It echoed softly in his chest before it came to us. I made meager attempts at telling jokes; they were poorly timed. I sat quietly in my skin that I wanted to shed for five minutes: I wanted to be expat white, I wanted to be seen.

We finally spoke. We had both started to sing along to an old nineties song. That's one of the divine gifts of developing countries. They play you pop culture remnants that you've forgotten, like Men at Work, Phil Collins, Ace of Base, or in this case Mr. Big. As we crooned, we smiled, turned our chairs toward one another and began the real introduction. Where was I from, where did he work, where had I been, how long would he be here, where to eat the best shrimp, what book was he reading. And then he was mine.

There was not much time for courting. Anders was the logistician for MSF clinics and had to think of every detail required to get people the assistance they needed. His mind was filled with vaccines and how to keep them cold, beds, bandages, people's hours, local staff, security, anesthetics, procurement of medication. But he wasn't weighed down by it. He thrived in the organizational maze that was his head. He got doctors and patients what they needed, made thoughtful decisions in seconds, soared in dire crises. And in the midst of it, he loved me.

My greatest misstep, perhaps, was that I wanted to replace it all. That was love, to me. To be in a drug-like haze, to have vaccine orders come a distant second. Because that's what I felt. The orphans, the friends, the political drama, the burning tires, the intermittent electricity—none of it mattered unless I was telling Anders about it. But he loved what he did, and nothing was more important to him. Not even me.

I was haunted by him and blame this country for it. It's so damn sensual here. People are either killing each other or making love and creating another child. The sun a sizzle, the breeze like silk in the evening. The rain so thunderous in its monsoon that after a few years of living here, you can distinguish the scents of flowers wafting toward you in a downpour.

During the moments of R&R Anders and I were allowed, we explored this part of the continent. We tried foods, got lost on hikes, found secret waterfalls. We ate in random villagers' homes. We smiled at their children, felt guilt in accepting their generosity. We hid under mosquito nets and ate each other's faces. My lips were never not bruised from kissing him.

I loved his clean hands, his square nails, the fact that his fingertips had been everywhere on my body. Behind my knees, around my ankles, even against the roof of my mouth. I got oddly aroused when we were in social settings and he was signing a bill or shaking someone's hand. I saw those hands doing those functional things, then coming home to me. An intimacy people couldn't fathom.

We forget what our bodies look like here without full-length mirrors. But Anders made me see myself. He would sit on the bed, smiling, and I would parade around naked, thighs jiggling, breasts swaying, juices leaving trails as he looked and looked at my most common of movements. I was fleshy and wanted.

In this unstable place our lives took on an air of predictability. We would spend ten days working on projects and synchronize our days off. Anders cobbled contract after contract to remain in the region. As long as he was meeting with his shrink back in Sweden who cleared him, things were great. Dengue, sleeping sickness, malaria—he dealt logistics like a ninja, going from sickness to sickness with strategic precision.

If I could, I would relive those years in an endless loop. I've never been so goddamn alive. Not when I was pregnant, not in my marriage. Eating curried goat or salted fish on a polluted beach with Anders, followed by frenzied undressing, is a euphoria I wish I could recycle. Going to the market, watching him cup a giant fruit in his hand. Picking up emergency phone calls and jetting off in his Cruiser with a focused look in his eyes. Smiling at the children chasing his car. The way he would wave at them, with those slender fingers. I would give anything to be there, watching him do the most mundane things.

It was him. His sincerity. The generosity of him not knowing he was generous. He was the first foreigner I met who made genuine efforts to know the local faces who surrounded us. He differentiated them from one another; they weren't one giant face contorted in anguish. It was through him that I learned words of dialect and made local friends outside of our staff.

Other humanitarians scoffed at us in envy, for we were solid. Transience is the name of the game here, everything a fleeting experience. People come and people leave. People are replaced. Permanence only exists back home. Relationships don't survive the frenzy. But ours did. At least for some time.

Things changed around the three-year mark. I brought Anders home with me to the United States. One evening, we were dining with friends of mine. While I had been away, their conversations had deteriorated to prices of real estate, home renovations, sports, celebrities. They had no idea about where Anders and I lived, no desire to map it. Those were the early Dubya Bush years, whom my friends regarded as a benign idiot. Their political commentary was basic CNN shit. They regurgitated, word for word, what they watched on giant screens in their oversized, bookless homes. They took trips to Palm Springs or Vegas, decidedly uncurious about the world or where their armies went. I found it entertaining how differently they lived and moved in this world. How cautiously they explored through guidebooks and consumer reviews. A world I could have been a part of but had managed to slip out of.

I remember looking over at Anders, as my friend Marnie told him about the celebrities she worked with and the endorsement deals she had gotten them. He nodded politely, looking crushed that such people existed—sticking faces to corporate logos as a profession—and that we had to engage with them. I tried to catch his eye and share a secretive smile. Only he wouldn't look at me.

He appeared to be sinking deeper into a malaise that every aid worker is well acquainted with. When life and death is our work, the first world is its parody. It's like someone is pulling our leg that people sit around reading magazines on how to decorate their living rooms. People can't really be lining up to enter shops on Black Friday when millions are dying, can they? Homecoming can be lonely. But this time I was with Anders, he was my country, he was my home. We could bathe in the malaise together, then towel it off.

On the way back to my parents' house, Anders suddenly veered the car to the side of the road and parked. It was quiet. I was afraid we'd get mugged. I was always more nervous about someone turning up with a gun in L.A. than in Likanni; I didn't have a protective logo on my car here. Anders looked worried. He held my hand, caressing my palm with his fingertips.

"Is this the life you want?"

"Like Marnie and Bill? Marketing and investment banking? Are you kidding?" I laughed.

"No, no, not like them. Do you want to come back? To the States?" Anders stared at me.

I thought he had known. That one day, of course, I would return to normality. Maybe to the U.S., maybe Europe, maybe Australia. To a place that was developed, where life wasn't so damn hard, where I didn't have to be on malaria pills that gave me nightmares, where I didn't have to see so many poor people without limbs, where I didn't have to stock up on food in case there was a shortage. I always thought of Likanni as an experience: one that would transform me, but that I would return from.

But I was nervous to say so.

"Maybe, one day," I said. "But I'd be just as happy moving to Paris or London or—Stockholm."

"So, you want to leave?" Anders looked at me as if every word coming out of my mouth weighed more than it should.

"Not now. But someday, yes, I see us leaving and starting over somewhere else."

Anders looked down at the gear selector. He'd been disappointed by the automatic car given to us by the rental company. Everything was too simple here, he complained. The transmissions weren't manual, the streets were in grids without the winding

25

romanticism that got you lost. Everything looked the same, franchises repeated every couple of blocks. Everything so easy, so predictable, that you didn't have to engage any part of yourself. People were so bored that kids brought guns to school or watched other people's dull realities on TV.

"I never want to leave. After this mission, I want to go to Chad or Sudan."

"Okay," I said slowly. "We can do that."

Anders fiddled with the leather bracelet on his wrist. "I'm not sure you understand. I want to be on mission forever. I don't mind going to Sweden for Christmases, but that's not my home anymore. Home is where the work takes me."

There it was. The curse of the elevated humanitarian: to view poverty and violence as the only moral place to inhabit. The desire to have no worldly possessions, to leave no footprint, to live in flux. I could see his addiction to the poor, the deprived. I could smell his rejection of all that could be construed as conventional and cosmetic; it scared the hell out of me.

"You're right. We can make a home wherever our work takes us," I said.

Anders kissed me. His lips stamping mine shut. Then, with his Scandinavian bluntness, he said, "I don't think we want the same things, Maya. You want children, but I don't want to bring any into this violent, overpopulated, materialistic world."

Everything felt like it stopped moving in my body. My cells, my blood, my electrons. Anything that pulsed or beat.

"But I love you," I burst out, like a child.

He looked at me with kindness, suddenly foreign. Suddenly patronizing.

"I love you too, but I don't want to depend on you and forget the important things I have to do. And I don't want to deprive you either. You want a family and that's normal, but I can't give that to you."

26

I could not understand why love or interdependence needed to be smaller than disease or war. Couldn't we be human and suprahuman at the same time? Why did one have to be severed for the other?

"You're my family. Where we live doesn't matter. I don't want anything more than what we have right now," I wailed.

Anders cried politely, as contained as when he laughed, wiping small tears neatly with his thumb.

"I don't want to hold you back, but I don't want to be held back either. This love—it will take us to a small place. A small flat, in a small city, with a small child. I don't want to live a small life." He shook his head resolutely and gripped the steering wheel.

We drove to my parents' house. We held each other all night and wept. I shivered uncontrollably and repeated that couples go through phases, that we would soon return to our exceptional shared life, but Anders never responded. I lied and said I didn't want children. I lied and said I wanted to move to Afghanistan, to Palestine, to any country that sounded perilous. I tried to phrase words perfectly, convinced that the perfect articulation, the right sequence of verbs and nouns, would preserve us. I stroked his back, trying to memorize the constellation of his moles. There had to be some calculation of touch and expression that would salvage us.

We flew back. I clung to him on the plane, at the airport, afraid to let go. I was pathetic. I tried to seduce him, tried to be funny. I tried neediness, levity. I spoke of our history with grandiose words; I showed him pictures and played songs to reawaken memories as one would with an amnesiac. I wore a low-cut shirt, flashing a lacy bra.

Two weeks later Anders told me he would be wrapping up his mission and going to Sudan. I was not invited.

Anders's dramatic departure stunted me for years. I wonder if I ever recovered. I still awaken from dreams where he's leaving me, the rejection a permanent horror. I blame Western culture, the transience it fosters. How it teaches us to start things, use them up, get rid of them, move on to the next.

With the people in Likanni, their bonds last a lifetime. Then beyond lifetimes in the words of elders, as stories to pass on. Only murder or adultery sever relationships.

When we first-worlders arrive with our broken spiritual bonds, our meditation podcasts and mindfulness journals, the easy way people connect here floors us. There are no how-to books devoted to fixing ourselves or broken relationships; people just are. That's why we end up staying. We're tired of the perfect fixes, thrust at us from every direction back home. Dieticians on TV, parenting blogs telling us how to talk to our children. Mindfulness instructors. Instagram weight-loss heroes. People recommending Botox to freeze lines of human expression. Others pushing fillers to puff cheeks to laughable proportions so we look like grotesque babies. Apps reminding us to breathe or sleep. Tips on how to fold shirts, how to rid ourselves of things we were told to buy. We have to be told to think of the present. We have devices strapped to our wrists telling us how much we've walked or whether we've slept, as if our bodies are alien to us. We have life coaches and influencers. Pundits and evangelical rock stars. They come at us in an endless barrage, promising us better, though our lives are plentiful. I've dabbled in it, sung from the twelve-step hymnbook. But the bullet point mantras are a false promise.

The young girls here want to be "progressive" like us. They giggle when they ask what boyfriends are. I tell them boyfriends are nothing. They come and they go. We've given titles to the transitional. Don't take on our impermanent rites. When people can be open and shut like books, it's not progress. Stick to your long stories, your endless bonds that evolve as you grow into mothers, aunts, and grandmothers.

Eventually, I accepted Anders's departure like a death. It was the only way I could survive it. I talked about him in the past tense; I smiled at our memories as if I had buried him in Likanni's dry red earth.

It was after this loss that I dipped into the ways of the locals and consulted a shamanic healer. He made me drink herbal teas that made me sick. He told me I was not to be Anders's, that Anders would find a woman like his mother, tall and blond, and that if I wanted, I could wear a talisman around my neck to keep him yearning for me. During the two years I wore it, I never heard from him, except in sterile wishes on my birthday. One day I threw it in the river, hoping he would remain as unsettled as the tide.

Anders is now married to a tall Romanian named Natalya; they have no children. They bounce from country to country and have a home in Hanoi. He writes me once a year. The emails are short and polite, typed by fingers that were once inside me so long they wrinkled. But I know it's not really him, that the real Anders is in fragments in the village's soil. That that him decayed when he left me. This guy is a cheap imposter standing in for our memories.

That's how I started hating this place. I realized the problems would never end: they would swallow me whole. My country would become foreign. My lovers would disappear. My friends would seem superficial. I'd be left observing the endless pain of others, like a tired voyeur. I had to get out.

———

We roll up to the hotel. Philippe pulls the car onto a dry patch of dirt, and I tell him to pick me up at four in the morning. He's going to find a quiet spot and sleep in the car. He saves every cent of his per diem, all the drivers do. A night without a hotel room means a few more dollars in his pocket. I wonder where he uses the bathroom. He always looks clean and smells nice.

The hotel is as decrepit as always. There's something comforting in this. I enter the makeshift lobby, its wooden table strewn with papers. One of the table's legs has a piece of cardboard tucked under to stabilize it; it's been this way since I first stayed here fourteen years ago. I ring the brass bell sitting on the table.

A new face appears. He's young and looks like he was sleeping. He proposes to carry my suitcase; I decline, worrying his bony frame will teeter over. He has acne. I don't think I've ever seen anyone with acne around these parts. I get the Wi-Fi password from him and walk to my room while he watches my every step. He makes me slightly nervous, in that way that every man observing me makes me nervous. You never know whether it's dull curiosity or a plan for assault that sits behind an onlooker's eyes.

I think back to my security training and a cautionary missive: never take a room on the first floor to avoid being attacked from the window. Whoever wrote that script never slept in Somoko.

The first time my suburban self read the security training manuals, I panicked. Learning how to negotiate if I was kidnapped, following the stars if lost, building shelters in trees, finding safe drinking water by observing the currents, dealing with bandits: this was the stuff of movies.

What the manual failed to acknowledge was that we first-worlders wear a protective shield: we're foreigners, the majority of us white. That protects most of us tucked in Africa and the Americas and Asia. Even in conflict, rebels and soldiers honor the white skinned. In civil wars, where people mutilate each other, we come in as intermediaries, witnesses, authority. Most foreign photojournalists survive on front lines, while those around them fall. Those of us who aren't white take on their symbols. We roam in SUVs with powerful logos, we wear clothing that leaves no doubt of the pedigree of our first worldliness. The rebels and the militaries let us pass checkpoints in their towns and villages as we give polite and dismissive waves.

There are, of course, targeted attacks on rich hotels every now and again. Kidnappings, beheadings, killings of healthcare humanitarians. I have to be careful because Brown and Black skin is easily accepted as collateral damage. It is mostly the local aid workers who die, the ones without obvious protections. But I'm American, that's my shield. No one wants to deal with the consequences of pissing off the white armies. Everyone's seen footage of Iraq. Messing with white people can mean complete annihilation.

I enter the room, she's a rebel against time. I tug the string attached to a Hitachi tube light; it buzzes for ninety seconds before it turns on. Anders used to laugh at its anticlimactic nature: it buzzes and buzzes as if some great illumination will follow. Instead, a yellow blur is emitted, barely enough to read by. The flowery bedsheets are the same from years ago. The pillows still the chunky bits of separated foam so that when I rest my head, it will fall straight to the bed. I feel Anders everywhere. We often met in this room, me coming from my hood in Likanni, him from his in Mwawere.

I take off my shoes. Microscopic ants crawl on the floor under my swollen toes. The same floor upon which Anders used to put his bare feet. This touch separated by time, and (hopefully) swipes of Javex, gives me a small shiver. I sit on the bed and turn on the laptop, my rite of passage. My mother has sent a picture of my daughter eating ice cream. A daughter who bears no resemblance to me, having caught her father's genes in the battle between my dominant and his recessive traits. Chloe's genes know what's best for her. She's light-haired and pale: she'll never have to prove her first worldliness.

Survival of the fittest.

I miss her and how her small frame finds mine like a magnet. We are like a lugubrious creature with two heads, always intertwined. It's cumbersome but glorious that another human can own me in this way. That she can pat and touch any part of me for safety, my flesh the pinnacle of generosity. I force my thoughts away—I can't afford to be sad or sentimental. Being here can sever one from that kind of history. I stare at the filthy corners of the room, corners she's never seen, and Chloe feels so unrealistic in this space, that my motherhood evaporates. Flowery bedsheets take over.

Are any remnants of Anders and me in here, are those remnants together? Is there a younger me floating in a dust ball somewhere? Is that me happy?

I scroll through emails. Shoe sales, furniture deals. Nothing from my husband. There are work emails, one from Burton flagged *urgent*. I open it knowing it will stress me out and there's nothing I can do about it at this time of night.

Maya,

I trust you've arrived safely. The situation is deteriorating—protestors have surrounded the project site. One of the drivers was assaulted on his way to work. We have requested that Marc remain in the office until things calm down. We trust you have an evacuation plan in mind and will advise us on how to proceed. We count on your expertise to be responsive to the aggrieved beneficiaries while protecting the brand.

Yours,
Burton

I can almost hear the forced calm of Burton's voice. *Protecting the brand* looms, a symbolic flag above my head, a banner by which to swear my allegiance. Protecting the brand means protecting vulnerable lives, those of the people we serve. But also those of our bosses, of our colleagues. Burton knows. He is the Britisher-living-in-Geneva type, the bureaucrat with weekend games of tennis,

32

that proper kind of man who finds my Americanness too forward. He liaises with donors, ensures that folks in the field are complying. He takes a few trips to Likanni every year, during which he wears a crinkly safari hat. He ensures that everything looks good, that all we do can be documented on a glossy leaflet or in a poignant video while reflecting the benevolence of the human spirit.

I lie back on the bed. This is going to be hell. When the big guns count on me, they are not willing to risk their name. If I have to protect anything as large as a brand, the multitude of people it employs, the children it serves, the donors it courts, I'm in trouble. I should call my daughter. I should write my husband, tell him what a minefield I'm about to stumble upon. Instead, I write to Anders. It's one line, a raw invitation for something.

I'm in Somoko tonight. Maya

The words seem to tremble on my screen. I want an essay from him in return. About anything. A crack in a wall, a child suffering from some disease I've never heard of, memories of this place with me. Something vivid, to feel another's life. To feel him. Like we lived this thing, it wasn't just in my mind.

I don't unpack. There are too few hours to sleep. I put on a pair of flip-flops to take a shower. There's a black hole in the ground for a drain. As the water runs, bugs scramble to and from it. I see a roach lurking in the sink, its antennae shuddering.

I put my clothes back on, take the busted pillows and line them up like a body. I close my eyes and lean against them. I ignore the thought of dust mites and remember the hairs that Anders and I left on these pillows long ago, and think of all the men and women who have sought a rest stop. Visitors, like me. I embrace them with all my might.

My phone pings. It's an email. Anders's name on the screen. What a rush. Those letters next to each other forming the most sacred of names, in the most casual of ways. I await a gem. Instead, it's one line in return.

Cool, is that blind dog still hanging around the lobby?

Cool? You asshole. The blind dog? He knows me well enough to know I'm starving for connection. I shove the pillows off the bed, spread out in a star shape, and fall into an uneasy sleep, knowing it will only last a few hours.

There is no time for breakfast. I ring the bell and hand cash to the acne-marked boy. I use the last of my Wi-Fi to shoot an email to Burton, letting him know that I'm on my way and will report back as soon as I arrive. I shove a squished PowerBar, brought from California, into my mouth. Philippe is already here. He's always here. I climb in the front passenger seat and force myself to talk to him as he looks tired and the road to Likanni is winding and dangerous.

The sun is rising, everything has a hopeful glow.

5

There are dirt roads and then there's just dirt. The road to Likanni cannot be called a road, but it's bloody glorious. You're jerked from right to left. Your head crashes against the window. You can't carry on a conversation because you're being thrashed about, and if you have birthed children, you can end up with pee-stained pants. But what a rush. It makes you feel like a real adventurer.

You pass through the green; you drive through rivers where young kids are doing their washing and bathing. They splash, wave, and cheer. The water rushes by in brownish hues. Open the car door and you see it, the current of the river—hopefully not too fast so the vehicle can cross, and not too slow, indicative of drought.

You pass through small towns, where children walk barefoot in oversized T-shirts, clothes beige from dust, from chasing cars, from chasing tires. Sometimes I look for T-shirts I recognize, mine, my friends', given away over the years. What bodies they eventually land on, how long they last until they disintegrate.

In busier villages, children hold metal trays over their shoulders, tapping car windows, ready to sell anything. Fruits, rubber bands, water bottles that look like they've been used, fried food, cracker-type things, nuts, citrus, soda. It's a constant play between driving through the bush, then finding a small stretch of road, passing through noisy towns and villages made up of huts and shacks, strolling goats. The high street of the village, if you will, is only about a hundred meters long, a loud, musical, colorful stretch before we are back in the bush, bouncing about, one reality to the next.

Being thrown about in the car makes me laugh uncontrollably, which has irritated my colleagues in the past. I try to contain it but cannot. Soon, I'm laughing maniacally in the passenger's seat, clinging to the handle, tensing all my muscles, trying not to fall onto Philippe's lap. I'm embarrassed; he's embarrassed for me. In broken words interrupted by the vehicle's leaps and climbs, I manage to sputter, "Can you turn on some music?"

Philippe flicks on the local radio. We're accompanied by mellow, happy voices, drums, and lots of synthesizers. There's something about listening to music in the place it is birthed. When the landscape and music match, it's like being on a drug-induced high. Every shape accentuated, every color bright. My work in high definition. Everything makes sense. The grass seems greener, clumps of floating butterflies take on mystical charm; children and women walking miles to collect water look like they are swinging their hips and babies to the beat. I'm laughing, swooning, almost peeing my pants, clutching the car handle, seeing as though I've been blind, and I feel something huge. I think I'm happy. I think I am full. A ball of sensory overload. No room for thought or analytics. I'm subject to this place, its tones, its shades. It has been so hard to feel things, this is nothing short of a miracle.

The road worsens, our vehicle slows, the green lessens, the brown takes over. We're getting closer to humble Likanni where there is a severe lack of water.

Likanni is a large village that sits strategically at the border of two overpopulated provinces far from the nation's capital. It's a thoroughfare, witnessing movement of people from east to west. I've often wondered how the hell the charity I work for found this place to begin with.

Our office is housed in a two-hundred-year-old monastery dormitory. We painted the wooden doors and shutters a cheerful green. It is the only large solid structure in the village, with a sizable field that extends before it. I've never seen anyone mow it, but the grass is always razed to the ground. During winters when the days were cooler, we would play soccer, and the locals would watch us shyly until we invited them to participate. It became a friendly winter pastime that we all looked forward to.

But today, as we roll onto the driveway, things do not look friendly. About fifty people stand on the field in a colorful array of T-shirts. They look upset. I've never seen people gathered here in anger. The only crowds I remember witnessing were during droughts, when food or water was urgently needed, or during festival celebrations.

Chantal stands at the front door, her hair tied in a knot on top of her head. She shields her eyes to look at my vehicle. The Cruiser rolls toward the building, leaving a trail of dark dust in the stagnant air. There are angry yells as we approach.

My stomach churns.

Philippe parks in front of the building and I step out, feeling rusty. Chantal almost runs toward me and clutches my arm. Without any greeting, she tugs at me and says, "Let's get inside." It's odd to see her this frazzled.

I'm about to respond when I hear a loud "Bigabosse!"

It's been awhile since I've been called that. I turn to see Paulsie, waving wildly in the crowd.

Bigabosse is how I'm known here. The nickname came from a Bollywood reality TV show, *Big Boss*, which the locals gathered to watch each week. With me looking Indian, and being in charge of the office, some of the villagers jokingly started calling me Big Boss. With dialects, accents, new TV interests, the name evolved to Bigabosse. As Bigabosse, I bargain unapologetically in the markets, laugh harder at lewd jokes, have bigger arm gestures.

Paulsie breaks from the crowd and runs toward me, her feet sliding in broken green flip-flops. Her toes look enormous. As I turn to meet her, Chantal grabs my arm.

"Let's talk first—before you meet with them," she whispers.

I see Paulsie, the excitement pulsating in her face. Ignoring her would be the worst thing to do.

"I have to talk to them. That's why I'm here," I say through clenched teeth, so nobody else hears. Chantal drops my arm.

"I've already been briefed. I know what our official position is. Let's go talk to Paulsie and the others and sort this out," I say, rubbing my arm, straightening my shirt.

Chantal shakes her head. "You go talk with them. I'll wait in the office. Come meet me when you're done." She scurries toward the entrance before I can say another word. I barely have time to register our awkward greeting, with Paulsie upon me.

"Bigabosse," she exclaims, grabbing me into a bony hug. "You've come to help. I knew you would come. Oh, bad things, such bad, bad things have happened," she says in French. She shakes her head, three meager braids swing.

Paulsie looks even skinnier, her eyes bright and wide in her lean fleshless face. She used to clean our offices, which is how I met her. She had twelve, maybe thirteen children at the time. Never a husband in sight. Just Paulsie, working, children on her back, children at her breast. I thought of her as having an inexplicable power that allowed her to always be in motion, through pregnancies, through childbirths, through deaths. I once went to her home, a room of caked mud, where I sat on a straw mat. Her children sang for me. I wept. Paulsie could die of poverty but never of loneliness. Actually, no one here could die of loneliness even if they wanted to.

Everything feels charged. Chantal so curt, Philippe hurriedly taking my luggage and disappearing around the back of the building. The villagers eyeing me with skepticism. There's tension in the air, as if anything could erupt. And we're walking right into it, straight onto that field of grass where they all stand in fury, Paulsie and I holding hands.

It's hot. Someone yells something rude in dialect.

"It's Bigabosse. She is come to help us. She always helps us," yells Paulsie, gesturing for people to sit.

There is a cacophony of sound. Arms pat my shoulders. I'm drawn into the crowd, into the smell of sweat. How long have they been standing here under this scorching sun, facing our office in defiance? One man starts clearing the root of an old tree for me to sit on, the only spot that is slightly elevated from the ground. We foreigners always get the seat. Is it because we're weaker or because years of subservience have trained the locals to put us on a pedestal, even when they are angry?

I sit on the root, keeping a watchful eye on the giant ants racing on it. The others sit on the ground in a large circle, as if at a community meeting. I wish I could sit with them, but I do not want to offend the respect they've bestowed upon me.

There are many new faces. A lot of young men. They must have been the teenagers that ran to and fro when I lived here, now adults. There's distrust in their eyes. I see the sweat dripping down everyone's foreheads. I hand a water bottle from my bag to the first person next to me. He, oblivious to the remnants of my ChapStick or my germs, takes a small swig and passes it to his neighbor.

"Go," says Paulsie, waving off the lingering crowd. "This is Bigabosse, she will help us. Let the elders of the community stay. Shoo, go do your work." Everyone stays put.

"It's alright, Paulsie," I begin. "Thank you for welcoming me into this conversation. Some of you know me. I'm Bigabosse. I know most of you, and some I knew as children—you've grown up too fast." I give a nervous smile and continue.

"This village was my home for many years, and I don't want bad things to happen here. I'm here to listen to you. I want to understand what has happened. I want us to work together to make things better. There shouldn't be two sides to the story. There is only one story, the truth, and I'm here to obtain it."

I take a breath and continue. "The people who work with me"—I gesture toward the building behind me—"also want to support you. We want our work to continue so that children remain safe in this community. So please, let us help you. You can tell me anything, and I'll assist in any way I can." It doesn't feel like I've spent hours in a tumultuous ride. The words slide off my tongue in French; this is what I was born to do.

Paulsie translates what I've said into local dialect. One of the older men tears up; I see his slight frame trembling. Another, beside him, looks at me with kind eyes. The younger men stare with hard looks. There is one guy in particular: his skin is almost purple in rage; his piercing eyes, bloodshot. He hasn't said a word. He is wearing a blue, white, and red flannel shirt in this heat. While the others have looked down, maybe played with a blade of grass, he has done nothing but stare unflinchingly at me.

Paulsie ends her translation, and the older men and youngsters get up and congregate a few feet away. Some people walk off. I'm confused, and Paulsie becomes my de facto cultural interpreter. It frustrates me that after all my years of working here, there are moments when I have no idea why people are saying or doing the things they are.

"They are removing themselves to give the privacy," explains Paulsie. "The discussion is on a girl's dignity. Out of respect they will protect her honor and not listen to any words of abuse."

A smaller circle is formed around me, of women and the angry young man in the plaid shirt. I recognize everyone but him. I'm hot now, really hot. The dizzying kind. A woman notices and offers me my water bottle, which by now has touched many strangers' lips. I awkwardly shake my head no and attempt a polite smile.

"Fanon, go, go to your work. The elders will speak with Bigabosse," Paulsie says to the angry guy. Fanon. An apt name.

He doesn't move and stares me down. "This is about my sister. I do not trust anyone else to discuss this matter."

Ismail, an elder, pats him on the back with affection. He whispers in his ear and takes Fanon by the arm. They stand a few respectable feet away.

A plump woman sitting next to Paulsie plucks dead grass, chews it, and spits it out noisily. She says, "Bigabosse, do you remember Lele?"

Of course I do. Lele, bright-eyed and rambunctious. I knew her first as an annoying teenager, following me around the market, asking me to teach her English, teach her about office work, teach her anything. She didn't ask in an endearing way. She pestered. She hovered while I studied vegetables in the market, bombarding me with questions. She stood outside our office, followed me to my car. She wasn't content with learning a few expressions or words. She wanted all of the English language in her head. This went on for months until I finally agreed to have her volunteer at the office. That day, her face lit up in a way I cannot forget. She was quiet for an instant, rare for her, then babbled at how proud she would make me, how hard she would work, how she would be indispensable to our work. I had to laugh. She asked if she could tell her parents, and once I agreed, she sprung off, braids flying.

Her parents, in true ceremonial form, arrived at the compound with a box of sweets. I was taken by the seriousness of it. What I saw as menial filing and stapling was a moment for her father to wear his finest, to inaugurate the beginning of his daughter's working life. He bowed as he handed me gifts, thanking me for the honor I had imparted on the family.

Lele is the Chief's daughter, though that title hardly means anything nowadays. The Chief is as poor as the rest, his role replaced by municipal governments that the colonizers instated back when this place was part of the French republic. The Chief is so in name only. He shows up at funerals and weddings. He appeases family conflicts. He's at meetings where people like me interview him and pretend his endorsement matters to our work. It doesn't.

The Chief has the demeanor of an eighty-year-old elder, though he's much younger. He walks slowly, he talks slowly, he bows his head much more than he needs to. He's a shy fellow. His thoughts, like everyone else's, are focused on how to ensure food security for his family in the hungry season.

During Lele's first few weeks at work, I helped her use her rudimentary reading for filing and showed her how the office worked. When she wasn't being taught something, she was asking questions. Where does the building get its electricity? What is electricity? Why doesn't the rest of the village get electricity? Who even found electricity? What color is electricity? The questions were endless and drove me batty. I tried to pawn her onto other staff, but she always found her way back to me.

After a few months of working with her, I made Lele a deal. If she could upgrade her reading skills, I would teach her how to use the computer. There she would meet a Ms. Google who could answer all her questions. Lele nodded, a serious look in her eyes, and shot off to another corner in the office. I had respite for a few weeks, before she returned with several books and reports she had found lying around the office.

"Test me, kindly," Lele urged. I looked up at her from my desk, confused.

"I can read all of these," she said.

I wanted to encourage her but was doubtful she understood the content of human development reports and the dull books on demographics she was carrying. Nonetheless, I opened a report randomly and handed it to her to read. She did. Then I asked her to explain what she had read. She did. In eight weeks, the girl had taught herself and improved her comprehension in English. She cross-referenced various documents to understand what certain terms meant. She carried a notebook in which she translated every word she came across, which she then memorized and used in sentences. The phrases were sometimes awkward, adjectives after nouns, but she knew the meanings of words she used. She was only thirteen.

I was astounded by her talent. Lele was one of the promising ones. She possessed a photographic memory. She spoke French and Portuguese in addition to two local dialects and English. She could, it seemed, teach herself anything. She would take the slightest bit of offhand commentary and transform it into a grand lesson from which she drew concepts I didn't know I was teaching. Maybe it was her chiefly blood, but Lele walked around as if she expected only good things to come, sucking up information with every breath.

By the time I left, five years ago, Lele had become a reliable, punctual, steady intern who assisted with the administration of the office. I imagined that one day she would be running the place. That one day, foreigners like me could leave, and Lele would manage the office herself, working for and with her own people.

Paulsie and fifteen other women sit in the grass huddled close to me. From afar we must look like a group of friends, like college students on a grassy campus somewhere. Most of these women have never even been to primary school. Different worlds, different landmarks. There's an air of camaraderie though, and it's not an act.

Paulsie puts her calloused palm on my hand. She looks me in the eyes. My power disappears. We are just two women, sharing.

"You remember, Bigabosse? Lele worked in the office? Oh she loved working there. Oh and when you started her salary, how proud she was. My own children so jealous of the girl and all the luck. Oh but how she cried when you left, Bigabosse. Miss Chantal let her stay. And she continued to hard work. She teached other children English. Then my children were not so jealous." Paulsie chuckles and says in dialect, "When they receive the English.

"She worked, Bigabosse. She went to the school, she helped with the animals, she taught the children, and she work for Miss Chantal. But you know . . ." Paulsie pauses, looks down at her large feet.

I swallow. Please don't say it, Paulsie, I say to myself, please let us stay suspended in this space before you say what you are about to, and it becomes real.

"One day, Bigabosse, Lele came to the house in quiet. Not a word out of the beak, and you know how she is . . . chatter, chatter, chatter. Her mother say she fell on the bedding and lay there, no words, no sleep, only tears. For days, Bigabosse. She soiled herself. Her mother, she cried to her, she sang to her, she slapped her. They could not wake the child. Her mother, she knew by looking. She sent the boys out the house and wiped her with Dettol water. She wiped, and she sang the song of comfort. Bigabosse, when she touched the rag to the child's thigh, Lele screamed. The legs stuck together, Lele holding them tight-tight. She was shaking. Her mother, she knew. Bigabosse, he did this to her. He did this to her." Paulsie points angrily toward our office.

I bow my head against my knees, hugging them to my chest, rocking, as if I'm holding Lele. I purse my lips at the thought of her lying in filth, sealing her young thighs together. I swallow my nausea.

Paulsie kneels before me, holding my shoulders, making me look at her. My knees separate our bodies, her fleshy breasts push up against them.

"Five weeks, Bigabosse, five weeks little Lele lie saying nothing and crying. Her mother fed her the broths, held her in the arms. The brothers told her the stories and tried tickling and slapping the feet. The healer came. The toubib came. After five weeks, she spoke. At first the mother could not hear, because she whispered. But then she said his name again and again."

I hold my breath.

"'Monsieur Marc,' 'Monsieur Marc' is what the child would say." Paulsie points at our office. "Monsieur Marc. He raped our child. He took our honor. He betrayed our elders and our kindnesses. He did this, Bigabosse."

There.

The words I did not want to hear float in the air between us. There is no breeze and so they hang. My eyes water. They brought me here to be the professional, and I'm in the fetal position, welling up.

"How is Lele now?" I croak. From a few meters away, Fanon looks at me curiously.

Paulsie shakes her head. "Not good. She had the fevers. She hangs to her mother like a broken child. She cries. She's afraid of men's voices. Fanon sits outside the door at night, to protect her. She is broken, Bigabosse. We hear the cries at night in the village. Then we all pain with her. That happy home, Bigabosse"—Paulsie shakes her head—"it is finished. Monsieur Marc finished it."

Hearing Marc's name again stirs me to reality. This is a man I have worked with, lived in close quarters with, saved lives with. And so, the worst question must be asked, not because I don't believe, but because I can't afford to be wrong. I'm the expert, I must see it all. I have to probe, even if it's hurtful.

"Are you sure it's him?"

Paulsie looks at me with disgust.

I take her wrists in my hand.

"I'm not asking because I doubt what has happened. I just need to know whether Lele has said it's him in a full sentence." I salvage the situation.

Paulsie nods. "Yes, Bigabosse. When the words came, Lele told her mother. She even told her brothers. She said she was willing to carry the shame if it meant Monsieur Marc would be punished. Now you are here, I know he will get the severest punishment." Paulsie looks triumphant.

I am feverish. Talking about rape in this village is no small feat. I'm proud of Lele but know that she may now spend her life unmarried, childless, maybe a pariah. I'm also nervous to hear Paulsie speak of punishments. This is why they think I have come. To punish Marc. But I've been summoned to find out what's happened, to protect our charity from stumbling and breaking its jaw before the world. To stop us from being one more aid casualty that people can point at, or keep their precious dollars from. To keep our work going, to keep those children safe and thriving.

It's too much. The heat, the fatigue, the bumpy car ride, the thought of Lele getting attacked. I lean forward and throw up. It's not delicate or contained. I emit phlegmy sounds purging myself of everything. A few strands of hair get caught in the spray. I ungracefully lean forward on my hands and knees. The villagers rush toward me, one of them with my sticky water bottle. I steady myself and sit back on my heels, wiping my mouth with the back of my hand. They watch. Paulsie looks up at everyone and yells, "You see? Bigabosse is one of us. Lele's suffering is her suffering."

Fanon walks toward me, reaches out, and steadies me. I smell like vomit and sweat. I'm self-conscious of his proximity, but it doesn't seem to bother him. For the first time, the guarded look in his eye is gone. He looks at me with concern.

"Ça va?" he asks.

I nod. I turn to the group and produce the most generic of words. "I'll go rest for now. But I'll come back to you in a few days. Please do not worry. I will help as best I can."

Paulsie's lips stretch into a huge smile. The other villagers look relieved. Vomit and tears have sewn me to their sorrow. They vacate our front lawn.

I lean forward to get my bag, but Fanon already holds it. He walks me toward the office. He and I both know I cannot let him into the building, not when things are so tense. Fanon stops a conservative distance from the door and hands me my things. As he does, he holds my hand in an informal handshake, then brushes away flecks of bile stuck on my knuckles. We are the same height and I peer straight into his boyish eyes. Without the anger, he looks like a different person.

"Thank you for believing my sister."

I'm quiet.

"You rest, and when you have time, please visit the family home. You will speak with Lele," Fanon says. I nod and walk toward the brightly painted door, which Chantal quickly opens. I disappear into our air-conditioned fortress, leaving Fanon, Paulsie, and the rest to the heat.

6

The first door shutters behind me with a creak; it's wooden. The second one, made of heavy metal, closes with a gentle thud, sucking the hot air out. The lobby is as it has always been. On my left, behind plexiglass, sits a bored-looking guard who takes names and IDs through a small semicircle window. I don't recognize him. On the right stands an armed guard, his hands on a weapon, ready to check people's bags. I don't recognize him either.

Faded posters hang on yellowed walls. The largest poster greets visitors with images of happy kids, hugging, smiling ear to ear. Many very white teeth. There are others of farmers working a field, children sitting in school, infants getting vaccinations from a smiling Western doctor. Over the years I've wondered how old these kids are now, whether they are from Likanni, whether they know they are printed on thousands of posters set up at registration desks in conference centers around the world—whether they receive royalties from poster fame. Fat chance.

Chantal gives me a hug. She backs up, laughs, and says, "Oh, you smell." There is a forced levity to her, as though we are students, happy to see each other after a long summer away. As though our reunion hasn't been precipitated by a crisis. We've always gotten along, but it's been polite and distant, not much teasing about scents.

Chantal is striking as always, the consummate Parisian even in the bush. She's in a simple white buttoned shirt tucked loosely into a pair of denim-colored linen pants. Her face looks fresh, anchored on high cheekbones, unharmed by Likanni's violent sun and dust.

"Let me introduce you. This is Madame Maya Burnett. She is the regional director, and my boss, so we have to make a good impression." She smiles at the security guards and winks at me. "Maya, these are Cyril and Benoit. They've been deployed from the south and joined our team a week ago." She gestures so widely I have no idea who is Cyril and who is Benoit. They nod at me with restrained, cautious silence, as if they are nervous to say the wrong thing.

"Thank you for joining our team. We appreciate your services at this challenging time," I offer.

I give my passport to the Cyril or Benoit behind the plexiglass and offer my bag to the other one for inspection, but he gestures for me to go into the building. I'm not perceived as a risk.

Chantal takes my arm. "Ouf. I have no idea how you got rid of the protesters. They've been camped in front of the office for days. We haven't been able to go in or out. We've been living off the vegetables you insisted on planting in the courtyard." She gives me another smile. Flattering my meager gardens. She wants me to forget how she greeted me. I should say something polite. But I'm still nauseous and can't bear to ask how she's doing and get an honest answer.

"Looks like you got the air-conditioning fixed" is all I can muster.

"Are you okay?"

"I'm tired. And I feel sick. I think I'll feel better after a shower and a nap."

"Of course," she says. "Let's go to your room, you must be exhausted." She grabs my bag, while I wheel my small suitcase. "How's Chloe?"

"Good," I say. Chantal does not have children. She asks out of politeness, for Chantal is a free woman. She goes places without planning the survival of another.

The building became an office a long time ago but still has the priestly dormitory feel. Early office managers had the good sense of keeping four bedrooms intact for guests. The lobby leads to a set of steep, wide stone stairs, which split into two corridors running in opposite directions. One can imagine boys running to and fro, in knee-length navy shorts, schooled by priests in long robes. The floors are tiled an odd blue that must have been all the rage among French administrators in the 1950s; the walls are a smooth yellowed plaster. It's dark and cool in these corridors, like the sun has never risen. Anywhere else, this darkness would be a curse; here it's a blessing.

We walk to the end of the corridor, passing half-open office doors. Things are abnormally quiet; the rooms are deserted. I'm about to remark on this when Chantal says, "We've sent all the staff home for leave. It was too risky to keep them here. The guards and drivers are the only ones left." I'm surprised; nobody from headquarters informed me of this decision.

My room is the last one in the hallway. I suddenly worry Marc's is next to mine.

"Which room is Marc in?" I ask.

Chantal looks flustered. She fumbles through keys on a large ring. She extracts one and hands it to me.

"He's in the kitchen right now. Do you want to speak to him?"

"No, no. I'm just wondering what room he's staying in. I'm guessing he hasn't gone home?"

"He's on the other side." She points left.

Good. As far as possible from me, the opposite end of the corridor. I don't think I can bear sleeping on the other side of a wall from him. And I don't want to worry about him overhearing my conversations.

"Thanks, Chantal. I'm sorry I'm so out of it. I'll be back to normal after some rest."

Finally, alone.

The room is simple. Tiled floors, plaster walls, an old single bed with a wooden frame that could be a hundred years old. There was a time, a few years ago, when I cared enough to dress these rooms with local artwork on the walls, a large basket woven by women of the village, a colorful batik sheet at the foot of the bed. Small things to cheer up the space. To make us forget the priests and whatever they may have thought while in here.

I unzip my carry-on and pull out some clothes.

I have a sudden desire to talk with my husband. I want to tell Steven about what Paulsie has said, about Lele, about Chantal's odd behavior, the pressure from headquarters. It has been so long since I have expected anything of my marriage that this feels like a breakthrough. I rifle through my bag looking for my phone. I'm a bit excited; this chaos can give us something to talk about. I check the time. It's five a.m. in California. I hesitate for a moment. Surely he won't mind me waking him—he'll feel needed.

I call the landline and imagine it ringing in our pristine kitchen. Steven likes white, so everything is white in our home. White, clean, minimalist, little trace of human life. It rings and rings, until my own voice greets me. I keep dialing; I keep hearing my voice. I call his cell. It goes straight to voicemail.

I throw the phone on the bed, deflated. Doesn't he know that I'm in a dangerous country? That bad shit can happen to me? That

51

he has to be reachable while Chloe is with her grandparents? That bad shit can happen to her? That he has responsibilities as a father and husband that don't just disappear when I'm away?

I shove my suitcase and pants to the floor and crawl into bed. I should wash off the throw-up. I should brush my teeth. I should zip up my suitcase so bugs don't crawl into my clothes. Instead, I fall asleep in the fetal position with curses on my lips.

A roll of thunder awakens me.

I see dramatic flashes of white out the window, but there's no sound of rain. At first, I don't know where I am. I'm sticky. I check my phone for the time. It's a little past midnight. I've slept a long time. I'm hungry and out of PowerBars.

I throw on sweatpants and feel something crawling in them; it could just be my mind. I unlock the creaky door. The corridor is still and dark. From somewhere comes the electric hum of the generator. I feel around for the wall, familiarity rushes in, giving me comfort. These are walls I know.

I go down the concrete steps, hearing lizards scamper. There are voices in the kitchen. I push the door open. Marc is sitting at the table, lazily peeling an orange. He looks up nonchalantly.

"Want one?" he asks, holding up a slice.

The kitchen has always been a hangout for the staff. It's a large room with bright lights and a huge wooden dining table, usually covered with wrinkly newspapers that we read during breaks. On the far side of the room, there are plush maroon leather couches that outdate us all facing an old television set, VCR, and DVD player.

Marc looks sunburnt, expressionless. The red reaches all the way to his dirty-blond hairline. He's thinner than I remember, still with the robotic demeanor he's always had. He gets up and reaches for the mandatory hug. It's a strange embrace. Should I be embracing him?

The moment is surreal. Did I hear Paulsie's words correctly? And if I did, were those Lele's words, or the community's rendition funneling through Paulsie's mouth? Allegations, Burton had said. Allegations. And here's Marc, the way he always is, in a half-sleeved button-up shirt, even at this time of night, as if a T-shirt would be too disorderly, too unprofessional; his silver eyeglasses pinch his nose.

"Thanks for ending that protest. I was concerned they were going to get heatstroke," he says.

I extend my hand for a slice. Marc plunks the whole fruit in my palm and reaches for another from a black plastic bag.

"How are you?" I ask, sitting across from him. I don't know what else to ask a could-be rapist. Could be, until Lele says so. Could be, until I know for sure. Innocent until proven guilty, right?

"Pretty good, considering. You know how it is."

No, I don't know how it is, I think. I've never been accused of rape.

Chantal pops up from the couch. I hadn't seen her nestled deep in the cushions. She rubs her eyes. "Oh hi. I must have fallen asleep." She stands, stretches her lithe body, and joins us at the table. She sits next to Marc; he hands her a slice of orange.

"I'm so glad you're here," Chantal says.

Marc nods. "It's been very difficult, M. We've never encountered this type of situation before. People are spreading vicious rumors, and it has been impossible to do our work. I haven't been able to go home in weeks, and"—he looks over at Chantal—"I worry about her safety all the time. What if someone does something to her in retaliation?"

I don't know if it's the jet lag, but I'm utterly confused. Marc seems calm. Chantal, the same as she always does. Are we discussing rape? The weather?

"At the same time," Marc continues, "you can't blame them. Something has happened to Lele. Maybe someone attacked her, maybe it was a relationship gone bad, maybe"—he lowers his voice conspiratorially—"it's one of our local staff. Until we talk to her, we won't know."

Chantal jumps in. "That's where we need you. They trust you, Maya. They'll let you talk to her. You have to find out what's happened."

I nod.

"Have you had any contact with the family?" I ask.

"A few weeks after the supposed incident, I was in the market to get groceries. Some of her brothers and their gang of friends surrounded me and threatened to beat me. Most people hadn't yet heard the rumors. The merchants came to my rescue. Big Henri pulled out a gun and chased them off. Since then, the boys have spread word that *I'm* the one that attacked their sister and now the whole village is against me. So no, I have not reached out to them. It's difficult to talk to people when they've already decided I'm guilty of something I couldn't even imagine," says Marc, shaking his head.

Chantal gets up, pours palm oil in a frying pan, and turns on the burner.

"Since then we've only focused on security," she says, cracking two eggs into the pan. "We've sent the staff back home. It's me and Marc, the drivers and the guards. We've even gotten new guards from the south to make sure they don't have any allegiances or ethnic connections to Likanni. No one has been attacked per se, other than the local driver whose car was stoned, but they sit in front of the office day and night, waiting for us to come out. Today is the first day we've had peace. I've wanted to talk to them—"

Marc completes her sentence. "But I told Chantal, no. It's too big a risk. I told her to wait for you. No one's connected with the

54

locals the way you are. Chantal and I may be running the place, but this is out of our control."

"One of the proposals by senior management," I say, "is that you leave. It would have to be done respectfully, of course, so that the villagers don't feel as though we're sneaking you out of the country to avoid the issue. You *have* been here a long time."

Marc leans forward and frowns. "I don't want to leave. Not like this. Not when I've been accused of the most disgusting thing. We have to fix this. And"—he looks at Chantal—"we have new initiatives on the go that I'd like to see through."

I'm strangely impressed by Marc. I thought he would want to be on the first plane out of here. That he'd fold up Likanni like a cloth napkin at the end of a meal.

Chantal puts a plate of fried eggs in front of me with a "voilà."

I look up questioning and she laughs. "You look hungry."

There's a nice feeling in the room. The three of us up well past midnight, eating, sharing, in solidarity. Wanting to fix things for Lele. It's nice to be in common cause with other humans who aren't just in my head or on a screen. Maybe all is not lost for me.

"How are you?" asks Chantal. "How's life back in California? I always imagine you doing yoga by the beach and drinking smoothies."

"There's definitely yoga and smoothies." I think of Steven making himself smoothies in the morning, before his run, neglecting to make one for me. Then I lie. "Life's good. A kid, work, husband, you know. It's weird not to be in the field though, to be among the senior administrators, working from my computer in a coffee shop. It doesn't feel real."

"Sounds like heaven. Do you have a swimming pool?" says Chantal.

I laugh. "Yes. Yes, we do." It does sound like heaven. Why isn't it? "To be honest, I'm still reeling from my conversation with Paulsie. I hadn't realized the victim was Lele," I admit.

Marc grimaces. "They should have told you. Chantal and I gave headquarters all the facts so they could prepare you. This must be a shock."

"It is, but I'm even more determined to find out what's happened," I say.

"The trouble is we don't even fully know what we're being accused of. We hear bits and pieces," Chantal says.

I'm about to tell them what Paulsie revealed, when Marc yawns. He bites it back, his hand a polite mask over his mouth. "Mesdames, I have to get to bed."

Chantal gets up. I was hoping she'd stay and gossip, but I'm jet-lagged and she isn't.

"I can wash your dish," she says.

"No, no, it's fine. Thanks. I'll clean up. You guys head to bed."

Marc stops and looks back. "Let us know if you need anything. Thanks again for coming on such short notice."

I smile, surprised at the gratitude. I say good night and watch them leave.

It's nice to see them getting along. Marc never quite accepted Chantal when she was hired to replace me, effectively becoming his boss. He had worked under me for years, and she was new to the charity. He put up a stink, but headquarters remained steadfast. The optics of hiring a female director were far better. And frankly she was far more likable. Marc, though immaculate at his job, never exuded enough warmth to be the face of the work. Since then, he challenged every decision Chantal took, rubbing his Likanni experience in her face, making her second-guess all her choices. Every time I've visited them in the last few years, I've had to address their issues.

I wash the dish so cockroaches don't feast on my food remains. Marc seems to want to get to the bottom of this; he wants me to talk to Lele. Not a single gesture or look appeared suspicious. He's still Marc, not Marc-the-rapist. It's not any kind of proof, but it's something.

The dish soap is imported, like everything else. I shine the surface of the white plate. What joy there is in accomplishing a simple task. Something that can be started and finished without doubt. There's not enough of that in the world.

The situation here is messy; I'm going to have to navigate cautiously. My departure date is in three weeks and I want to resolve everything beforehand. I wipe my hands on a smelly dishtowel and pull out my phone. Time to start reporting back.

Dear Burton,

I've arrived in Likanni. Things are indeed quite tense, but I'm confident I can resolve the situation. Marc and Chantal are doing their best. I've managed to speak with a few villagers and gotten them to stop protesting.

One thing I ask is that you give me some time. I must speak with the local community and gain their trust. I'll make sure we do things the right way, that we give voice to the aggrieved, while still celebrating our work.

I will keep you updated.

Warm regards,
Maya

Firm. Confident. Masculine even. It's nice to be needed in this way. As though I bear answers.

I switch off the kitchen lights. The moths fighting to get burned on the naked bulbs are suddenly lost.

7

I chose this life of an aid worker, or a humanitarian, or whatever they call us these days, when I was twenty-three, after a classic coming-of-age European backpacking trip with friends. As we sat in youth hostels and met boys with odorous backpacks, we discovered how inconsequential we were, how little we had seen. Sacramento had been our whole world. It was nothing. A drop in a huge bucket.

Our fellow travelers had stories from Goa and Morocco. They had gone to Thailand, seen the kindness of the Tuareg. I had no idea where Goa and Morocco even were. The only thing I had been taught about strangers was not to trust them too much.

It was on one of those hostel nights in Amsterdam that I met Roanne, an American. She sat on the stoop, smoking incessantly, her hair a mess, loose and tangled, unlike my fellow American students who curled their eyelashes and created voluminous manes. She had just completed her first stint at MSF and was deeply troubled. She had fled to Amsterdam to lose herself in high afternoons and boozy evenings.

One such evening, we sat on the front steps of the hostel smoking cigarettes. She described how she couldn't erase the memory of a thirteen-year-old boy who had carried his sixteen-year-old brother on his back for three days to reach one of their clinics. The sixteen-year-old had been suffering from malaria along with malnutrition, and he died, from dehydration, half-way through the journey. The boy arrived at the clinic, dead brother strapped to his back, exhausted, disheveled, with blistered, bleeding feet, but full of hope for an antidote. He dropped his brother's body on a bed and waited for Western doctors to perform their famous miracles on an illness that was very much treatable. He sat hunched but expectant, unable to straighten his own back after the arduous trek.

Roanne knew the minute she saw them that nothing could be done. The doctors examined him out of politeness, but it was clear, the older boy was dead. And it was Roanne who had to share this news. She winced as she told me of the noises she had made, of the strange words she had formed to tell this young boy that his brother was no more.

The younger boy stayed in the medical camp for a day, lying on his side, silent, reacting to nothing. He stared at his brother's body until it was covered with a white sheet. Then he rose and left the camp, despite Roanne's protests, and began the long return home, alone, a new curl in his sad posture. His brother was buried in a foreign village without traditional rites, wrapped in the white sheet of permanence, donated by MSF.

Roanne smoked cigarette after cigarette, rubbing her eyes. She told me she had spent weeks trying to forget the defeated look in the boy's eyes. That kind of futility was something she couldn't grasp. It didn't fit with her American dream insides, of working hard and getting what you want. As she spoke of the boy's trauma, I stared at her with fascination.

This was a life worth living, I thought. I saw her biting her nails, grabbing at her hair, touching her face, looking oddly mature though she was only a couple of years older than me. Everything about her was sexy. The pained anxiety, the fidgeting, the buttons of her denim shirt carelessly undone, her hair flying as she moved her head, the cigarette lodged between fingers. Her frustrated low voice, saying she couldn't remember either brother's name. I wanted those stories. I wanted to do something meaningful. I wanted to be this careless with my body, this comfortable in it, taking it to far-off places. Mostly, I wanted to cradle that thirteen-year-old boy in my arms, comfort him, tell him he wasn't alone and that he had been brave.

I was naive.

———

I deal with orphans. That's what I do here. I oversee the orphanages in three countries to ensure they are meeting their milestones, making good use of funds. I review their programming, human resources, and communications plans. I look over their budgets and design for the future. My charity is an internationally recognizable brand, whose clever catchphrase everyone knows. Hollywood stars speak soulfully on our behalf. We're not the UN but are well respected. We have clout. Our emotional commercials on late-night television make people cry. And yes, they show skinny children walking barefoot in rubble, because that makes people send money. And money is what we need to make it all happen.

A few months into this job, I was posted to Likanni. It was not where I wanted to live. I wanted to be in the hubbub of the capital, where I would mingle with expats and other first-worlders in an exotic context. I wanted to have hard days but social nights. The capital had gyms, it had clubs, it had writers' festivals, along with a light genocide. It had men to meet and lots of foreigners. It had Le Paradis. Every third car was a Land Cruiser with a painted logo—Médecins du Monde, GIZ, WHO, WFP, OCHA, UNDP, UNOPS, UNICEF—a vehicular alphabet soup in which the city swam. It felt alive. Like I didn't have to give up everything to live in this country. Like my Western brethren was still around.

Likanni, by comparison, was like descending into a quiet tomb. It had wide open spaces that swallowed up sound in its sleepiness. Its poverty wasn't the frenetic sort of the city, where people are piled on top of each other in noisy, vibrant shantytowns, the kind that artists and musicians emerge from. It was the kind that scrapes at the soil where nothing grows. The kind that's sparse and slow and has been the same since the last millennium.

My first week in Likanni, I stepped outside our office one morning to do yoga. There was a largeness around me; I felt I could touch the sky. With so few people, it felt private. As I grew tall into tree pose, a local woman, toddler in tow, walked toward me. I stopped and smiled. She smiled back. There was a large gap between her two front teeth and what looked like a tattoo on her forehead. Her eyes were gray, which I've since learned is a sign of semi-blindness caused by cooking over smoky firewood, but at the time looked exotic.

I was charmed. New job. Stretching in the open air. A curious village woman with mystical eyes walking toward me. A bumbling toddler holding her skirt, following along. A quiet serenity holding us in. I said hello.

She gave me a wide smile, her face almost vulgar in its teeth and bone. She came close, grabbed the toddler, and extended him to me. I laughed. Maybe this was a thing. I had seen many first-worlders posing with local children for pictures. She must have thought I wanted to do the same. I held him awkwardly, repulsed by the white crust at his nose and eyes.

61

She turned and walked away. I thought it was cultural misunderstanding, some joke or tradition I was missing. Maybe she needed a babysitter, maybe the child belonged to one of our groundskeepers. I stood there uncertain, stuck in place, afraid I would offend by calling out and afraid not to.

As she got further, I realized this wasn't a joke. She was walking away. She wasn't turning around; she wasn't waving. The toddler wriggled in my arms and stuck a dirty palm on my cheek.

"Hey," I called out to the woman. My voice loud, booming across the open field, then eaten by Likanni's stillness.

She began running.

I ran after her, the child bopping uncomfortably in my arms. He giggled. He slowed me down. I didn't know what side to shift his weight to. I'd never run holding a child before.

"Hey," I yelled again. That woman was fast. That little woman, those teeth and bone, she ran like I've never seen anyone run, her frame becoming a dot on the horizon.

I was out of breath, and she'd had a pretty solid head start. Frantic, I returned to my office and stormed into my then superior's office.

"This woman, she handed this kid to me and left," I exclaimed to Natasha.

She barely looked up from her screen, her hand curved on the mouse, brows knitted. "Yeah, that happens sometimes," Natasha said, clicking away at numbers on a spreadsheet.

That was my introduction to Likanni.

A few months in, overwhelmed by the sight of mothers leaving their children, pretending they were orphans, I decided to be brave. Burton was visiting our office. He was the head in Geneva. During one of our staff meetings, despite being new and the youngest, I said, "I've noticed a trend of women leaving their children because they have no means to support them.

Perhaps we should start preventative programming focused on mothers."

Burton and Natasha exchanged bemused looks.

"Stick to the mandate for now. There are a plethora of organizations working on maternal health and women's opportunities. *We* must focus on the orphans," Burton said.

A few years later, when raiding gangs raped local women and created a surge of unwanted pregnancies, I insisted we needed to work on reconciliation and peacebuilding. Burton scoffed. Those issues were too big. We were to leave them for the larger organizations—ones with soldiers and diplomats. But I had no faith in those institutions. They spoke of ceasefires and treaties, not of little bodies that we had to deal with. What would diplomats say to stop marauding child soldiers who were taught to rape? What would diplomats say to child soldiers who were creating scores of their own babies in battered women and villages? Charities like mine, we could hold up those babies of mixed ethnicities to child soldiers' faces. We could show them these infants with eyes and mouths that were the aftermath of their acts. I was convinced that if a child soldier peered into a smaller life wearing his facial features, something would change. But Burton ignored me.

Then I went on about poverty. "We're getting so many orphans because people are poor. They don't know what to do with these children. We need to help them create jobs, earn a living."

I was told not to duplicate the work of other international organizations, to avoid stepping on their toes. So I did. I protected the invisible toes of UN bureaucrats, of well-wishing aid groups, of Western countries' diplomatic corps. Meanwhile, the number of toes in our care quadrupled.

When I was told for the fifteenth time that our-donors-are-telling-us-to-work-with-orphans-so-work-with-orphans-for-god's-sake, I stopped asking. I followed the mandate.

I started this career wanting to heal the world of its ills. I've since learned that when you make a career out of helping the starved, you somehow become part of whatever is starving them. It's impossible not to—being the one with air-conditioning and safe drinking water, laughing with fellow first-worlders, only screwing first-worlders, while the ones you want to save live in the periphery. You take their photographs, dramatic close-ups, catching every crease of their foreheads, every bead of sweat, every expression of desperation, but you're the one holding the camera. You empathize in the moment. You feel their pain, in the moment. You interview them, talk about them, maybe you write their stories, in the moment. Then you get up and walk back into your own life, abandoning their pain like orphans.

A few decades before I started working in Likanni, a well-meaning missionary working for our charity decided to open the gates of adoption. He was often approached by American couples wanting to adopt. They wanted to save kids, show that Blackness could meld with Whiteness, that the desolate could be welcomed to the rich world.

To hell with the mandate, I imagine Jean-Michel Toussaint thinking. And so, with blessing from the board, he started a small parallel organization to match kids with loving families. A win-win situation, truly the work of God.

The program worked beautifully for a few years. Then strange things happened. There was the couple who discovered their child had a physical disability and left her on the tarmac at the airport of the capital city. They had wanted to leave her earlier, in Likanni, at the hotel, at the restaurant, back at the orphanage, anywhere really, but they didn't want to face any follow-up questions or their guilt. And so, they left the baby at the last possible place, near men wearing protective earmuffs, loud propellers, people waving goodbye to planes. In the chaos of travelers with their numerous children in frilly dresses and oversized suits, overflowing multicolored canvas bags, no one noticed Janie Sanders delicately placing a Moses basket on the ground as if stopping to tie her shoelace and then rushing onto the plane right before the doors closed. By the time the child was discovered following the mayhem of departure, no one knew who it belonged to. The airport was hardly high security. There weren't any cameras around to document the appearance of the mysterious child clothed in an imported onesie.

Janie Sanders cried the whole way home. She had never thought of herself as someone who could abandon a child, especially when she had tried so hard to conceive. But she knew a child with a lifelong disability was not something she could handle. Her husband, Charles, felt both tantalized and disgusted by what they'd done. Their marriage broke up a few years later. It was a relief that their ugly secret would no longer be reflected in each other's eyes every morning over coffee. After Janie signed the divorce papers, she wrote a letter to Jean-Michel Toussaint confessing what they had done, albeit anonymously.

I imagine Jean-Michel distraught, disrupting his practice of biscuit dipping in coffee, and pulling out all sorts of tan-colored files to identify the child and parents. I've been told he never knew which child had been abandoned. Resigning himself to the will of God, he concluded that this had been the child's fate to begin with. Besides, he had bigger worries. Roger Allens, a British man and generous donor, who had assisted him in finding adoptive families all over the U.K., had just been charged with pedophilia and child slavery. Apparently, his immaculate estate in Surrey had contained a child prison, laden with stuffed toys and beds on which he could teach children the arts of human desire.

Jean-Michel Toussaint began to thoroughly detest adults and children. One night, he walked off with a wheelless suitcase. He left his files, his books, his photographs, his Bible, his crucifix. He took his clothes, a pair of thick leather sandals, a thermos someone had once brought him as a gift, along with all the money in the organization's bank account to which he had access. It wasn't too large a sum, but still.

When this all came to light, the mandate hammer came down hard. My organization, which had affiliated itself with Jean-Michel's, broke all ties and ceased involvement with international adoptions.

Meanwhile, Jean-Michel Toussaint's departure left devastated couples around the globe. There were hopeful mothers and fathers readying baby rooms, announcing the news to their colleagues, sharing cake with family, cheersing champagne. Many had received presents, shared tears of joy at their impending parenthood. In one instant, Jean-Michel's departure swiped their aspirations bare. There was no way to refund prospective parents or ease their pain with new adoptive arrangements.

Rumor had it that Jean-Michel left the suitcase of money in a church. There's no evidence of this ever happening, but it added to the lore.

I blame Jean-Michel Toussaint for the restrictive mandate I inherited. I also feel sorry for him—imagine believing you're doing something good and finding out it inflicted devastating harm. It must be impossible to believe in anything after that. I wish he had some way of knowing that decades after his disappearance, we received a letter written in shaky handwriting, a mea culpa, as well as a sizable bequest from the Janie Sanders estate, which ended up supporting so many orphans. Some good did come out of his work.

As for those families that never received the children they had paid for, some simmered quietly, others came with private investigators to unearth what had happened, some wanted to sue. Many complained about the organization to the media, tarnishing the brand and reducing donations. They had all gotten screwed by the few who had messed up the adoption food chain.

I guess that's the part that is too much to stomach sometimes: that anything can be made ugly. And somehow, unwittingly, we can become a part of it. I imagine Jean-Michel Toussaint, smoking a fat cigar somewhere, shunning God, keeping a stash of money in a wheelless suitcase. He's in Spain, he's in Greece. He's rich, he stopped caring, because what's the point?

Or I see Jean-Michel Toussaint the night he left, walking slowly toward the river. His eyes weeping rivers of their own. He clutches the suitcase full of money and walks into the river. Like most men of the village, he does not know how to swim. He and his suitcase sink in the darkness, drowned, because what's the point?

8

The roosters are loud this morning. There's the eager one that starts before daybreak, showing off. Then the others join in a cacophony that endures even when the sun is visible to all. There's a frenetic energy to it, of getting the day started, of not missing a moment of sunlight. Of rising with the rest.

I lie without moving until my own rooster caws: it's my mother on Skype. I should pretend I'm not available; I dread being summoned to that world when I'm far away. It's much easier to pretend it doesn't exist. But one parent has to be accessible. I answer.

She appears, strawberry-blond hair in the same short curls she's had for forty years; her eyeglasses hang precariously on the tip of her nose. She looks down at the keyboard, her eyebrows furrowed, befuddled. Her face is rosy, almost cartoonish in this room.

"Mom, I'm here."

She looks about.

"Up here on the screen," I say.

"Oh hi, honey." She looks happy, marveling over the miracle of technology that brings me to her, no matter how many times she's used it before. I look at her plump reddish cheeks, her small blue eyes, and remember that in the eight years I lived here, I never once let my parents visit. They wanted to. But I was too worried about their security, the hardship of traveling on dirt roads, of being too far from a hospital. Likanni for them exists only in the mouthful of words I gave them. Words that came in long streams and colorful adjectives in the first years, then dried into curt monosyllables near the end of my tenure.

"What's up? It must be late there."

"It took so long putting Chloe to bed today. She kept telling me one knock-knock joke after another." Mom laughs.

I think of Chloe's fair body tangled in cozy blankets, kicking sheets with scrawny limbs. I blink out the image.

"Yeah, she does that. Everything good otherwise? I hope she isn't tiring you out."

"I gave in and let her sleep in bed with me and Grandpa," she confesses.

"That's okay. Your house, your rules."

"So, the reason I'm calling is"—she pauses and takes off her glasses—"a little girl in her class was talking about adoption."

"Okay."

"Chloe was asking me a lot of questions—whether I know someone that has been adopted," she says nervously.

"You can tell her the truth, Mom."

"I thought you might want to have that conversation. It's one of the big ones," she says.

"Oh, we've already talked about it. She's probably just confirming what I've told her. Just tell her your part in the story, after all you're the one who did the adopting," I say. My parents scooped me from Bangladesh when I was three. My mother was a hippie;

I was a kid with thick curly black hair who didn't speak. I don't remember a thing about my life there, the language, or the people. I just remember an airplane. Something immense and alarming.

"You sound so powerless when you say that," she says sadly.

"Don't get defensive. It's not a big deal for me. I want Chloe to know that there's nothing taboo about adoption, and you're so good at describing things. You should tell her how you found me. She'll love that story."

"What if she doesn't think of me as her grandma anymore?"

I laugh. "Come on. That'll never happen. Besides, it's slim pickings for her right now."

She laughs uneasily.

"Just be honest with her. There's no reason why my adoption needs to be secretive—or shameful."

That gets her.

"Oh honey, I'm not ashamed. I just don't want her to worry. You're gone so much, and Steven is so busy working, I don't want her to have any fears that *she'll* be abandoned. And I'm nervous. What if she starts to wonder what her biological grandmother is like?" The well-intentioned remark stings in so many ways.

"Well, given the life expectancy in Bangladesh, this hypothetical biological grandma is probably dead, so I don't think you have much to worry about. And Mom, are you okay? We've just talked for five minutes without you bringing up Obama."

There. That gets a giggle out of her and walks her away from the subject at hand. Mother, the Obama fan, can always be distracted. Since his recent second inauguration, her admiration is out of hand, and I'd much rather she harps on him than my absentee parenting.

"You should have seen him at yesterday's press conference. What charisma, what eloquence. I don't know why you want to be sitting in a war zone. It's a new dawn here, honey we are ushering in a true postracial society! You should be a part of this. There is so much to do right here."

I think of Trayvon Martin. Nice people like my mom love a Black president but easily forget Black children. I can tell she's about to start a long discussion on the virtues of our great country.

"I have to get my day started, and you should go get some rest," I say, stifling any chance for more talk.

Those early years of mine are a black hole of memory. They must be the reason why I don't fully understand how to mother a four-year-old. They must be the reason I can leave a daughter behind, while other mothers wouldn't dream of it.

My parents gave me a family, a country, a language. They gave me a sense of being and a story. The sperm-and-egg parents left me nothing but this dark skin. A skin I don't know. When I meet people from South Asia, they want to connect, talk about food or Bollywood; they want to find their familiarity. I have nothing to offer. I wear this skin like exotic fur—a fully, deeply, WASPy American with a mink coat that I wish I could shimmy out of. This skin has only given me a feeling of not knowing. It's the color of my abandonment, a promise of foreignness no matter where I go.

My parents tried, I think, but how could they connect me to a culture they didn't know? Once, they almost took me to a Bangladeshi restaurant. We drove to tacos instead. How would they introduce me to foods they couldn't pronounce? I was relieved. Questions were what I dreaded, and a waiter could ask about my heritage, what languages I spoke. I wouldn't have any answers, my lack of story becoming painfully apparent, especially to myself. In other circumstances, this skin rendered me adequately invisible: the Brown woman in a white world, an extra but not the lead role, your pharmacist but not a poster on your wall, functional but not desirable. It made me hide in plain sight, keeping my gaping histories to myself.

In Likanni, foreigner status was stamped and gifted to me. I was slightly more noticeable among Western peers. Between the binary of Black and white, I was the oddity who stood out, but in a good way. The locals gave me the same appreciation they gave the other first-worlders and I was finally living with white freedoms.

I stand in the shower and hum. I try not to look at the mold that has proliferated on the mildewed tiles. I manage, with drips of shockingly cold water, to wash out the bubbly shampoo bought in a Californian drugstore. It smells artificial, like invented fruit that exists only in plastic bottles. I'm finally released of the stench from the day before.

Things feel possible this morning. I need to get organized, call a meeting, devise a strategy. I put on a shapeless tunic and pants. The largeness of it swallows me, so my body cannot be assessed. I'm neither young nor shapely, but with men's eyes, you never know. They see things you don't. Their gaze lingers in places you wouldn't think. Every risk must be minimized in the field, so I float in a sea of cotton.

In the hallway, I see Chantal stumbling into the corridor from her room, half-asleep.

"Hey," I call out. My voice echoes off the tile and plaster. She closes her door, waves, and walks toward me. She's in her pajamas, a tank top with her nipples protruding and short cotton shorts. It's odd to see her padding about half-naked in what is usually a professional workspace.

"It's very early," she says, yawning. "Why are you up?"

"Jet lag. And the roosters," I answer.

"I'm going back to sleep. Tandi's been kind enough to leave us a bottle of milk and some groceries at the back door every day before dawn. She doesn't want any of the others to know she's helping us, so I try to get them before anyone sees the basket."

I check my watch. It's only a few minutes past five. "Why don't you go back to bed? I'll grab the food."

She looks relieved. "Thanks, M. I'll see you later in the day."

"Actually, let's meet at nine thirty in the boardroom. Please let Marc know if you see him, or knock on his door around nine. We need to get started," I say.

Chantal nods and heads back to her room. She seems surprised by my official tone.

I head downstairs and unlock the heavy metal back door. It creaks open, and I'm in a painting.

It's early, and though workers in this village are quietly at it, the morning is intimate, like it's only mine. Instead of grabbing the basket, I sit on the back steps. Goats and chickens roam about; who knows who they belong to. There is a relaxed disposition that can only be found in this part of the world, where resources are scarce but no one seems fierce over their possessions. The grass is a pale green, the sky white. A few scraggly trees dot the horizon, dramatic in their curves. There are six vegetable gardens out back, all of them raised, all of them first planted by my bare hands many moons ago. There was an Italian guy, Francesco, working with the Food and Agriculture Organization. He loved the earth and small gardens; he inspired me when he spoke of the miracle of growing things.

Two kilometers east from where I sit is a small enclave of huts and houses. That's where Chantal and Marc have their homes. Theirs are made of stone walls, roundish, to emulate the shape of the local mud homes with thatched rooves. One-bedroom homes, simple and comfortable, with all the amenities, large porches, open enough to the breeze and people calling in, surrounded by

73

gardens. Because of us, the neighborhood has modest drainage and plumbing. The founders of our charity insisted that staff live among the people, and for the most part it has served us well. Our employees live nestled in cozy communities, homes surrounded by green on little dirt roads. Places where neighbors speak to one another in the mornings about when it will rain, if it will rain. And even though our employees have more in their bank accounts than their neighbors, they are accepted.

I think of my own house back in California. A boxy structure of large windows and steel. A modern house with no history or ghosts, one that veers off the winding road into a private lot so that it's held secret from those driving by. Neighbors are not people you bump into, but people you make a plan to see if, oddly, you wish to. Otherwise you honk at them congenially when per chance your entries and exits onto long driveways co-incide with one another.

I inhale deeply. It's the smell of soil, of manure, of a fire crackling somewhere even though it's hot, probably to clear land or burn garbage. Giant birds swoop in the sky. *National Geographic* material, but here commonplace. Life back home withers away. I'm wearing the morning on my shoulders, engulfed in its magnitude. This place, it eats you up with its harsh softness.

The office in Likanni serves as a hub for four orphanages a hundred kilometers away in each direction. They are run by local staff who take care of the children, feed them, clothe them, educate them, entertain them, embrace them. They are all women except for the security guards and groundskeepers. Most of the women are spinsters, infertile, divorced, or without kin, women unable to find security with a man or family. The children become their everything, the orphanages become their home. We design it that way, leveraging their misfortune into dedication to the most vulnerable.

The Likanni office is staffed mostly by foreigners with two

or three locals for administrative tasks. It's the nerve center where budgets and school curricula are drafted, health and diet plans designed, supplies from beds to books procured, decisions made, policies designed. That's what I used to do: run the nerve center until I passed my baton to Chantal. I'd visit the orphanages once a month. It was my favorite thing to do, to go into those buildings with the colorful lettering, have the children run up to embrace me, clad in matching uniforms we had made for them. Those children were products of human disaster, but those places, the people who nurtured them, put them back together, piece after painstaking piece, so they resembled the sights and sounds of any other vibrant kids.

I would sit in classrooms, hear children recite their times tables. I would listen to staff complaints and appease them. I'd marvel at juvenile art and watch them play strange versions of tag. I'd monitor the state of bedrooms and buildings and hear stories about "problem" kids. I'd hear the children call all the women that worked there "Ma," and I'd feel that spread of warmth, that afterglow of charity. When I would drive back to Likanni after these oversight visits, I was convinced that our work was good; at the very least, we were giving these children a chance to laugh, to learn, and to call someone Ma.

And during that time, I hired Marc. It was me. How could I not? I saw how plain he was and recognized a man who wanted a legacy. This one would be a workhorse. He'd want a concrete thing to attach his name to, point at and drop into conversations: how he had saved a village, how he had carried orphans. That personality type is ideal for this line of work. The desire for a heroic-self story can make people move mountains.

Marc comes from an unremarkable place in France. Not Paris, or damp coastlines, or the ever-fragrant Provence, but somewhere in the middle of the country. Not quite a city but not a quaint town either—a manifestation of some urban plan from the seventies.

He spent the first few years after his university education in the French army. His mother, I believe, is a travel agent; his father works for an insurance company. Marc needed something to strive for, an antidote to the insignificance. I could see it in his eyes, even though I interviewed him through a laptop screen. He was ready to have a story, this man who was so orderly and structured.

Most of the first world guys who come here are pretty messed up. The women, they come with good intentions. They are troubled by the way the world works, the injustices, the suffering. They want to apply their university degrees, want to craft the future into something better, confident they can serve the world. They stay with diligent hands on stethoscopes, on trees, on children, until they realize they have to go back or they'll miss their window of fertility. A war zone is no place to conceive babies. Men in war zones do not make good fathers. Even if they are there as saviors.

The men. That's a different story. Some arrive fleeing predictable futures, chasing adventure and adrenaline. Others, incapable of functioning in a conventional lifestyle, want to move constantly, feeding off every human experience, evading boredom like a disease. Then there are the romantics, the poets at heart, sorrowfully passionate about the deprived, wanting to connect with the spirit of humanity to feed their own bottomless existential crises. They depart with many scribble-filled leather journals and black-and-white photographs. Others, meek in the first world, come to these poor parts to exercise some form of power. Those are the dangerous ones. They flex muscles they didn't know they had. They think of themselves as the rescuers, the experts, the ones who know better, and see the people they help as pitiful, weak, powerless.

It's not that any of these men have poor intentions; many are warm and generous. But there's always that common thread: hunger. They are hungry for experience, for adventure, for recklessness and intensity, which a structured and lonely Western life cannot deliver. Sometimes they don't even know they are lonely until they live here.

At first, they land good stories to impress their friends back in D.C. or London. But after a few more years in the field, more wild rides, more foreign experiences, they become unrelatable to their peers back home. They return with more stubble, more eccentricities. They've built latrines, gotten drunk with locals, learned about tribal traditions (the source of many a tattoo), and soon they belong to no place at all. They miss war but despise it. They hate violence but photograph it. They know the perpetrators but dine with them. And that hunger, it keeps growing, keeps gnawing until they end up adrift with an inability to connect with others.

They get used to saying goodbye to their families, to fellow expats who get transferred to other countries, to the locals, to passing loves. After a while, the quest for more unique experiences rings hollow, perpetually unsatisfying. For what is more intense than seeing normalized cruelty?

The Western world, where we come from, becomes a bore, unreal, like a shopping channel. Danger zones become exhausting. Conventions like raising a family or buying a home become mere clichés. In the face of chronic suffering, the desire for life slowly depletes, leaving behind a disagreeable shell of a person who can no longer go home and can no longer empathize with those around them. You've touched God's darkness when every oppressive thing has been seen and ceases to move you.

Yet Marc stayed the same. No tattoos or journals. No stubble even. As long as he had a purpose, an objective, he dove forward, seemingly satisfied, our work a permanent carrot before him. He ended up being more resilient than I was. I began to tatter, began to question, began to not feel.

That's why I'm going to get out of this work. I've carved my own little life in California. I embraced the conventions before it was too late. Those who come for my elaborate dinners, with ornate place settings and brass cutlery, don't know of the grand things I've witnessed, both beautiful and horrific.

It's lonely not to be able to share the world with those who inhabit it. People speak with such authority about the news, other countries, the good guys, the bad. Inside, I laugh a little. You've never been there, I whisper to myself. You don't know. But I've transitioned to Western normalcy with its small talk, orderly queues, loud news stations, and I stay quiet when I need to. Because you can't describe a village to people who think they know the world.

9

Marc and Chantal file stiffly into the room, a little late. Chantal, a hair taller than him. Marc looks like a suburban French dad, always in a short-sleeved button-up shirt, with the very top button undone, his Adam's apple bobbing in the gap. I'm at the table with my laptop open. They sit in chairs across from me. Chantal leans forward, while Marc sits back, arms crossed. It's a far cry from last night's amicable ambiance. I wonder what's happened, whether they've had an argument.

"Thanks for coming. Chantal, do you want to take the minutes?"

She looks around for a pen, frazzled. She should have come prepared. She's not usually this unprofessional.

"Here." I slide my laptop across the table to her. "Please use your discretion." Conversations loosen when not imprisoned on paper. "Alright, guys, we clearly have a situation. Thank you both for managing the best you can despite the circumstances."

Marc nods.

I continue. "I want to get back to business as usual. I want to see our staff return so that there aren't any gaps in our programming. But first we have to address this crisis."

They look at me expectantly. I shuffle papers. I'm unprepared as well, but I pretend.

"Our priority must be to address Lele's situation and reconnect with the community. Let them vent, argue, whatever they need; we need to hear them out. I'll meet with Lele's family, with Lele herself, with the elders. I can organize a community dinner. It may take some time, but that's the only way to exorcise the anger they have toward us and decrease any threats. We must plan for Lele's physical and mental health recovery. Paulsie said Lele is not speaking much. Her testimonial is what will drive whatever we do from here on out."

They nod in agreement. Marc looks more relaxed. A project, a purpose, that's what he's built for.

"Our second priority must be bringing the culprit to justice. Marc, I know this will be uncomfortable, but given the circumstances, you will not be a part of this process. I'm including you now for disclosure of the procedure, but from here on, Chantal and I will be handling community partners without you."

He winces, and I continue quickly. "We'll follow our standard protocols, of course, we'll interview every intern, every tech guy, every program officer, every driver—in other words, show the community that our staff is not above the law. The final decisions will be made at headquarters with HR and the board. But to be honest, I feel they are too removed from all of this. While the protocols do not encourage this, I think we should also interview any suspects in the community. There may be domestic factors at play."

I lean back in my chair, short of breath. I spoke faster than I intended, jumping into things without appropriate buildup. It's a strange thing. To discuss the assault of someone we know around a conference table. A conference table that she once sat around, with the accused across from me. How fast the words pool. How desperately I give violent actions a logistical bent and shape. No one says anything. Chantal types furiously while Marc looks at his hands.

"I understand where you are coming from, M," says Marc. "I agree, I shouldn't be a part of these conversations. But let us be clear. I have not been accused by Lele, it's her brothers that are making these accusations. We are just assuming that she's in agreement with all this."

"Unfortunately, that's all we can go on for now," I reply. "This is what we need to protect the brand from. If this story leaks, it'll go from allegations to perpetrator in a matter of seconds in the public's eye. Then goodbye donors, goodbye work, and God help the orphans."

"You don't think that treating a staff member like a rapist will hurt the brand?" Marc looks at me from behind his glasses, calm but angry.

"Whoa. When did I do that? You know the protocols as well as I do. The accused should not be involved with anything to do with the victim. And, of course, if Lele clarifies that you have nothing to do with this, then the point is moot. But the locals are buying this narrative, and we have to probe further as to why, and what we can do to address it."

"And how are we supposed to chase a culprit in the community?" Marc asks. "What right do we have to accuse someone? We're not the police, we have no jurisdiction, and if you don't find someone, then in everyone's mind, I'm the rapist."

"I'll work on it," I promise, realizing I haven't thought through any details. And Marc loves details.

"How? You haven't been living here, Maya. You don't what's going on. There's all sorts of Black awakening stuff on the radio, there are groups that want all the charities gone. This is the context in which we are operating. We have to be cautious that accepting the slander of one colleague doesn't put all the foreigners and aid work at risk."

"I'll follow a process where everyone is heard, that we are as fair and transparent as possible. I would never put any of our colleagues at risk."

Marc is quiet. He's giving me that destabilizing look: he doesn't believe in what I'm doing.

"When I informed headquarters that this was happening and suggested you be brought in, Burton told me, quite clearly, that headquarters will deal with the crime only if it was committed by a staff member. What they want *you* to manage are the relationships, the security, and the goodwill of the locals."

I'm his boss's boss, but Marc has a way. Suddenly he's telling me what my bosses want me to do. I lick my lips, annoyed. "Of course, headquarters doesn't want to get too involved in the crime. But the fact is, a girl says she's been violated by one of us. If we want to have any legitimacy in the future, we have to overtly demonstrate justice." I tap my pen noisily on the table. "If we get ahead of this, we'll look better to our donors, to the community. Our staff will be more respected in the long run. We need to set an example, show them that this won't be like the other rapes, that there are real consequences."

"No one is stopping you from doing that," says Marc. "But you should be diverting attention away from this crisis through incentives and opportunities, rather than have the whole village following some wild goose chase. Build them up instead of fracturing them further. We'll end up with vigilante justice and I'll be the one crucified."

"Maya's right," Chantal interjects. "It's not enough to just give them gifts of livestock; we have to find the person that hurt Lele."

"What a surprise," sneers Marc.

"Oh come on," Chantal explodes.

"No, you come on. The procedures are clear. Our mandates cover our staff and people on payroll. In case of wrongdoing, a superior is to investigate, and a safeguards officer is to be made available by headquarters to ensure everyone's rights are protected. HR and the board are to determine validity of claims, that's it. Nowhere are we told to chase people in the community like Sherlock fucking Holmes—we have no policing mandate. It's dangerous and puts us at risk."

"You don't see the giant hole in these procedures?" Chantal argues. "HR will recommend a decision to the board on evidence, and where do you think they will get this evidence? Who knows when this safeguards person will come? It may take months. By then, everyone will have forgotten the details of what happened to Lele. And what about Lele? Doesn't she deserve our help to keep her safe in her own village?"

They bicker and I watch these colleagues of mine that I have known for so long. A vein protrudes on Chantal's otherwise smooth forehead. Here we are, the three of us, fumbling with things we don't quite understand. Rape and justice and reconciliation and jurisdiction. Their voices get louder. Marc wants to use this crisis to give the locals more schools, community gardens, anything they've ever wanted even if it's outside our scope; he's sure the board will give in times of crisis. Chantal accuses him of trying to buy the community's silence. Her outrage sets off another fiery back and forth. They tumble into their Frenchness. I'm fluent, but this language is their own, there's slang, the exaggerated *pffs*, *putains*, and arm gestures as if they're fighting over a parking spot.

I study Marc. This job, it makes us good at knowing one another. We've seen each other at our worst, through illnesses and trauma, through embarrassments of running to find a toilet after we've had worms in our guts. We've seen each other's frailties, been repulsed by them. We've been moored to this bizarre isolation. It's not like other workplaces where one can be surprised that a colleague turned out to be a rapist. We really know one another. I know Marc's ugliness. I've seen it before. I've also seen the good. The man is smart, he's dedicated to his work, he'll spend hours trying to solve any problems we've run into. I've seen him undermine women, but I've never observed an ounce of predatory behavior.

"It's my name on the line," he says. "While you two run around playing detective, everyone is accusing *me*. I don't have time to wait around for you to find a possible suspect. I need things to calm down now." He points at me. "You have to talk to Lele and find out who did it. If it's one of ours, then we deal with it internally and fire the bastard. But we can't go after men in the community. Let's focus on healing rather than disrupting."

"I can't work here knowing there's a rapist in our midst," Chantal continues, smacking her hands on the table.

"I know this is a difficult topic, and all the more challenging because we care for Lele and one of us is being accused," I offer.

"Not one of us. Me," interjects Marc.

Chantal shares a guilty look with me.

"It's been hard, Maya. People think I raped a girl! I'm not sure what Lele has said or why. I don't know what my colleagues are thinking, whether they believe me. I can't leave this building. I can't even go to my fucking house." Marc holds his head in his hands.

Chantal looks at Marc with sympathy.

Did I forget about him in all of this? I need to change tracks. "Maybe you guys should walk me through exactly what happened that day. It might give us fresh ideas about what to do next."

Chantal has faint circles under her eyes. I've been too rash. This is a finer matter. I cannot be abrupt.

"Should we get some coffee before we begin?" I ask. It's one of the habits of working here. Before getting into substantive matter, people break for coffee. It's annoying when most get to meetings late and immediately break for long coffee sessions to socialize. But right now, we need this bit of Likanni tradition.

I push my chair back, but Chantal says, "Leave it, we'll get it." They disappear out of the room, Marc taking long strides toward the kitchen, Chantal trying to keep up. I hear their voices colliding, getting fainter as they go down the corridor.

I have a lot of questions. Why is Marc being accused? Did Lele actually say he did it, or did she just say his name? When did it happen and where was he during that time? Where was Chantal when all this was going on? Were there witnesses? Did anyone see Lele leave the compound? Could any of our other colleagues have done this? I received such a curt phone call about the whole thing. Burton could not even recall who the victim was. To him, in his office in Geneva, where he was most certainly getting ready to go to lunch in a restaurant with crisp white tablecloths, the foreign name was unimportant. What was important was the accusation and the threat to the brand.

I draw my laptop back to me. The wallpaper is a sunny picture of my smiling daughter. Chloe's face looks alien in this boardroom. How she's learned to smile this much is mystifying; happiness feels like such effort.

I browse online to connect to my own world. There's an email from my husband, the first since I've left, asking where the housekeeper has stashed the vacuum cleaner. The query itself, its intentions are questionable. He's never vacuumed a damn thing in his life. He sent it at nine thirty p.m. his time—what did he break? Maybe a champagne flute he was sharing with his mistress? He probably doesn't even know that you're not supposed to vacuum glass.

Rage climbs my body. It claws its way up, bit by bit. It hangs in my blood vessels, spreading into muscles. I feel myself swelling. I'm surprised. I haven't felt much of anything about this until now. I haven't felt much of anything for so long. This thing with my husband, it's been there, but hasn't, lurking behind me like a tail I can't see. I'm thousands of miles away, inhabiting another time zone; I'm going to be discussing rape over coffee, yet I see broken glass, a man hunting for a vacuum, a blond giggling in the background. His email condenses me to utilitarian purposes, the person who tells you where stuff is in the house.

My hands are in fists when Chantal and Marc walk back in. I'm so enraged I barely recognize them. They look like shadows, as though I've stared at the sun too long. I focus myself back into this space.

This boardroom. With its large, worn-out fake leather chairs with massive armrests that stick against one another. The table, chipped veneer. In Likanni, this is a five-star conference room. By other standards, it's a joke. The outlets hang out of the walls, held by colorful cables. Yellowed posters promoting our work curl on the walls alongside a large map of the area. I often think of the first newcomers who mapped this region, from high peaks to valleys, from thick foliage to sparse dry lands. Did they walk it inch by inch? Did they know which dirt paths turned into streams in the rainy season? I imagine they were Spanish or Portuguese with big fifteenth-century swirly hats, wondering how low these valleys go. No, they were probably French, well-heeled and short, with compasses and protractors. With the moral imperative to civilize.

"Voilà," says Chantal, as she places the tray on the main table. "When in Likanni . . ." referring to an old joke she and I share. When she was first hired, I had to traipse her from meeting to meeting to introduce her as my replacement. She was struck by how much coffee she was forced to consume, along with dry biscuits and countless spoons of white sugar, the Likanni way. Today, her tray contains three chipped white cups and saucers, a coffee pot, a plate of stale digestive biscuits, and a bowl filled to the brim with sugar.

Marc is empty-handed, desolate. He takes his spot beside Chantal again, as though we are in an interrogation room, me as the interrogator. I shut my laptop, pull out a chair next to me and rest my feet on it, as if we are all hanging out, shooting the shit. Trying to lessen the tension.

After pouring herself some coffee, Chantal asks, "What would you like to know?"

"Everything. Everything you have experienced, in order of when it happened."

Chantal clears her throat. "Well, it was a Wednesday, about eight weeks ago. I don't know if you know, but Lele has been helping us develop the weekly bulletin. Her reading and writing are quite strong now."

I beam inwardly—to think that Lele is advanced enough to write professional communications products.

"Every Wednesday, she would run from office to office to interview everyone. She then sent updates to headquarters to be printed for the Friday weekly bulletin. That day, she and I were running late. We had to go to Magania to meet UNICEF. We returned by five and only then started catching up with our work for the day. Lele told me that she would interview me last so that I could attend to my other work. But she never came back to my office. I saw her interview Tahiry. I worked till eight thirty that evening—I went to her cubicle to find her before I left. I thought she was being lazy, that if I had to work late, she should too. I was the last to leave that day. I told the guards to turn off the lights and went home. The next day her family sent word that she was sick. I was surprised because she had never taken a day off before, but to be honest I was so busy with completing our grant proposal, I didn't follow up," Chantal says, sheepishly.

"Then what happened?"

"She didn't come in for a week. I was going to follow up, but then the donor visits started and all of us were busy taking them around to the orphanages and selling our five-year plan. Tandi told me Lele was still sick. I told her to make sure that Lele saw the doctors we use and we would pay for it. A few weeks after that, Marc and I were accosted and that's when I found out what had happened," Chantal explains.

Marc clears his throat, then says in a gentle voice, "She did interview me, so whatever happened to her must have happened after my interview. Lele came into my office. She made fun of how neat everything was. She sat down, asked me questions for about five minutes, then left. I told her about the pilot training program we're setting up with the national university, and that was it."

"You guys didn't hear anything? No sign of a struggle? Any raised voices? I know it's not PC—but did she seem okay? Did anyone see her crying or acting any differently?"

They both shake their heads.

"Did you ask the guards if they saw her leave?"

"Yes, I checked. They said she was in a hurry. We assumed it was because it was after dark. They mentioned she forgot to say good night," says Chantal.

"Do you know who she interviewed after Marc? Chantal, you said you saw her interview Tahiry . . . Was this before or after Marc?"

"Tahiry was the first person she interviewed. We've asked the staff. Marc was the last interview," says Chantal.

"You can see why I'm suspected," says Marc. "She left my office and there were at least forty minutes before she left the building. Something happened in that time."

"And you checked the time of her departure with the guards?" I ask.

"Yes," they respond in unison.

"What about any video footage? Are the cameras still installed in the lobby?" I ask.

Chantal nods. "We've seen the footage. You can have a look if you want."

"And—" I pause, choosing my words. "How does she seem?"

"It's hard to tell. The video is fuzzy. She's holding her purse to her body, passing through very quickly, maybe a little hunched," says Chantal.

"What did Tandi say when you sent her to see Lele?"

"She said Lele was ill, and it looked serious, but that her family did not accept the contact information for our physicians. I was about to visit myself, but you know, with donor visits it's hard, you're busy with them all day and then for dinners—I had no time. Before I could visit, a group of local people showed up to the office demanding to see Marc. I thought they wanted his advice on some matter, so I let them into his office. They began yelling and throwing things off his desk. One guy kept saying, "I know what you did!" They left after trashing the place. We were so overwhelmed, M. We called the capital for more guards. Luckily the donors had already departed. It could have been a disaster if one of them was attacked."

"A few days after that," says Marc, "I was at home and people started throwing rocks through my windows. I contacted headquarters and moved into the office."

"Did you know why you were being targeted?" I ask.

"No. There's a new group stirring anger toward NGOs, trying to make it look like we're all a bunch of racists. I thought it was because of them. But when I checked with the other charities, they said they had no problems," he says.

Chantal chimes in, "It's only when I went to the market a few days later that the village women cornered me and told me that Marc had—he had hurt Lele, and they demanded I do something about it. I came back and talked to Marc. He had been accosted by her brothers that very day. Other staff members were verbally abused at the bar. I panicked and sent everyone home and called Burton. We didn't know how far this anger could go. I didn't want to risk anyone's life."

"And the orphanages? Are they running as they should?" I ask.

"The local staff is doing what they can, but we've had no oversight. We haven't visited or dealt with their procurement needs in almost three weeks."

"Did you hold any community meetings?" I ask.

"Of course not. I was afraid of being mobbed," Chantal says.

"So, there's been no communication between you and the community? What about some of the sister organizations? Have they offered to act as intermediaries? I had someone from the Danish ministry ask me about this. Word is getting around. Who have you told outside of the organization?" I try not to sound critical.

"We haven't told anyone; I have no idea how the information has leaked. It's probably Lele's family. As for the community, we can't talk with them. Since we've sent the staff away, there's been a mob standing outside the building protesting. In all my years here, this is the most frightened I've been," says Chantal.

"I don't think you understand how stressful this has been," says Marc. "Before trying anything, we asked headquarters for advice, which is why they've sent you. Any day now people could beat down the door."

I think of how easily Paulsie and her friends walked away. How they shared my water bottle.

"Has headquarters suggested a leave or suspension for you?" I ask Marc.

Chantal jumps in. "There really hasn't been a formal complaint brought forth by the community; we're not even sure what the accusation is. Till now this has been more like a community uprising against us as a whole, rather than an accusation of sexual assault."

"What sort of formal complaint do you expect Chantal? They are protesting outside of the building. If that's not a complaint, I don't know what is."

"Well, we have partnerships with the community leaders. No one came to speak to me. We have local staff. They haven't reached out either," says Chantal.

"The local staff could have been nervous to bring it up when it's one of their bosses being accused. Did you interview the staff?" I ask. I'm irritated at them, at myself. I feel like we're handling this awkwardly, not thinking of the things we should be.

"Of course. I have notes from all the meetings if you want to read them. I conducted them alone, but feel free to do your own."

"Has headquarters conducted an internal investigation of the rest of the staff?"

"I'm not sure who they've spoken to. They spoke to Marc and me extensively, and said they would send you in for support. A safeguards person will come eventually. That's all I know," Chantal explains.

There are a few moments of silence. Marc hasn't touched his coffee.

"I hate to ask you this, Marc, but did you and Lele have any friction, any relationship of any kind?" I ask.

Chantal shakes her head.

"What are you insinuating?" Marc asks me.

"Marc," Chantal warns.

Marc puts his hand up. "I'd like to address what Maya is afraid to ask." He leans forward and stares me dead in the eyes. "Lele is a child, like the other children we care for. The only relationship I've ever had with her is a protective one. The same as you've had with her. I'm a senior colleague. She is starting her career. I've always made sure that she has been treated equally by the international staff. I've been her counsel when she has needed it; I've given her advice about what to study down the road. It's a shame anyone would sully our interactions." Not a blink, not a flutter. He looks hurt.

"Was anyone on staff treating her badly?" I ask.

91

"They had a tendency to pass menial tasks on to her, or not invite her to social events." Marc pauses. "But let's clarify something: I've worked here for ten years, ten years during which you have observed me closely. I have never had any kind of romantic or physical relationship with any local woman. To be frank, that is simply not my preference. I'm an easy target as one of the white men around, despite the fact that I have no interest in these women."

I'm taken aback, but where to start? The selectivity of his desire? The revulsion within it? It's a comment I've heard in the field, often from Europeans, usually after a few drinks. But the race thing doesn't seem right. Nobody messes with white people here, except for thefts or kidnappings for ransom. Anger against Westerners usually comes out in vulgar graffiti on some broken wall. No one has time to set up an elaborate scheme to frame a staff member of a charity. But I haven't lived here in five years; maybe the tensions are worse.

"I'm sorry," says Marc. "I want to understand why this has happened, why have they come after me." He takes off his glasses and rubs his abnormally red face.

The three of us sit quietly. I'm lost, deluged by guilt. Guilt for Lele, guilt for Marc, guilt that I'm not handling this as I would if I didn't know the people involved.

"Why don't we break for the day? Chantal, can you send me the staff list with their contact numbers? I'd like to interview them. Let's convene again after I've chatted with the family, and we can go from there."

We slowly rise, picking up our cups and saucers. Ordinarily there would be small talk, some jokes at the end of a meeting. Today there's none of that. We've resolved nothing; I've led them to nothing. One of us is suffering more than the other two and I don't know what name to give his pain.

"Does anyone have a cigarette?" I ask.

"I thought you quit. What happened to your healthy California lifestyle?" Chantal smiles.

"I'm taking a break from it. I think we all deserve a smoke in the open air," I answer.

"I miss the open air," says Marc as we file toward the kitchen. I feel a twinge of guilt.

"I'll go grab smokes from my office," says Chantal.

Marc washes our cups, which is a meticulous affair as we have to conserve the water we get from the tank. I watch his slender body, his precise movements, trying to detect any hints of rapesmanship. He's right: I have had years of observing him. When he's lashing out, when he's covering for a work error, when he's proud of what he's accomplished. I know his tells.

I lean back into the leather sofa in the kitchen and close my eyes. I fall asleep. It's the kind of sleep where I feel I died a little, my organs collapsed, drool went free, everything surrendered. I have no dreams; I disappeared from the arc of time. When I wake up, it is dusk outside, and five cigarettes and a lighter sit on the dining table. I've missed the whole day.

10

Night here crashes in, obliterating everything. It's nothing like where I live. It is absolute in its inkiness. You walk in it blind, unable to see your own limbs. You live on sounds and smells, hoping your next step lands on something solid.

I want to go outside for a cigarette but am afraid of the monstrous bugs that could fly at my head. Not to mention the slithering of snakes in the grass. There are too many little big threats.

I walk over to the guards to find a creative way of discovering who is Cyril and who is Benoit. No name tags. They wear matching expressions, blinking in unison, looking bored. I half-jokingly tell them that I want to go out to smoke but am scared. The one I think looks more like a Cyril doesn't seem like he jokes very often, and he proposes to stand outside with me, with his gun. I laugh. "You can't shoot mosquitos," I say. He stares back.

The door closes behind me. It's like this place has a second life at night. Like the earth is breathing out, exhaling its sighs, its whimpers of pain, its aches from the broiling day. The crickets, the fireflies, a multitude of other forms of existence make their songs. I sit on the front steps and light my cigarette, relishing the sound of flame igniting paper. I don't even like smoking. I like sitting for a moment, inhaling, hearing paper burn. A pause, the cigarette an hourglass.

We are surrounded by villages that have no electricity. In recent years, there are new lights dotting the landscape. In addition to stars and oil lanterns, there are flickers from old Nokia cellphones, fires from camping child soldiers, solar lamps donated by some environmental NGO. Sometimes you can make out swirls of white cooking smoke against the black. It's romantic, the way the smoke dances into the darkness, then gets consumed.

The night is in its first act, unfolding slowly, when I see the outline of a human form walking toward the building's entrance. I panic. I'm about to bang on the doors to alert the guards. But there are video cameras and sensors on the driveway, and the one who looks like a Benoit swings the door open, bursting out as if he's in a Hollywood movie.

The person coming toward me shines the light from his phone on his face. "It's me, Fanon," he yells out.

"I know him," I say, uncertainly.

"Were you expecting him?" asks Benoit in a stern voice.

I wasn't, but I lie. "Yes, I was. Thank you, it's fine."

"Let us know in advance next time you expect a guest. We have to be vigilant," Benoit says in a quiet but frustrated voice and disappears inside. I did run this office for many years and know the security protocols inside out. I pretend not to be irritated. I miss our usual chatty security guards, who respected my authority. Who knows where Chantal found these killjoys.

I wave to Fanon. I can barely make him out, even with the greenish light he's shining upon himself. He's half swallowed up by Likanni's night, as if his head is free of his body.

"I see you," he calls out in a deep voice. I'm embarrassed. Of course he sees me. Fanon lives here. He's used to this darkness; his eyes become superhuman at night, unlike my citified ones. I'm from a place where our refrigerator, our microwave, our patio, everything has lights, as if any darkness will make us blind. We've lost the dark sense.

He walks over. There is an awkwardness between us. We are not friends, barely acquaintances, an embrace would be too warm, a handshake too bizarre. I quickly sit back down on the front steps and gesture for him to do the same.

"Cigarette?" I ask.

"I am too poor to develop cancer," Fanon answers.

I don't know how to respond. It's a joke, but it sounds like there's spite tucked in there. I light another one. I swirl the red end around and around, like a ribbon.

"You're right about the cancer. I don't really smoke. Only in Likanni," I justify.

"Why so?"

"I don't know. Being here, away from my home, feels like a break, like smoking won't affect my health," I say.

"Where do you live?" Fanon asks.

"In the United States."

"Is being here like holiday?"

I can't really see him, just an outline, a flash of teeth, of eyes. The steps are wide, he's sitting on one end and I'm on the other. He speaks properly, his French clearly enunciated. No dribbles of dialect.

"I've never thought of it as a vacation; there are too many problems. The militias, the violence, the hunger. But it's beautiful, I suppose that part is like a vacation," I say.

96

"Hm." His voice is low and velvety. He cocoons the sound in his mouth. One more night sound to accompany the others. I wonder what his concept of a vacation is. Probably visiting an aunt in their ancestral village.

"You were here for many years. Why did you depart?" Fanon asks.

I don't want to answer this question. "It got too hard."

"How so?"

This is a strange conversation. I don't know why he's here; I don't know why I'm answering. But as all things Likanni, it's unfolding, without planning. There's an honesty in these parts one has to surrender to.

"I suppose I was lonely . . . Friends were always leaving. Children kidnapped by violent gangs, witnessing the never-ending hunger— that was painful to see. It felt like every day I was starting over, and every day felt hard."

"Yes, we would like to depart at times, but there is no manner to escape."

"I felt guilty when I left. I had a choice but friends I left behind didn't."

"Do you have friends in the village?" he asks.

"Of course," I answer.

"No, no, I do not mean the foreigners. I mean friendships with villagers. People you write to? People you invite to America?"

I didn't have local friends after Anders left. I hid from them, my rejection too obvious, the empty space Anders had occupied too blatant. I had neighbors, I had the girl who cut my hair, the guy who owned the bar we hung out in, the guy who fixed my car, the local staff. I had people like that with whom I would share smiles and pleasantries, but that I would forget the minute I sat on a plane. Like extras in a movie.

"The problem is the white people all stay together. You would have a better time if you met with us. But it is comprehensible; you have your culture."

"I'm not white," I say.

Fanon laughs buoyantly. "That is true. You are not white or Black. You do not belong to us or to them. You are a true foreigner." His baritone words sting. My white daughter, my white mother. Surely I must belong to them?

"The foreigners must laugh at us," Fanon says.

"Why would we do that? And what about you? You must laugh at us with your friends."

I feel him shake his head.

"C'mon, tell me," I say, stretching out my legs and putting out my cigarette. "What do you and your friends say about us? What do you laugh about?"

Fanon laughs deep and long. I feel the air around his body change.

"Many things," he replies.

"Give me an example."

"No, no, I cannot."

"Why not?"

"I do not wish to offend," he says.

"Oh, come on. Like you said, I'm neither from here nor from there, I won't take offense. And I won't tell anyone," I say.

"Then you will have to do the same," Fanon says.

I pause and remember Ari, a director from an international agency who after a few drinks told me that Black people's fingers were too fat to use a computer. I remember Gabby the well-meaning activist who talked about social justice but would rant about people being entitled if they asked for anything. There was Eddie, part of some environmental group, who told me it was useless to give locals any tools because they would break them. I could never even whisper those words.

"Deal," I lie.

"There are many things. Many I cannot say because they are improper about women. Where to begin? You have a lot of belongings.

You have belongings for the belongings. You Americans have the most things. Very large knapsacks with dirty shoes hanging. And the American girls. Aie yai yai. Their voices are very high. The voice come from the nose, not the mouth. And when they speak, they smile very much, as if it is the most important conversation, but they will not remember you the next time you meet. The British and the French speak sternly like we are schoolchildren. The Australians, no one can understand their French. The Germans and the Dutch have strange pants but are comfortable everywhere, even in the most private settings where they may be trespassing. I've seen Dutchmen at funerals asking people questions about traditions during the lamenting and the mourning."

I burst out laughing. "You're right about that. And the pants, it's like they are always a little too short," I sputter.

"But I am correct about the Americans too," Fanon urges.

I see the American volunteer girls in my head, with their top-knots and bandanas. Looking badass and earthy, smiling. I'm not like them. "You haven't said anything about the Italians."

"The Italians. They are friendly. Sometimes they like our women too much."

The mention of foreigners liking women quiets us. I think of Lele, of what must have happened in the building behind me. I miss the cigarette and want to light something else. I toy with the lighter, flicking its wheel, until a click turns into flame. Suddenly, I see Fanon clearly, and he, me. I am startled by his face and proximity. The easy camaraderie is broken. It was possible in the darkness, when we were just voices. With faces, it is clear we are strangers.

We sit in an awkward silence.

"So, what are you doing here?" I finally ask.

"I endeavored to speak to you. It was not a clever plan as I know the office will not allow me. I was hoping that perhaps a guard would take a message. But you are here," says Fanon triumphantly.

"Fanon, where did you learn such proper French?"

"We go to school." He sounds offended.

"I know that," I say, apologetically. "But you speak differently, like you've gone to school outside of the village."

"Radio. RFI. France 24. Books, and yes, I went to the capital for schooling. And with Lele—we spoke all the time," Fanon says in a quieter voice.

"I want to visit her. Is that possible?" I ask.

"Yes, certainly. This is why I have come. My family wish to prepare a feast for your visit. Will it be acceptable in two days?" he asks.

"Oh no. I don't want to trouble anyone. I thought I would pop in, talk to her, preferably without too many people around."

"You know the traditions, Bigabosse. My family wishes to honor your visit. Please allow them. It has been long since they have celebrated anything. It will be good for Lele as well."

Of course, I know how it is. The poor of the world somehow have great generosity for the rich. They spare no expense to feed the guest, even if the guest is coming with a full stomach and will consume their month's ration. Still, I cannot fight hospitality.

"Sure," I submit.

There is another moment of silence interspersed with crickets, lizards, choirs of nighttime song. Fanon gets up to leave.

"I remember you. I remember you giving Lele her first work. This is why I believe you now. This is why I believe you will help her."

"I'll do my best. I need to talk to her and understand what happened. I know it will be difficult for her, but it is the only way if we want justice."

"It is only in respect for you and this office that we haven't beaten Monsieur Marc." Fanon's voice becomes threatening.

"Thank you to you and your family for remaining calm. I just have to talk to Lele first and find out what really happened," I say, nervously.

"Do you doubt it is him?" Fanon towers above me somewhere

in the darkness, his voice heavy like a hammer. I'm not quite scared of him, but he's different from the person I was laughing with a moment ago.

"I need to talk to Lele to get all the facts. You understand, right? She is the only person I can believe. I am not saying I don't trust you, but her word is the most important. I promise that I will do everything in my power to punish the person who hurt her. There is no way I'd defend anyone who hurt that child."

"I apologize for speaking loud." Then he laughs, his voice butter again. "You know she is not a child anymore."

"How old is Lele now?"

"She is twenty."

Twenty. Time had passed. She wasn't that thirteen-year-old running circles around me. I wish I had a drink. Fanon fiddles with his phone and looks at the time.

"Do you miss Likanni?" he asks.

"I suppose," I answer. "I miss who I was when I was here. Maybe I miss my youth."

"You are not old," says Fanon. "You are maybe thirty?"

"I'm thirty-nine," I say, wondering again why I am telling him these things.

I hear him make a noise as if stretching his back. "Is it true that everywhere else, in America and Europe, things are going much better?" he asks.

I think about that. "Yes," I say, getting up and dusting off my bottom. "It's not perfect, but there aren't soldiers in the streets, entire villages aren't starving to death."

"Then you must be very happy in America?" he asks.

I freeze. The last time I remember being happy, really happy, the explosive kind of happiness, was here. It was when I was in love with Anders, when I woke up with a sense of purpose every morning, when days crashed into one another, and I was busy and hungry and in motion.

"Yes," I lie. "Good night, Fanon. Please tell your family that I will come in two days."

I enter the office.

The clicks of doors opening and closing, the sensation of leaving the night outside inevitably takes me. Though I fight it, the memory, the one I have been quashing with all my might, stretches monster-like before me. So much of my attention, for the last seven years, has been spent holding down that quaking door in my mind. It's because of it that I used to hold my baby over a white cot, and instead of marveling at the plump arc of her cheeks, I would clamp my eyes shut, trying to block the past from penetrating the decorative serenity of the nursery.

11

It was spring, seven years ago, when the mining guys came. It felt like summer to them, because of the heat. They were handsome. Or maybe they just seemed that way because they were clean-cut, overgrown boys in tidy clothes—geologists, mining engineers, scientists, environmental assessment men. They didn't live in these parts like us. For some, it was their first big work trip after graduate school. They had offices in bigger, more developed cities, and every now and then they would be contracted to do their due diligence before Canadian or Australian mining companies came to drill for treasure.

We, the rough aid workers living in Likanni, found them charming in their awkwardness. They weren't used to staying in shitty hotels where bed bugs chewed their ankles; they were accustomed to minibars. They had briefcases containing scientific contraptions; they were professionals.

One thing was affirmed with their visit: the ground was fertile. Likanni's land housed treasures as rich as the people were poor. Wave after wave of environmental and social assessments only confirmed it: yes, indeed it was safe, sound, and even desirable for mining companies to dig up and extract these riches. This country's treasures would mean wealth for everyone—the villagers, the country, the world. Likanni's gifts would power technologies whose impact would trickle down to every kid on the continent.

They found us—and by us, I mean all the women from abroad who were working on children or health or water or peace or refugees or agriculture or environmental protection or AIDS or sanitation—heroic and strange.

We found the first batch meandering in a nearby town where we went to drink on Thursday and Friday nights. They followed us into what was, for all intents and purposes, a bar. It was a space held together precariously, with makeshift walls of tin. The owner, Mickey, stood behind the bar and laughed with everyone who walked in. Two girls and a cheerful young man worked there; it was our hangout. We would blast whatever music we wanted, although there was usually West African or Caribbean bass pounding the little structure. Teens and twentysomethings crammed in, and it was one of the only places where foreigners and locals comingled, enjoying a common experience, although at separate tables. We would joke and dance with the locals, and they with us, and for a few hours our realities blurred and blended. As soon as we'd exit, the differences would surface. We would enter our 4x4s, as obtusely as if we were climbing into spaceships. They would begin their long trek home, laughing, smoking, roughhousing with each other in the dark.

Our gang at the table in the corner was ever-changing, as new first-worlders would come, then go, as researchers and journalists and diplomats and humanitarians would visit, then leave. It was the white corner. It was a sure place to make friends when you were new and uncertain, wondering what the hell you were doing in this country, and how you were going to survive your term. This was how we met the three Canadians: Andrew, Matt, and Todd.

Two of them wore baseball caps. They sauntered in looking lost, presumably having read about this place online or in a *Lonely Planet* guidebook. It was probably not what they'd envisaged. Ilse spotted them and waved them over to sit with us. She was a six-foot-tall, freckled Dutch girl that no one would ever mess with. She could dig wells and fix vehicles and exuded raw strength.

The Canadians were friendly, as per the stereotype. They tried to sound worldly by telling us stories of backpacking through Europe. We were arrogant and scoffed at them. We had seen so much more of the world; our R&Rs were for real travel, not lining up at museums or churches; our work had taken us to the remote. When they asked for no ice in their drinks to avoid hepatitis, we laughed. We were weathered. We had local know-how. We could smell the weather and give accurate predictions; we weren't soft like these charming newbies. Ilse took Todd home that night. She said he was adamant about putting up a mosquito net before having sex.

The boys were starting out in their careers, which would involve trips like this one to far-off places. So far, they had only worked in Suriname, which was far more developed than where we were. They lived in Toronto, wrote reports, worked in cubicles. They handed us business cards with beautifully embossed silver logos. They were the first emissaries of mining.

They stayed in Likanni for six weeks. In that time, they walked the terrain, met a multitude of villagers, learned a few phrases of local dialect. The locals were charmed by their politeness and desire to hike. Todd, innocent in the ways of how relationships worked in this part of the world, told Ilse he would be back again the following year, despite the fact that he was a little frightened by her. It wouldn't have mattered, because by the time he came back, Ilse had gone back to Amsterdam and applied for a job with the Red Cross to go work in a "real war zone" in Iraq.

Once Andrew, Matt, and Todd had written their neat reports in font size eleven; signed, sealed, and delivered the news that geologically the underground was rich, rich, rich and could be (should be!) exploited to give local people jobs, the companies swiftly moved in.

They came with fanfare. There were free training sessions. Umbrellas with logos were handed out, along with branded water bottles, solar flashlights, pens. More shiny, spiffy guys with names like Tom and Tyler arrived, building excitement, roads, and architectural plans for schools. There was an enthusiasm for the future; it was contagious. Even the environmentalists were charmed by these men who seemed removed from everything ugly. These guys were office dudes, not cynical field folk like us; they talked about sports, told jokes; they were easy, nonpolitical; they were efficient and scientific. Even the warlords held back, strategizing on how to relate to these powerhouse companies, which were clearly bringing a new future to the country.

Monstrous construction began and, yes, employed many of the local men. However, before digging could begin, four villages had to be moved. About thirty thousand people were told, and not by shiny men who passed out water bottles but by local criminals, that they had to leave the premises. When and how the companies hired these attackers to do their dirty work, we did not know.

We were caught in an awful situation. We had to witness the displacement of villages that had existed for centuries. Local bullies showing up with machetes to kick out those who would not leave by eviction deadlines. Women and children crying. There was no replacement land allocated. The rush meant that villagers had to rebuild their lives atop existing villages where there was already overpopulation and a shortage of water and food. The friction grew.

Those of us with international charity status weren't a part of this, and yet it didn't matter; in the eyes of the villagers, we were like the white folk who had started this mess.

Ilse Skyped Todd in desperation to tell him what was happening with his famous mine, hoping he'd be able to do something on his end.

He sympathized. "That's terrible. But I don't think the company has anything to do with this. This sounds like it's a local management issue."

Ilse fought back. "Of course it has something to do with your company—who do you think is paying these criminals?"

"It must be the warlords. I heard they got involved. You know they are the source of all trouble."

"You're so bloody naive!" she shouted at him.

Todd argued with her, told her about the CEO of his company. That beacon of light, a man who had hospital wings named after him, a man who would never condone violence. Why just tonight he would be speaking at a benefit at the Four Seasons in Toronto. Ilse disconnected the call, cursing in Dutch.

I imagine Todd celebrating the virtues of what he did. Mining, as he had explained to me once, wasn't about stealing land or hurting people to unearth gems that old ladies wear on wrinkly fingers. It was the stuff that went into computers and phones and connected us. It was how democracy was born: it was what connected Africans to Americans; it allowed global conversations. It's what the Egyptians used to show the world what happened at Tahrir Square. That was mining. It was the earth gifting resources to build a better future. His company was merely sharing the gifts of the earth, creating a more connected tomorrow.

How nice it must be to believe so deeply in your mistakes.

On our end, things worsened. People got hungrier, there were more IDPs (who had time to say internally displaced people) flooding our village, and local management of the mine was in the hands of a warring faction known to speak only by force and weaponry. My charity was given executive orders to help as much as we could. We tried, but this was hardly international news. It was just something happening in small villages in the middle of nowhere, a battle against corporate interests which interested nobody. We took our existing resources that were already scarce to begin with and tried to manage the exploding population. Yes, new roads had been built, but only to the mine. Some guys were hired for labor, but the wages were very low. The men working the mine were perpetually dirty, some without hard hats, many with new coughs and sicknesses. What came out of the mines, we never saw, but apparently it was shipped all over the world, achieving technological greatness.

I was working day and night delivering programs for children in the tents, trying to manage relations between village elders and those from the newly displaced villages, smoothing disputes on relocation and settlements.

One night, as I was leaving the office with my flashlight, I saw fire brightening the night sky. I stood paralyzed, as the dark lit up with red and smoke, illuminating trees and land around me. Birds flocked noisily to the skies in chaos. I forgot all about standard operating procedures and began running toward it. I felt someone running next to me; it was Marc. We were joined by Adrien, my French-Lebanese intern, then my neighbor Faima, then Feta, and Ilaba from the neighborhood. We ran and then stood still. There were no firetrucks, no fireproof suits, no 911s to call. The International Red Cross was miles away. We stood in horrific silence as part of the camp of internally displaced people flew up in angry flames. Children's screaming pierced the air. For years, I would be reminded of that sound whenever I heard white noise or the crackling of a romantic winter fire.

When sense took over, I grabbed fistfuls of dirt and flung it at the goliath of flames. With my neighbors and hundreds of villagers, we went as close as we could. We dragged people out, helped those fleeing with their hair in flames, their faces twisted, unrecognizable. We patted their bodies as hard as we could; we singed our hands. Without planning or speaking, we created a human chain, passing people from the fire toward those nursing the injured in makeshift ways. I didn't know who was in front of me or behind me; I didn't know how the strength came but I carried women, men, children, like we were in a mosh pit, our faces burning, our eyelashes and eyebrows melting from the heat. I saw Marc carrying wounded after wounded. This went on for hours with the smell of charred skin, plastic tents going up in flames. I vividly remember a USAID "From the American People" tarp burning, the words disappearing as if by magic. As the fire grew, we moved back to avoid smoke inhalation. From time to time, the people at the front of the line would stumble off, exhausted, smoky, in desperate need of water.

There weren't enough bandages, enough water, enough blood, enough ointments, enough bloody cotton balls. There wasn't enough of anything that night, except for misery. None of us wore gloves or had antiseptic. Disease and germs passed from wound to wound. We all became healthcare workers, blowing on burned skin, fanning half-baked babies. Mothers, fathers, siblings, children, grandparents were separated. The mosques where dead bodies' final ablutions were performed became hospitals, churches became clinics. Open fields were resting spots for the dead and burned. Somehow, by the time I got back, MSF had appeared and erected what looked like a professional clinic on our front lawn. I recognized my friends, friends of friends, people I had laughed with at the bar. We didn't smile or share woes; we were moving constantly, in horror, but moving. There was no time to think. My three interns, Adrien, Mohamed, and Lele, were running back to our offices, filling cannisters with water from our tank, rushing it back to every temporary clinic. Marc turned into sheer strength, carrying men and women upon his slender shoulders, his face knotted and focused. Everywhere we turned there was moaning and screaming; every second we heard someone shrieking for someone lost. "Has anyone seen Adel?" "Mariam, have you seen Mariam?"

More than half of the IDPs died that night. No. More than half of those mothers, fathers, children, friends, grandparents, aunts, uncles, poets, artists, citizens died that night. The other half had the fire singed onto their skins and minds in a distortion that would never be normal to look at. Hands did not look like hands. Eyes hung out of sockets, skin burnt back to the bone.

A few years later, Todd visited a nearby region to conduct a preliminary assessment, and decided to drop by Likanni to see the school his CEO had built. He told me he remembered reading about it in the newsletter prepared for shareholders and felt proud that kids in the region would be getting an education because of the company he worked for. Especially the girls. The girls needed that so that they wouldn't be forced into child marriage; he'd seen a documentary about that.

"It's a big problem, these child marriages."

When he got here with a new colleague whom he was trying to impress, like a veteran of the developing world, there was no school to speak of. Just footings with "nique ta mère" scrawled on them.

Todd shared his disappointment with me one night over a beer. "These people—you can't help them. You can't help a people that destroy their own things."

There was so much I could say, but the words would not come. I didn't even know where to start. That was the real problem: Where was the beginning of all this pain? Did it start with a logo on a water bottle? A few hundred years before that?

The fire became its own story. The great fire. People spoke of it as a temporal event, "before the fire," "after the fire." It wasn't linked to anything other than to itself and time. There was never any blame, only mention of misfortune. Everything happened in such fragmented pieces that seldom were connector strings drawn between events. It was its own monster. People would talk of where they were during the fire. They recounted the miracles, the people who survived. They relived the losses. They had anniversaries. And time kept going. The fire had nothing to do with the Todds or Toms, their umbrellas and baseball caps, or the fact that a mass movement of people had been forced, increasing risks and pressure in a small dense location. It had nothing to do with the fact that my mutual funds back home, which I'd set up when I was eighteen, had investments in the mining company that Todd worked for. No, the fire was what it was. An unfortunate discrete event. Like Lele's rape.

12

I see why Marc and Chantal are edgy. On the front stoop there is nothing but memory; inside it's claustrophobic, haunted by the silence of a muted office. I should go somewhere. Maybe to the bar, shoot the shit with the new first-worlders, discover whether they are German or English. Whether they went to Oxford, a grande école, or Yale.

I go upstairs to Chantal's room and pause outside her door. It sounds like she's watching a movie. American accents and sounds of explosions pop beyond the door. I knock. The movie is quieted. I hear shuffling. A male voice.

"Coming," yells Chantal. She opens the door. "Hi," she says breathlessly.

"Can I come in?" I ask.

"Of course."

The room looks very lived in. Clothes hang on the backs of chairs and the bedframe. The two single beds in this dormitory room have been shoved together in the corner under the window. Chantal kicks a huge orange duffle bag out of the way to make room for me. Stacks of books sit in a corner, as if she's been here for months rather than weeks. There is a smell, not quite sweat, but that of dry, flakey skin. Marc sits in a wooden chair facing Chantal's laptop. She hops onto her bed and pats for me to sit with her.

"We're watching a movie," she says. "I was going to ask you to join us, but I thought you were still asleep."

I have no desire to sit in a stuffy room watching an action movie. "I'm wide awake now. Do you want to go out for a drink with me?"

"That doesn't sound safe," Marc says.

"For you, it probably isn't," I say, "but Chantal? I think you'd be okay."

"I don't know," she says.

"I'll let you drive." I wink.

Chantal laughs. "Because you've forgotten how to."

"Please? You saw how it was with the villagers. I think it will help if they see us out and about among them."

She scratches her head. She looks worried. "Okay. Give me fifteen minutes and I'll meet you downstairs." That Chantal, always a good sport.

"Is it okay if we leave you?" I ask Marc.

"It's fine, although I think it's a terrible idea." He stretches his skinny arms high above his head. "At least I can finish the movie in peace. Chantal talks incessantly." She throws a pillow at his head, which he catches. She grabs her toiletries bag and heads out to the hallway with a towel to use the communal bathroom. They gave me the one room with the attached bathroom. The boss room.

I lock my room and wait by the foot of the stairs. Chantal comes down, a spring in her step, her hair freshly washed and scented, in a loose T-shirt and long jersey skirt. She looks like a nervous animal about to leave her cage.

"You're sure about this?" she asks.

"Don't worry. By now everyone knows I'm back, and you're with me." I sound more confident than I am. I have no idea whether we'll be safe, but in these parts, you never know. Just follow your instincts, your mantra of privilege, and off you go.

We leave our bags and wallets behind, shove a few bills in our pockets for possible bandits, bribes, and drinks, and head to the security booth. Chantal has a convoluted conversation with the guards, telling them we'll be out. They advise against it. Benoit and Cyril look at me with disapproval, wearing matching looks as if they've been practicing the art of synchronizing expressions. I'm seen as the source of trouble. I smile boldly at them.

Chantal grabs the keys and we walk into the darkness. She flicks on her flashlight as we head toward the cars, parked behind the building on the eastern end of the property. She walks rapidly; I, cautiously. I'm impressed by her know-how of the terrain, which I once had. Her canvas shoes curl expertly around uneven rocks. She doesn't trip or stumble. That's the sign of someone who belongs here. Her family owns an apartment in the sixteenth arrondissement of Paris that she has posted a million pictures of online, but her feet know this is her home.

I've always been in awe of how Chantal does this: how she marries that Parisian to Likanni. Back home, she drinks great wines, dines with intellectual friends, rides mopeds, then returns to this dusty mayhem. Somehow she remains the same, there is no France-Chantal or Likanni-Chantal, no spliced identity that has to be worn or shorn. No Maya and Bigabosse. She's at home everywhere. Maybe because of the skin that houses her, the skin whose status is understood by all.

We slide in the Cruiser and she guns the engine. The smell of diesel and fake leather seats fill me with an unexpected thrill. Chantal eases the clutch and maneuvers the stick gracefully. We're propelled into darkness. Under us, tires crunch rocks in soft bursts. I'm reminded of a hundred Friday nights. I'm in my twenty-six-year-old body for a moment, the body that was in perpetual excitement for the next thing.

The headlights are weak, but Chantal barely needs them. The road to the bar is mapped in her. She knows which turn to slow at, where landslides tend to happen, how to avoid hitting villagers gathered under a starry sky. I squeakily roll the window down. To physically roll a lever in circles, a joy my daughter will never know. The night air floods in, touching our skin, disheveling our hair.

"It's nice to be out," Chantal remarks.

We drive quietly to our destination. I hear the music from a distance. Good old Bob Marley has crossed more borders than he probably ever imagined he would from his small island-state. People put on his accent, don't quite know what he's saying, but sing along. Here he is tonight, like a lion in Zion. There are two jeeps announcing the presence of first-worlders like us, but something seems off. Quiet, even though it's not quiet. These are the nuances we learn to sense. The eerie under the noise.

Chantal leans over my lap to roll up my window, which I've forgotten to, like an amateur.

"You haven't left anything in the car, have you?" Chantal asks. "Don't want our windows smashed." I show her my empty hands and we slam the Cruiser's doors with loud clangs.

I step into the bar and am hit by a surge of nostalgia. The place smells the same. The music so loud it alters the heartbeat. There is a new waitress shuffling about in a tight black top and jeans, her hair in a perfect afro, large hoops in her ears. The cast of characters seems to have changed. Maybe it's that the kids who were kids when I was last here are now grown-ups moving their ripe bodies around tables. There are fewer people than I remember. There are three blond girls sitting at a large table, and Chantal gestures me over to them, but I'm interrupted by Mickey, the owner.

"Bigabosse," he booms, his voice cutting through the music. He comes from behind the bar to kiss me on both cheeks. I'm genuinely happy to see him.

"Where have you been, ma belle?" Mickey asks, throwing his arms up in the air.

I haven't been to the bar in years. My missions over the last few years have been quick visits to worksites. I've reviewed strategic plans, discussed funding, and been back on a plane before adjusting to the jet lag.

"It's so good to see you. You haven't changed one bit." Mickey's face and hairless head shine in the outdoor lights, clipped to the tin walls.

"But you. What is this white hair? You've gotten old." He points to the three gray hairs that have sprouted at my temple, which I imagine would be invisible in this dim light. I laugh. I don't know whether I love or hate the tendency of always speaking the truth in these parts.

"Well, it had to happen. Becoming a mother and living with a philandering husband will do that to you," I say carelessly. How easily pain rolls off my tongue. It's the first time I've uttered anything like this, even to myself. I'm instantly ashamed.

"No, no, no." He shakes his head and clicks his tongue. "You are too young to be looking like this. And the husband"—Mickey takes one hand and slaps the other palm with a loud snap—"you bring him here, I will set him straight." He gestures for me to come to the bar. I lean over the sticky counter while he makes a cocktail intended to impress; it will likely taste like watery fruit juice concentrate.

Mickey is at least thirty years older than me but looks my age. The music has not deafened him. He has the short stocky body of a doer. Of a guy who decides to stick some metal sheets into the ground and create a social scene that has lasted decades.

"What's going on here?" I ask. "It seems quiet."

"Things are not good. There are fewer foreigners now; they have more important places to be. Hah. They've fucked up other countries pretty good now, so all the kids are going there. The militants are stupid boys with no good sense. One day, they showed here with AK-47s demanding I pay them tax. I took a stick and hit one of them so hard, he started crying. I told them if they bugged me again, I'd see to it that none of them got another drink for the rest of their miserable lives. That taught them a lesson. I'm the only one with good booze for one hundred kilometers. If they want to drink shit that makes them go blind, be my guest. Can you imagine? Blind soldier boys running around shooting AK-47s. Ha!" Mickey laughs heartily at his own jokes. I've never known how much of what he says is true; he's always been self-congratulatory. I doubt he smacked a kid with an AK-47, but then again he has survived numerous regime changes, militant groups, and even the American military.

"The kids that come now, they are not like you lot. What a good bunch of kids that was." Mickey shakes his head. I imagine he says this to every wave of visitors, if there ever are any. He's like an old school principal, welcoming alumni fondly. We took our first uncertain steps in his establishment, made friends, and began relationships in the midst of his metal scraps.

"Do you see my colleagues often?" I ask, hoping he'll gossip and I can get a whiff of the rumors about Marc.

"You know me." Mickey pats himself on the chest of his tight collared shirt. "I never know who works for what. All I know is those American boys get drunk and start fights."

Mickey sees through my question and dodges it. Of course. He hasn't survived this long by getting involved in the politics around him. He's at the center of it, hosts the interactions, but never participates.

He hands me a cocktail with great flourish. A purple paper umbrella fastened to a toothpick is the crowning jewel.

"On the house." Mickey beams.

As I lean over to take my first sip, I hear a familiar voice. "Well, hello there, old friend," Tommy says as he slides an arm around my shoulder. "I thought you might be coming round these parts."

The first time I met Tommy he told me his father had gotten so drunk when he was born (with happiness, followed by alcohol) that he had chosen *Tommy* as the first name on the birth certificate. Not Thomas. Not Tom. Tommy joked of the trauma of becoming a man with a child's name, forever infantilized. I wouldn't describe him as childish, but he is unabashedly sincere. He and I became instant friends.

A New Zealander, Tommy settled in these hard parts with his Pakistani wife, Seher, whom he met at an Australian university. They have given themselves completely to this country. They learned local dialects and even went as far as applying for citizenship. When they submitted their paperwork, the two bureaucrats at the immigration processing department, located in the corner of an old post office, laughed hysterically, holding their stomachs. Why on earth would these two want a nationality that would give them nothing, passports which required visas to travel everywhere in the world, voting rights in a country where there was neither voting nor rights. But Seher and Tommy were insistent. If they were to live here, build a home, be a part of the society, they had to suffer the same travails as everyone else. "You have to live your politics, otherwise you are bullshit," Seher said in dinner party conversations, her strong Pakistani accent and defined *T*'s making *bullshit* more pronounced, like a slap to the rest of us.

Seher was dogmatic, heavy-handed, but deep down we admired her. We just couldn't live up to her expectations. There had to be a limit to how much we could endure. Would it really help anyone if we became citizens of a failed state?

Seher and Tommy were antiwar, as are most first-worlders living in war zones, but they were vehemently antimilitary. They often ruffled the feathers of those with even mild tolerance for military action. Their frequent dinner parties with other first-worlders often ended in raucous, angry debates.

Hannah, an American teacher working in the region, would argue, "Not all soldiers are evil."

"No," Seher would say, "but every soldier is trained to kill. Every soldier is trained to take human life on command. All soldiers are the same: they are taught to blindly follow orders, to murder for whichever country has sent them."

Hannah, often drunk mid-meal, would rant, "What about World War II? As the granddaughter of Italians, I can tell you we are thankful for the service of those young, brave men. If they hadn't saved us, Mussolini would have destroyed Italy!"

While passing us delicious curry, Seher would look Hannah straight in the eye and say, "World War II and the Holocaust would not have happened if humans were not militarized, turned into Nazi robots and soldiers, and trained to follow orders. Now the *résistance*, that is something worth admiring. The only honorable soldiers are those forced into such roles, who didn't join out of free will. For everyone else, if they die, it's their choice. As far as I'm concerned, they are all terrorists. Someone's dying for a god, someone's dying for a president."

By now Hannah would be sweating in fury. "My maternal grandfather died in the war! Are you comparing him to a terrorist?"

"It always has to go back to someone's grandfather, doesn't it? That's why we can never progress. We are too busy justifying our grandfathers." Seher would sigh.

"What about the greater good? You can't honestly say that people defending freedom around the world are the same as the boys looting widows or blowing themselves up in a hotel."

"If you are given a command to take human life and are not

allowed to question or refuse it, then as far as I'm concerned there is no greater good. You are following orders. You are a terrorist serving someone's agenda. The guy killing someone for a chicken to feed his belly, in my opinion, has a higher purpose than a guy being sold some bullshit about exporting a freedom you can't see, feel, or touch in any of the places it has been forced."

These conversations were always the same. The rest of us would be soaking naan into Seher's flavorful curry, quietly eating as much as possible. We endured the debates because Tommy and Seher's house was the only place that felt like a real home, with board games, picture albums, CDs, homecooked meals.

I had a strange fascination with Seher. I wondered what it was like to always say what you think, to live what you believe, without fear. She was a rather unattractive woman with a large pointy nose, her hair a short curly mop. She too was a perennial foreigner, but she laid roots. She spoke in a calm but resolute manner, and Tommy would gaze admiringly at her, unafraid for her, unembarrassed for her. He set the court and she would shine. She was so cynical about the world, its power imbalances, but so deeply happy in it, planting her gardens, speaking disappearing dialects, furrowing her nose in fading traditions, gathering so many of us.

I would watch Hannah, this young American teacher, her brown hair frizzy in the heat, adding to the electrical charge of her words. There she was, so absolute about country, her grandfather, honor and freedom. Believing in righteous wars. Wouldn't it be nice to believe in something's purity so much? Then I would look at Seher, so unafraid of seeing our grandfathers, including her own, as sinners. Wouldn't it be freeing to be so historically untethered, to not be defensive of the past? To accuse, even the ones we love.

Seeing Tommy reminds me of those nights.

Maybe my own marital failure occurred because I compared my life to theirs, to those dinners where people came with ideas, arguments, food. Where a man beamed at his wife as she challenged her guests on their core beliefs. Maybe Seher had the courage to be honest because Tommy accepted her social transgressions. Steven would die if I insulted the politics of any of our guests. Not that I ever would.

Tommy and I exchange pleasantries and kisses on cheeks. Before I can catch my breath, he gestures for us to sit at a table for two and says, "You know he did it, right?"

"What?" Maybe I didn't hear him right.

"Come on, I know why you're here. I went into Likanni last week. I'm sure he did this."

I lean in closer. "What makes you say this?"

"The guy is a creep, ay? Never talks to any of us. I've never known why he's been keen to stay here this long," he says.

"Just because he doesn't go out for drinks with you and the boys doesn't make him a rapist." I laugh uneasily.

Tommy grunts. "He just seems like he could have done it."

"You can't say that based on a feeling!"

Tommy laughs.

I say, "Look, I know he can rub people the wrong way with his particular ways—"

"Particular ways? He's downright rude." Tommy puts his glass down. "Do you know that I once saw him yelling at a pig farmer? I was giving a demonstration nearby and your chap came along and began spewing nonsense about how the farmer wasn't adequately managing his sow, and that's why the piglets were dying off. Man doesn't know a damn thing about farming, let alone on mating pigs or their diseases. The farmer was trembling and Marc had no qualms or embarrassment that I'd seen him do that."

"That's terrible, and please know I'm not justifying his behavior. I just want to be careful that we don't accuse him of being a criminal just because he's unlikable. And, isn't it better that he acts like a jerk in front of others? At least he doesn't hide it." I take a sip of my drink. "Do you remember how he was after the Likanni fire? He was a machine. I don't think he took a day off for eight months straight. He went to thousands of burn victim families to see what we could do for the kids. He's the one who single-handedly got money from donors and kickstarted the burn victim school in Twadid. He can be a real asset."

"Fine, let us sing Marc's praises for doing the job he's paid to do."

"He went above and beyond, Tommy."

"Did he? None of our work here can possibly fit in some notion of deliverables or time-bound results. Everyone here"—he holds up a finger—"wait, let me rephrase that. Everyone here that is truly committed is going above and beyond all the time. That's the nature of aid work." He shakes his head. "Anyhow, what's Lele said?"

"I haven't talked to her yet. I'm meeting her in two days. I have to be careful in how I manage this—I know Marc can be perceived as, well, a bit distant, and I don't want that opinion to cloud my judgment. I want to be fair."

"You agree then?" Tommy laughs. "He is an arsehole?" He winks.

I laugh back. I look at Chantal, who is sitting with girls I don't know at the back of the room. She raises a glass at me across the distance. I cheers back. The paper umbrella tumbles out of my glass.

"It's tricky. Any pronouncement on my part can affect these people's lives forever."

Tommy leans forward. "You know I think you're a gem. But you can't be impartial, it's impossible. Who are you living with? Marc. How can the accuser and accused be heard equally when one gets more airtime than the other? And what kind of pressures are your bosses putting on you? I reckon you're out here making sure the charity looks good, because if people get wind of this, then all those vulnerable souls you've been working to protect are left to the dogs. You're in an impossible situation."

"Thanks for the vote of confidence," I say.

"I don't envy you." He takes a sip of his beer. "Your bosses sent you because they know you're attached to the work, to Marc, to the beneficiaries. You won't want to drown all of that. For them, it's just a game of numbers. Lele is one victim, the orphans are in the thousands, not just here but globally. If you support her publicly, you risk losing all the work. They know that."

I pick up the paper umbrella off the ground, opening its parasol until it breaks in my hands.

"I have to talk to Lele first. Once I know what's happened, I will do the right thing. Lele has grown up before me. I won't stand for anyone hurting her," I say, slightly hurt.

Tommy leans back in his chair. His long golden arms rest on the sticky table. He looks so different from Marc, like a true humanitarian, wide shouldered, strong. Like a man someone could rely on. Colorful string bracelets slide on his wrists, giving him a youthful air.

"You'll have to see this for yourself," he says. "Just promise you won't let this little shit get away with it. Even if it's hush-hush, let Marc get what he deserves. The women here should be able to work with us without being taken advantage of."

"How's Seher?"

"Splendid. She just returned from a family wedding in Pakistan. She's jet-lagged, but come see her if you're sticking round."

"I miss those dinners at your house," I say.

"We have fewer of them with your lot, more with the locals. With the foreigners, you start developing relationships, and before you know it, people have gone to the wop-wops. It's too fickle, always starting over. And people are such dimwits when they first arrive. I suppose we were too." He flicks his thumb toward the girls sitting with Chantal. "I don't even know their names. I'm just the cranky old kiwi round these parts. But it doesn't matter. They'll be gone in a year or two."

"I'm glad you're still here, even though I'm one of the fickle ones."

"Nah, Maya, you were never fickle. Like I said, you're one of the gems. You must be doing splendid things back home. People remember you, though they've forgotten the others. Too many of us coming and going, but Bigabosse lives." He winks again.

I think of my immaculate home. Of folding white towels perfectly. Of yelling at Chloe, so nothing looks out of order, so nothing looks like it has life. Everything so beautiful it's fragile. So much for doing something worthwhile.

"How's your work going?" I ask.

"Fantastic. We bought fifty or so hectares of choice bush behind the house five years ago. We started a small sustainable agriculture project, with financing from an Italian organization. It's completely community-run and people have started testing climate-resilient varieties. We've even got them planting small, fast-growing forests that they'll be able to harvest for firewood and stop chopping the damn trees. It's been the perfect confluence of good donors and participants who've been keen to get agroforestry training from us."

"That's amazing. And there's been no violence?"

"Because the lands are on our private property, the militants have kept off. Amazing that they are ready to pillage their own, but the minute they smell foreign blood, they bugger off." Tommy scratches the stubble on his tanned chin. His blue eyes shine.

"I hear there's been racial tensions?" I ask.

"No more than usual. Some groups are louder, talking about decolonizing aid and how they have to become independent and self-sustaining. Frankly, it's been fantastic to see this revival of spirit. It makes colleagues from our part of the world very nervous, because it means we should all bugger off. Which, at some point, we should. The question is when and what we leave in our wake. But it's not a violent movement by any stretch."

I feel a tap on my shoulder. It's Chantal and her friends. She holds up her phone. "Sorry to intrude—hi, Tommy—we've just gotten word from security that two warring militant groups are going to block the road to Likanni at dawn. They are beginning to set up now. Maya, we should go."

We shoot up from our seats. Every foreign-looking face gathers their belongings. We wear the same focused look. It's what we've been trained for: how to avoid danger. We're one graceful animal, different parts moving in coordination. I glance at Mickey; he waves me toward the exit. He knows. The other patrons do too, when they see us leave in unison.

There is a curious problem when we've been informed by militant groups of their upcoming violence: they tell us to avoid disrupting our work and putting us at risk, but we are not allowed to warn local people. If we do, the militants will shoot down our projects, depriving the villagers of any support we provide. It forces us into terrible choices. Do we let people die in an ambush today in order to keep providing services tomorrow? Or do we save people today and let them die tomorrow when we are no longer here with our meager offerings? In a sense we collude, knowing where the militants will strike, warning the innocent only through silent gestures and innuendos. It's a disgusting weight to carry.

Our eyes speak to the patrons. They don't know where, but they sense there will be trouble. I share as many looks as I can with as many strangers as possible. I'm telling them to go home. To protect themselves, their children. To stock up on food and drink. The din in the bar increases in volume, people looking around nervously. As we near the exit, a group of boisterous guys enters. One of them grabs my arm. "Hello, two times in one night!" It's Fanon.

I shake my head at him. He looks confused.

I lean in and say the words I'm not supposed to. My voice is barely audible, barely louder than my breath. "Leave," I say.

"What?" Fanon asks. His friends look at us, josh, make quips about me whispering in his ear.

I look at him intently, then get closer to his ear. "Leave now. Go back home."

I get jostled out of the bar and look back to see him standing in his neon-pink T-shirt, staring quizzically.

Chantal is at my neck. "Did you tell him? What if he tells his friends that we tipped him off? What if one of his friends is connected to the militias?" Her voice is high.

I climb into the vehicle.

"That's Lele's brother. I'm showing him that he can trust us."

"Oh." Calm smooths the creases on her forehead. Chantal revs up and we drive silently for a few minutes.

"You and Marc seem to have become friends," I remark.

"Ouf, he was so arrogant when I started, I didn't know if I could manage it. But I've discovered how to work with him. He's very sensitive, you know. And he's dedicated to the people here. Every time we're told that there is a budget cut for something we want to pilot, he finds a way because he knows it's necessary. That's what really matters, no?"

"Did you doubt his innocence at any point?" I ask.

"Not really. I was in the building when the rape supposedly happened. My office is right next to his. If there was any scuffle, any movement even, I would have heard it. I always hear the horrible music Marc plays in his office, even when it's at low volume."

"What was the rapport like between Marc and Lele?"

"It was friendly, but distant. You know. We all treat Lele like a younger sister. Marc is the same. He teases her. He makes fun of her hair or her dress from time to time. All very innocent."

"Her hair? Are you serious? Did she ever complain?"

"Oh no. She would giggle and make fun of his fuddy duddy look."

"His mood really changed from last night."

"He's been under a lot of stress, which is understandable. He hasn't talked much about it—I think to protect me. I've been frantic, Maya. I panicked when the protestors came, and Marc has had to take on a lot more responsibility to compensate for me. Today was the first time I heard him complain. I think he needed to vent."

"I've seen him in crises before. He's very efficient, but he does get short-tempered," I say.

"He's been good until now. He wants to go talk to Lele and he's frustrated that he cannot help her. You really see the character of a person in these situations. Headquarters has offered him an evacuation on a silver platter, and most men, they would run away. But not Marc. He's adamant about proving his innocence."

We stay quiet for a few moments, enjoying the night air streaming in from half-opened windows.

"I want to go back, Maya. I don't want to do this anymore." Chantal keeps her attention focused on the road ahead, but her voice quivers.

"We'll get through this," I tell her.

"It's not just this."

I want to tell her that going away won't help, that she belongs to this now, that nowhere will feel right again, that the madness here is fuel, that it's life. It is life and death and struggle and trying, and sex and babies at breasts and backs, but it is life, fully charged. It is the consequences of everything and everywhere, of people buying diamonds in a London jewelry shop, of people taken away on boats hundreds of years ago, of French corporals coming and making people into citoyens de la république but not really, of the liberation movement that became its own monster, of boys being sold Kalashnikovs produced by companies in my schoolteacher mother's mutual funds, of our smartphones we use for selfies that house the deepest parts of Likanni, of greedy men who eat and sell every part of their country so that their children can attend the finest Swiss schools and British universities and drive the shiniest

127

red cars. Everything here is part of everything elsewhere. We can close our eyes, switch the channel, get on a plane, but we are still part of it, making it happen in some way. There's no escaping it.

I don't say any of that.

"I know how hard it can be," I offer.

"Headquarters won't want to lose international staff in the middle of a crisis, or maybe they would, who knows. Maybe they need a new person to come in and pretend like we haven't been accused of the vilest thing."

"You know that you haven't been accused of anything, right?"

"It's the same. Whether it's Marc, or me. We're the face of our charity here. If they have the audacity to accuse Marc, they are accusing me and my work too," Chantal says. I'm surprised by the solidarity. Her vouching for him means something; Chantal is one of the clear-headed ones. If there's one person who has borne Marc's stubbornness, it's her.

"If you're sure, I can get the ball rolling on your exit. But I will say this: you're an asset. You understand the people and the culture. You know how to manage local staff; you've cultivated very strong relationships with donors. I know how it is—to one day realize that it's too much and that there is no reason to live life in constant struggle when you don't have to. I'm sure sometimes you see pictures of your friends at cafés and concerts and wonder why you've chosen such a harder path."

"Yes, exactly. And it's not fair. The UN, the other charities, they come in for three years, four years tops. We're the only ones expected to stay this long to make a difference," she says.

"You have made a difference." That's something we all want to hear, even when it's not fully true. We need it to validate our time, to know our good years weren't spent in vain.

"I don't know," Chantal says.

"Of course you have. Under you, over a thousand children have received primary schooling and care."

"What good will it do if they wind up shot, or child soldiers, or slaves in a mine?"

"What good does education do anyone? Maybe some mobility, maybe a better understanding. Maybe they'll be able to leave one day. Maybe some will form a pacifist group, recognize friends from the orphanage and refuse to fight them. At the very least, they can read or write stories to distract themselves. All we can do is give hope for a better life. You've done that."

"I should do something like you. Live somewhere else, come in and out, have a real life," Chantal says.

"It's not that gratifying. I come here and feel removed. Then I go back to my own life and feel absent in that as well. It's no-man's-land," I confess.

We roll onto the driveway slowly and Chantal parks the car and says, "Maybe we just have to accept that we don't belong anywhere, and that's our place."

13

Two months after that terrible fire several years ago, Burton sent the staff shrink to Likanni to make sure we were alright. In the immediate aftermath, adrenaline had kept us running. But after a few weeks, some of the staff fell ill, others looked defeated. Everyone but Marc and me. Something had shifted in me after that tragedy. I looked the same: I was organized, I called meetings, arranged care for the sick, and dodged the shrink Burton threw at me. Yet I didn't feel much. It was like a newfound strength, an armor, as if I were encased. No horror could touch me. I could see it in Marc too. We were steel.

But one day, I was at my desk and couldn't move. I had to go home; it was getting late. The strength to click off the monitor, to get up, to put one foot ahead of the other would not come. Was this paralysis? Some neural disease? I saw dancing black dots. Marc knocked on my door—he was the only other one left at the office—but I couldn't answer, and he left. I trembled so hard I shook, the black dots erupted, multiplied, changed shape, moved faster. My thoughts, my motions, every link in the mental chain felt undone, disjointed.

Marc came back. He knocked again, and when I didn't answer, he barged in. He looked at me, sitting there shaking, my mouth ajar without words. He called my name. I saw him, swimming black dots marring his face. He said things I didn't hear. He swiveled my chair around and put his hands on my shoulders. I saw his lips move but could not make out the words. Then he said something that I heard.

"You need to go back home Maya and take care of yourself. Don't worry. I'll take care of things while you're gone." My head crashed to the desk, tears streamed down my face: I was released. Marc called Burton and told him I had to go on leave; he called my assistant and told her to book flights. He grabbed my bag and drove me to my house. He shouldered me to bed and called a female colleague to come spend the night with me. I felt safe. Someone was looking after me.

I landed at LAX like an alien. Everything felt loud, shiny. There were so many people, so many faces, ads, screens everywhere, the news streaming like the voice of God from every waiting area. iPods had been new when I first left; now there were all kinds of things people were looking down at. So many phones, tablets, things. People in skimpy clothing. I felt like I couldn't see. The customs officer, after asking where I had been and why, said, "Thank you for doing the Lord's work. Welcome home."

My parents stood in the arrivals lounge, nervous smiles on their faces. How battered does a person with PTSD look, I'm sure they wondered. I still wasn't sure it was PTSD, but it was something.

I spent weeks sleeping and indulging in packaged junk food I had been denied. I watched copious amounts of television. I soaked in soap operas, watched sitcoms, reacclimatized to American humor. It was glorious. This is how people lived. They went to work, came home, watched friendships on TV, went shopping on the weekends. Everything was about the next entertainment, the next purchase. It was great. I sucked it in like a glutton. I avoided the news like the plague. I walked in malls with noisy fountains. Bought ridiculous things I didn't need. I bought stilettos that would have sunk in Likanni's dirt. I bought a handbag for a price that could feed a Likanni family for ten years. I bought hi-tech gadgets at big stores from men with nametags. I wanted everything. I met old friends and mimicked what they did, laughed when they did, slid into the backs of their SUVs in short skirts. I talked about what everyone did over the weekend, whether they were going to Tahoe or Vegas. I ate appetizers, went to happy hours. I became a happy hour, killing off the self-deprivation I had lived.

When a family wedding invitation arrived, a few months later, I felt groomed to attend. I was excited: to dress up, to dance like American humans move, to forget what's happening elsewhere. To throw my arms up in YMCA. That's where I met Steven.

I must have done something to charm him that night. I'm still not sure what. He was a dozen years older than me, with the beginnings of silver hair. The kind of man who is universally considered good-looking. The kind you would trust in a hospital or politics, one who should be with a bosomy blond with gleaming teeth, not someone like me.

Steven was a corporate lawyer, a man who can't be conjured without a suit. He had already been divorced once and was ready for a new family, for children, for some steady adventure, for something interesting hanging on his arm but not as aggressive as the women he worked with.

I was interesting. Global but not foreign. Well traveled. A different shade but the same culture. I could tell stories of places he'd never been. I was ripe to experience every goodness of the first world—I had been hungry for so long. And Steven loved that joie de vivre about me.

He was funny as hell and had more friends than I ever did. He had biting observations and made me laugh. We spoke of movies and food; we met with his friends. The world and its sins were confined to news headlines he browsed online. He felt light. He knew about the bad stuff, sometimes we spoke of it, but he didn't wear it. The crimes of the world weren't his duty to resolve. They were floating distantly, removed from our lives.

We traveled to Paris, to Prague; stayed in hotels instead of hostels. We ate at expensive restaurants. He found the manners I had cultivated with diplomats to be utterly charming. I found everything delicious. I wanted to feel it all, and he loved to provide. Skydiving, sure. Scuba diving, why not. I was ready to swallow anything that wasn't sad. Steven didn't feel guilty about everything he touched, and with wonder I watched him, joining him under that tent of insouciance. Life was finally easy.

We bought furniture for his home; we spoke of politics. Not in the life-or-death way, but in the cable-news way—throwing opinions about. The politics of posture and imagery, liking some guys, hating others; the world a clear story of trickle-down economics. We had a lot of sex. It was different because he was older, and I became a plaything. I raised his status with my youth. I was the prize and he made me feel it. I could not believe a man like that, so accomplished, could want me, and with such ferocity. What a pleasure I suddenly became; I was a thing to be seen and eaten. What power to know that I could destabilize this powerful man with a look, or with the slow peeling of my clothing. To go from person to object, what glorious gratification. Every place became an adventure in hedonism. I turned him from distinguished gentleman to animal in seconds.

Steven had a small boat. We went out every weekend. I marveled at every wave, at every sunset, at the fact that I was so far away from Likanni that I couldn't even imagine it. I was like a villager seeing a city for the first time. He loved my wide-eyed admiration. Other women around him were jaded and dry, unsurprised and unimpressed.

Steven was comfortable in a different way than I was. I grew up with two schoolteachers: there was never any shortage of anything, but neither was there excess. I grew up in a comfortable split-level home, and until Steven, I wasn't fully aware of how expansive wealth could be, how large it made one's world. My experience with luxury was with diplomats I met in the field. I was impressed by their grand homes, cursive invitations to dinner, the numerous plate settings, the books and artwork—most of which would stay for the next round of diplomats to occupy those homes. That's what I understood as wealth: being rich and foreign in a poor country, with all the cultural symbols of a civilized being.

Steven possessed American wealth. This breed did not come with impermanent three-year postings or with collections of books accumulated from different parts of the world reflecting cultural capital. His wealth came from ownership: homes, investments, numbers skidding across the bottoms of screens, wrapped in corporate codes. The son of a judge and lawyer, Steven never had to rebel or transform. There was something peaceful in his continuity, the flow of something that didn't require a revolt or reform but could trickle the way it always had. With him, I didn't have to adjust myself or learn the lexicon of manners, as I did to fit in with French or British diplomats. American wealth was easy to be fluent in. All you had to do was buy the right symbols, and you were in. You didn't have to know about Baudelaire, Proust, or Goethe—you needed the right purse. And I had one now.

When Steven proposed a few months later, on the deck of his boat, with oysters and champagne, I couldn't help but think of Anders. At how he would look at these two people. The corporate lawyer and his gluttonous fiancée. How he would see Steven's boat as a vessel to transport families fleeing war. How disappointed he would be if he knew it was just for pleasure, a place to dine, for no other purpose than to enjoy the movement of waves.

Steven presented me with an impressively large ring, and I bit back the desire to ask which mine the diamond came from.

Instead, I said yes.

After the proposal, I called Burton and told him I wanted to leave permanently; I had already been on leave for almost a year.

He asked me to go back one last time to close my books, transition a replacement, and phase out Marc from his acting role. He proposed that I take on a supervisory role. I could work from home in California and be responsible for three countries. I would have to travel a few times a year, for short visits, to check that everything was on track, provide strategic assistance and oversight. I'd be his eyes and ears and give advice to the offices. Despite cold sweats at the thought of returning to Likanni, I agreed. I've spent the last five years straddling worlds.

14

I wake up the next morning to my husband calling. It's a pleasant conversation. He tells me he went to have dinner with Chloe yesterday, that she should be enrolled in tennis, that the roses I planted are doing well. I disrupt the niceties by asking, "You didn't ask why I had to leave so urgently."

"I assumed something was wrong with one of the orphanages? Or one of the kids?"

He hadn't been listening when I told him. His eyes were shut, probably thinking about some email he had to write. Not like in previous years when my stories captivated.

I invest some of myself in the conversation. "It's more messed up than that. One of my colleagues has been accused of raping Lele."

"Shit." He whistles into the phone. "Did he do it?"

"I don't think so. But the guy in question, Marc, is not exactly warm and fuzzy, so it's easy for people to believe that he could have."

"Wait—you don't think he did it? Isn't that the same guy you've worked with forever, the one who drives you nuts and argues with that other lady?"

"I didn't say he didn't do it. I just can't assume he did right off the bat."

"Who's saying he did it?"

"The community. Her brother, among others. I don't know if that's just their interpretation."

"Interesting that so many people are accusing one guy."

"I'm not saying that he had nothing to do with it," I repeat, frustrated. "You don't get it. Things are complicated here. He could have pissed someone off, one of the radical groups could be trying to delegitimize us so we leave, then they can turn all the kids into child soldiers."

"Right. I can't understand a girl being raped by a superior," he says wryly.

"No, I didn't mean that. It's just that there are different considerations out here."

"You know that that stuff happens here too, right? That we have gangs, just like you have your militias and child soldiers. It's not like what you are going through is too complex for me to understand."

Nervous breathing reverberates in my chest. It is a familiar sensation that arises when I've said the wrong word or phrase that sends our conversation careening. I'm usually so careful; our conversations are so fragile. I've been irresponsible.

"I'm sorry, I didn't mean that. I'm just under a lot of stress so things come out wrong."

He harrumphs in the phone. "You know, I get that you're Ms. World Traveler, you've seen it all, but that doesn't mean I'm an idiot. The rape of a girl by her boss is the biggest cliché of all—and let me guess, he's a white man and she's Black?"

"I don't think you're an idiot at all. I'm sorry. It's just that the politics are messy. With all the kids we support, the stakes are really high. I can't afford to make a mistake."

"Just don't become part of the problem," he says coolly.

"What's that supposed to mean?"

"Just that as much as you think you get the people there, you're also an outsider."

I feel like hanging up. This guy doesn't know a thing about my life here. I've worked here for over a decade, I've *lived* here. I've had parasites in my fucking guts and malaria like everyone else. I have a different fucking name here, I'm Bigabosse, people have made me part of their community. But how would he know that? He's never even been curious enough to visit Likanni.

"When do you talk to the victim?" he says.

"Tomorrow," I say nervously.

"You'll be fine. You've done this a million times."

"I guess so, but I never personally knew the rape victims I dealt with."

He sighs, annoyed that I've contradicted him even in a slight way. "What's with you today?"

What's with me is that I'm in this country where I can occupy more space than that of my body; I can slouch, walk in an unrefined way. I'm not that paralyzed woman at home, tangled in my perfection, performing, always performing the mother, the wife for some accolades, a beautiful woman with the right words, a woman striving for recognition that Steven has been withholding from me. I'm strong here. I can tell men with guns what to do. I can be honest.

"Nothing. On another note, I noticed that our home security cameras aren't on while you're at work. Could you arm them?" I ask bravely. Likanni-brave.

"There's been issues with the alarm system. The cameras haven't been working. I'll call the security company as soon as I get a chance."

That lying sleazebag. Look at the speed of those lies. They come as easily as an exhale. I decide to taunt him a little.

"I can call them. I know you're busy," I say.

"No. No, that's crazy, you're in another time zone, dealing with a rape charge. And there'll be roaming charges to boot. Don't worry, I got this." He doesn't miss a beat. Steven changes the subject, back to Lele. "Anyway, it'll be emotional for sure, but it'll help the girl to talk to you." There's a flicker of affection, or is it deception? The trickle feels good, like we can argue but safely get back to us. I'm about to delve in, about to sink into a soft place, let the words tumble out about so much, when he ends our conversation abruptly. "Good luck, honey. I've gotta get to sleep. Let me know how tomorrow goes."

With those words, I'm silenced, relegated to a distant second in a race I didn't sign up for.

I get out of bed and let my feet touch the floor. One more day till I meet Lele. I make a list of the staff I have to call and interview. I'm annoyed that they've been sent off to their respective quarters in the world, out of my reach, in other time zones. And I hesitate. Shouldn't Lele's words be the first ones I hear on this matter? She can be the only authority. The interviews, the corroboration, can come after. Until I see her, everything is in stasis.

On my phone, an email blinks in, causing my stomach to lurch.

Maya,

It has been brought to our attention that you have taken it upon yourself to police this matter. That is not why you have been summoned. The proper disciplinary action, if

needed, will be taken by headquarters, if and when necessary. Please call in at nine a.m. Geneva time so that
we may discuss this matter and clarify your responsibilities on establishing an evacuation plan for staff, and
determining the communications efforts required to liaise
effectively with our beneficiaries.

I trust you are well.

Best wishes,
Burton

My face is hot. It must have been Marc.

Dear Burton,

Thank you for your email. Rest assured I am not trying to
police anything. As you know, I have a history of working in this community and am aware of the steps needed
to make people feel heard and valued. Kindly trust my
expertise in the region.

Between the two of us, you should remind Marc that
by organizing community meetings I am representing the
institution's interests. I am trying to salvage broken trust
through a collaborative and participatory approach—as
is mandated by our mission statement. The evacuation
and communication plans can only be effective if I honor
and include the community's concerns.

I'll try to speak at nine a.m. but as you know the
internet connection is unreliable.

Warm regards,
Maya

Two can play this game. Marc can tattle to my boss, but I speak bureaucratic language like my mother tongue. I'm two hours ahead of Geneva, nine ahead of California, living in their later hours, in their future. I switch off my phone, disappearing from contact. If you can't reach me, you can't scold me.

I thunder down the stairs, emboldened, and burst into the kitchen. Chantal is making some sort of juice and Marc is sitting at the table reading a local newspaper. Elections will be held soon is what we've been hearing for nine years, and the paper, as always, reflects smiling pictures of future criminals who will be running for regional elections. At this point, it's impossible to keep track of who is running for what, much less whether voting will ever take place.

"Hi," Chantal begins, but I walk straight past her and slam my palms on the table and stare at Marc.

"Why the hell would you go to Burton behind my back?"

"I don't agree with your approach." Marc looks up at me, his calm honesty infuriating.

"Then talk to me about it."

"I did," he responds. "You didn't listen." He turns a page of the newspaper.

"Listening is not the same thing as agreeing," I say. "I listened but did not agree. I'm the expert that's been called in to fix your little mess. So let me do my job."

"You're not bettering conditions for them; you're picking at their wounds. Burton doesn't agree with your approach either. And it's not my mess. I didn't do anything. Technically it's your mess now as I'm not supposed to be part of the conversation."

"From now on if you have any issues with how I'm handling things, you come to me first. Do you understand?"

Marc says nothing, looks at me, then at the newspaper. He reminds me of my husband. Detached.

"Do you understand?" I repeat louder than I've ever spoken in the office. Maybe in my life.

He nods slowly.

"Good," I say and leave the kitchen, trembling. The intensity of the anger, its loud release, feels good. This is what honesty must taste like.

"She's an idiot," I hear him say.

"Shh. What the fuck, Marc? Why would you do that? Maya's been on your side all along," says Chantal. I'm touched by her loyalty as I lurk outside the door.

"On my side? She wouldn't be sneaking around with that guy last night if she was," Marc says.

"What guy? I was with her the whole evening. She only talked to Tommy. Maya has always been fair. She's not accusing you just because she's talking to people."

"Not Tommy, that boy who threatened me in the market. I saw her on the security camera when I went in to check on the guards last night. She was talking to him right outside our building. Why the hell was he here? Why didn't she tell us about him?"

"What are you talking about? I know you're stressed, but you can't treat everyone like an enemy."

I hear shuffling. Marc's voice is muffled, as if his face is in his hands. "I want this to be over. I want to do my work and live my life. I don't trust her. She lived here too long, she's like a native."

"Stop! I hate that expression. We should all be native. We live here for god's sake," Chantal says.

Without thinking, I turn back into the kitchen; she shouldn't have to argue with him on my behalf.

"Chantal, I was wondering whether you can come to the market with me," I ask.

"Of course, let me arrange a car and check with security. I'll meet you in a few minutes." She almost runs out of the kitchen while I'm left with Marc, who just shrugs, knowing that I've overheard him. He busies himself opening and closing cabinets as if searching for something. I don't say anything, letting him wallow in the discomfort of the moment.

━━━━━━━━━

I leave the building and walk toward the car. There's a heat haze as if every bit of life is being scorched into evaporation. The earth is parched, cracked. The insects are quiet, seeking shelter under rocks and bricks. The only sound is the gentle buzz of the sun pounding the earth dry.

The sun burns my hair into a wiry nest. I should have worn a hat. The older Americans and the Brits who come to the field have these awful khaki sun hats. They channel Crocodile Dundee even if they'll be in a Land Cruiser the whole day. We all adopt some strange role when we get here, a composite of images fed to us by Meryl Streep, maybe *Heart of Darkness*, maybe a little Indiana Jones, with the soundtrack to *The Mission*. The colonial dream of teaching, civilizing, connecting, seeing the humanity in the most foreign, changing oneself, becoming what was once other.

I kick a pebble with the toe of my shoe as Chantal walks toward me with a couple of baskets in hand, a satellite phone, and keys. We sit on scalding seats and she dumps her things in the back seat. I look ahead. The windshield is splattered with dirt. We drive. The fluorescent green of tall dry grasses passes us by like a film. On the side of the road, there are remnants of a drainage canal that was started and never completed. Its purpose was to channel water away during the rainy season to prevent floods. Now it's stuffed with garbage—old bottles, newspapers, plastic bags—making future flooding worse.

A few women walk by, hunched over, kilos of firewood on their backs. Many of them are permanently concave from a lifetime of carrying extreme weight. I've never given them a ride.

Somehow, assisting people practically, like giving them a ride, doesn't occur to us; it is not what we are trained for. Think of the security nightmare. Think of the culture of entitlement that could spread. Think of how you would have to decide who to give a ride to and who not to. What would be the terms of reference for that? Think of the cosmetic damage to the car, of branches and twigs scraping seats and windows. How complicated our helping becomes. How very particular and measured.

"As much as Marc thinks I'm his enemy," I say, "I'm not. I just want to do things the right way, without reproach."

"You have done nothing wrong here, Maya. He's the one—I can't believe he complained to headquarters behind your back. That's crazy."

I need these affirmations, despite being in charge.

The car hits a particularly large rock and both of our heads hit the ceiling; we laugh, without wanting to.

"What is it like to drive on paved roads again?" she jokes.

"It's boring. Sometimes I'm afraid I'll fall asleep at the wheel."

"So, what do you think really happened to Lele?" I ask.

"No idea, but we have to find out." She bites her lip. "Lele is so mature now. She has the same positive attitude, but the childishness is gone. She comes with me to meetings, leads on programming. I sometimes forget she's not part of our international staff. She's very bright. I can't believe this happened to her."

"I'm seeing the family tomorrow. You should come."

"I wonder how Marc will react," she says.

"That shouldn't matter," I say, a little too firmly.

"Of course not. It's just . . . We've been dealing with this crisis for so many weeks now, we've become a well-oiled team. I'll go. I just hope he doesn't see it as an attack."

I study Chantal's beautiful profile against the backdrop of the dry landscape streaming behind her. Her nose perfectly shaped, almost regal. I wonder if she has any nobility in her lineage, and if so, what they would make of her being here, working to help people whose ancestors they once enslaved.

"You're not accusing Marc by going," I say. "And even if he thinks that, who cares?"

She's pensive for a moment. "It's hard, isn't it, Maya, when we know both of the people involved? It would be so much easier if this were happening to someone else. We wouldn't even think about it, we would just know. But we do know him, and even if he drives me crazy, I've never felt unsafe around him."

"It is hard. But as long as we do our due diligence . . . That's all we can do."

We've arrived. Chantal parks on a grassy knoll and tugs on the hand brake, groaning us into place. She unrolls the window and calls a teenage boy over. She pays him a few crunched-up bills to watch our car and grabs the baskets from the back seat.

We've parked some distance from the market. It would be ostentatious for us to drive close to pedestrians. We're still within Likanni, far from any disruption the militants have planned. We walk up a hilly incline, then down again. Between two small hills is a long dirt path where the market is held each day. The local grocery store, if you will.

As we climb down to the path, I stop and smile.

"You look like a tourist," Chantal says, mocking me.

I do. There is a hint of a breeze on the hill, and looking down I see the colors of the market swirling around one another. If I squint, the people disappear. I see movement, liquids of color, mixing and breaking away. The entire region is wracked with violence, but the market feels happy. It's where people get their sustenance. It's where they count their pennies. It's where they barter. It's where they run into each other and catch up. It's where they do the mundane, and the mundane keeps us all alive.

Chantal looks nervous. These are the people she's been avoiding. I move closer to her, my arm grazing hers. She looks at me gratefully.

There are several types of vendors in this market. The poorest ones are the old women who lay ten to twelve fruits on a sheet. They sit on the ground, fanning themselves with a palm leaf, one leg outstretched, barefoot, white callouses on their feet. There are those who sell plastic odds and ends, made-in-China treasures, hanging on thin cardboard. Hair clips, kids' plastic guns, pencil sharpeners. I marvel at these knickknacks, at how far they've come, what Disney characters they bear, how they travel to places that don't even have roads. There are the fancier vendors: they've got carts on which they put their fruits, nuts, and spices. Some stalls are held up by purple eucalyptus branches, others by bamboo, covered by tarp, empty bags of rice or with remnants of aid tents. There are fruits, spices, toys, combs, buckets, salted fish.

At the end of the path is the second-hand clothing market, purchased from the excesses of the West. Piles of old clothing sit in small hills which people rifle through, finding the best denim, T-shirts with worn Armani logos. All over these parts clothing is reused and resold till the fabric can bear no more, chafed and softened from body to body, straight into disappearance. Creased, polished old shoes sit together on the ground, their laces tied, awaiting the next wearer. I've wondered where these articles come from, who wore them last, if their previous owners know that their threads belong to Likanni now; if people somehow intermix through the sharing of fabric. Whether some kid in Florida suddenly, inexplicably feels the fear then victorious laughter of a Likanni boy dodging militias, wearing his T-shirt.

The faces of the older people are familiar. As we enter the din, they take notice of me and gush. I am hugged and grabbed. I am kissed with parched lips. It's a grand entrance. One of the eldest women grasps me tightly by the hand, her labored palms scratching against mine. She pulls me down to sit with her on the ground and sends a little boy to grab me a coconut.

"Biga," she exclaims. "You are back, child."

146

I can't for the life of me remember her name and I hate myself for it.

"Marcel, vite," she yells at the boy. I sit on the ground next to her, Chantal next to me. "Oh Biga," she moans and puts my palm against her heart. "It is good to see you, my heart is calm now." Overcome by her affection, I grab her hand in mine and kiss it out of respect. It's so much easier to feel here.

"Biga. It has been hard luck. Look. The market has changed." She gestures around and shakes her head. She calls to another woman selling hair combs across from her. "Look, it is Biga." The other woman hobbles over and embraces me.

I'm surrounded. Women huddle near me, children climb onto their laps. They tell me so much. How hard times have been, whose children have been kidnapped by the militias, the strange Russian men who fly in on planes that land in the middle of fields. The foreign soldiers, how many people have fled. How rich men have gotten richer. Which politicians are being backed by the Americans. Which girls were forced into prostitution. The floods, the storms, the heat. The illnesses, the lack of medication. One finishes, the other begins.

Chantal and I listen. We touch women's hands. We put our arms against shoulders. For us, it's a torturous movie. We watch, we feel, we weep, we yearn, then we leave. The torture embedded somewhere in the cells of our minds. We can kind of remember, but we can also kind of forget, like this woman's name. This is the shame that lurks within me: that I can see, but that I can leave, like they are not real. Sometimes I wish they weren't—that they were holograms. Some twenty-first-century simulation to induce morality. How can any human receive such pain and survive, while others like me live in the parallel, in tired perfection? There are the women back home, the ones at the gym, the ones in my meditation class, the ones seeking work-life balance and trying to manage stress. They have pain too, but not this kind. Not the kind that involves the carving of flesh, the stealing of daughters, the sound of thunderous army boots.

Someone jokingly slaps me on the back.

"Aren't any of you ladies going to sell anything today?" It's the Chief's wife, Lele's mother, Nounia, smiling down at the small group that has formed around me, near the entrance of the market. The merchant women jump up and laugh. "It's Bigabosse's fault," one jokes.

"I can see that," says Nounia, with a smile.

I get to my feet and say hello respectfully, but she folds me into a tight embrace. She's the only one with her head completely covered in a wrap that juts out in various directions. I feel the stiff fabric of her sky-blue dress against my cheek and inhale her scent. She's strong. I think of Lele in this powerful woman's embrace, knowing that she can be held up. I want to be a mother like this, firm and embracing.

We look at each other, sharing more than an affectionate smile of women who haven't seen each other in a long time. We share sorrow for Lele. Nounia puts her hand on my arm. "We are looking forward to welcoming you tomorrow. We will give you a proper greeting as you have been away too long." She smiles at Chantal but doesn't make any gestures toward her. "You too, Madame Chantal, most welcome." Chantal mumbles a thank-you.

"Now, where have my children gone?" Nounia looks around. Two girls pop out of nowhere, younger than Lele, smiling with wide white teeth, shyly averting their eyes. I don't remember them. The older one carries a sack of rice on her head. They are joined by Fanon, who carries multiple bags. He grins at me like an old friend.

"Aah, Bigabosse. Look at the feast my mother is planning. I'm carrying all these items for your lunch," he says, laughing.

Nounia slaps him on the shoulder. "Is that a way to speak to a guest?"

Fanon grins wider, but when he sees Chantal, his smile erodes.

"Please do not go to this much trouble. I don't eat that much," I say, knowing it won't matter. The table will be full of dishes, and they'll spend more than they can afford; the guest is sacred.

"Nonsense. You look like you do not eat, so skinny." Nounia pinches my arm for fat. She leans in, puts both hands on my shoulders. "We will see you tomorrow, Bigabosse. Lele will be very pleased." We say our goodbyes, and Chantal and I attempt to get groceries.

It's a lengthy meandering walk through the market. We touch vegetables, talk with merchants; Chantal haggles the prices down. It's loud and we're loud. We laugh. We complain about the look of fruit. That transformative thing that happens to all of us in the field happens. The energy around us seeps in, changing our shape, changing our temperament. We become boisterous, funnier, more confident. We walk with wider shoulders, looser hips; we spread out like we've always belonged to this dirt path and its market. We walk a walk that we've never used in Los Angeles or Paris. We become the noise around us. This feeling, it's one of the reasons we live here. A freedom we cannot name. We matter here in a way we cannot back home.

Not much has changed, but I notice a lot more weapons. Even the poorest of vendors has machetes, metal rods. Life is going on as it always has; merchants continue to sell bananas but with added armament under the table. It's miraculous how people recalibrate.

Outside of war zones, people have a clear idea of who the good and bad guys are. They watch television and point at men with beards or accents and pronounce them villains, corrupt. In war zones, you cannot know. Freedom fighters can turn violent. Law enforcement can be despotic. Foreign democratic militaries can pillage. And people in the middle, they constantly readjust their compasses to the lesser evils of the day. Some try to keep their heads down. Others try to rise up. Those people in the middle can be good and bad, some situations demanding more bad of them than good, for survival. Then they return to themselves, their goodness. That return, I have seen it many times, especially in teenagers. No one is completely doomed. There is no permanent good and evil, just a spectrum people flirt along according to the sufferings of the day.

As Chantal and I buy cashews, the boy watching our car runs to us, tears in his eyes. He has a bruise on his cheek.

"They pushed me. Hit me. I'm sorry. I'm sorry," he wails. Chantal and I find ice for his face. He hands the money back to her, which she refuses to take.

"They broke the car," he whimpers.

As soon as he utters these words, Chantal and I hand him a few more bills, thank him, and rush toward the Land Cruiser.

"We shouldn't have come," Chantal grumbles.

"Let's see what the damage is," I say.

We walk rapidly through people, trying not to make eye contact, avoiding conversation. Thibault, selling bags of charcoal, calls out to me, a friendly smile on his face, beckoning me to buy a bag. I wave, yelling I'll be back, that I'm in a rush.

I look at Chantal, a few paces ahead of me, her neck stiff. I know what she's thinking. If the car is shot, we're stuck here for a while, and given the current circumstances, we could get attacked while waiting for our guards.

Chantal gasps. The windows are smashed. The hood dented in. I unlock the trunk, pull out a towel, and wrap it around my hand. I brush the shards off the front seats, but there's so much glass.

"We'll never be able to sit in there," Chantal cries.

She's right, but I try, hypnotically stroking the seat with my towel, now embedded with flecks of glass. Chantal calls the guards, while I swipe. Those walking by notice the very public display of our weakness, and a crowd forms. This wreck proves that we are not untouchable. That our stallion of metal and glass can be struck, and that someone is very angry at us.

"It was probably Lele's brother—did you see the way he looked at me?" Chantal says.

I stop what I'm doing and poke my head out of the car. "Who? Fanon? He was with his mother. Nounia would never allow him to act this way."

"That didn't stop him from threatening Marc and me earlier," she scoffs.

The crowd gets larger, the voices a little louder. No one offers to help, which they ordinarily would, but locals aren't allowed to touch foreign vehicles unless they work for us.

"Don't worry, security will be here soon. We'll leave with one of the drivers in the other car. They'll figure out what to do with this one." As I finish my sentence, I hear the clang of a rock against the car. I poke my head out. It's a kid, no more than twelve years old. He sees me and throws another pebble at the car. Another child joins him. Chantal goes white and grips my arm. The din gets louder. It's unclear whether the noise is frustration at the boys or at us, but the melee starts moving closer to us, more animated.

"What do we do?" Chantal whispers to me.

We have to look strong, unfazed, as though we are part of the group. The crowd gets louder, and I hear my pounding heartbeat over what everyone else is saying, rendering their words inde- cipherable. We should walk away to safety. I'm not sure where safety is in this open market. I'm acutely aware of my body sud- denly, of how not-strong it is, how I could be yanked by hair or by limb. Of how Chantal's phone could be grabbed from her, cutting us off from the office. I debate whether to yell at the kids like an auntie from the village, or join them in throwing pebbles at the car, turning the violence into a shared game. For maybe that's all it is. But I'd set a bad example, wouldn't I? Then they would al- ways pelt our cars with rocks. I frantically look into the crowd for familiar faces, for someone I can talk to. To demonstrate my connection to these people. But they are all strangers, and all men. So many considerations for a split-second decision, which has to be the right one, before the next pebble is launched.

Fanon walks toward us, out of the crowd, with more bags than he had earlier. I nearly collapse with relief.

"What is happening?" he says. He takes one look at the kids gathering rocks, yells loudly at them, and extends his arm as if he will smack them; they giggle and dart off. Fanon argues with an older man standing near the boys. It is in dialect, but I capture the gist: he's furious that the man didn't stop them. The man shrugs indifferently and tells him the car was already broken.

"Bigabosse, you are okay?" he asks.

"Yes, fine. Someone just damaged the car," I say, swallowing my breathlessness and minimizing my own fear. My heart is still racing.

Fanon clicks his tongue disapprovingly.

"Do you know who did this?" Chantal asks him, an eyebrow raised, a hint of blame in her tone.

"I do not know," Fanon answers, with anger. "Perhaps someone broke your windows because you work with a criminal. You should be satisfied they are windows. Most people here pay with their lives when the rebels come—you, it is only the windows." He spits.

This is what this place does. It only takes seconds for things to unravel. One moment there's laughter and familiarity, the next someone is spitting at you. Chantal has become a part of this. She's forgotten how to mitigate the outbursts. When everyone is living under heightened threat, everyone is subject to eruption. The eruptions feel good, like there is still a freedom of release allowed. But we have to be careful at how much release we allow ourselves, before we destroy everything.

Chantal is on the phone again, hollering at someone on the

other end. It's a frantic side to her I've never seen. Seventeen minutes later, the driver shows up with a vehicle and two other security staff people.

There's an odd efficiency in these parts. Public systems are collapsing, but magically our private cars get where they need to without tow trucks; they get fixed and we'll get a bill. Some invisible labor somewhere makes just about anything possible. Anything broken will get repaired—it might not look the same, but it'll be functional.

Chantal climbs into the back seat of the new 4x4, and I get in the front next to the driver.

"I'm sorry I took us there," I offer. "But on a positive note, those kids weren't throwing rocks at us. They were just aiming for what was already a wreck."

I feel ridiculous that I was scared. The freedom, the fear, the constant dance between the two, that's what it means to be here. The spikes of cortisol, the thrill of feeling threatened when not at risk, the victorious rush of leaving a situation unscathed—I had forgotten it.

"We were having such a good time before the car thing, I almost forgot everything else," says Chantal, her eyes closed.

It had been nice. Going into the village had felt like a home-coming of sorts.

We return to the office, and Chantal, in her role as the country manager, makes calls and notes the incident with the security services that monitor this stuff.

I decide to be brave in my own way. I call my housekeeper, waking her up.

"Hi, Miss Maya, are you back?" She sounds like she's patting a yawn.

I tell her no and ask her how the house is. She tells me that Mr. Steven said not to come this week. I say oh. Then I ask her to go in today and turn on the smart-home monitoring alarm in the house, the one with my code, that I'll walk her through how to do it over the phone.

She sounds doubtful. "Are you sure, Miss Maya?" Do I want to be able to see my own home while I'm away? She knows. And she knows that I know.

"Yes, Angela. Yes please."

"Okay," she says, "but only in the main hallway." This is as indiscreet as she'll be. She doesn't want the camera aimed at my bedroom door to be turned on.

I acquiesce.

There. If I can do that, I can face Marc and Lele. Fear, then freedom.

The door to Chantal's office, my old office, is open.

"I'm heading over to Seher and Tommy's for a couple of hours. I'll be back before dinner," I announce, not ready to see Marc.

She looks surprised, mouths "Okay," her hand cupping the phone.

15

If Tommy and Seher were surprised when I contacted them, they didn't show it.

"I won't be home, but Seher will. Come on over," Tommy texted back, as if me dropping by was a regular occurrence.

While the rest of the land is parched, Seher and Tommy's house, made of some earthy substance, is surrounded by lengths of hydrated green. They have built a greenhouse on the side of the house. I walk by and peek in; it's bursting at the seams. No room for humans in there, just botanical anomalies exploding out of a medley of colorful pots.

Their house looks like a barn and, knowing them, they've used science in the walls to keep it cool. It looks organic and comforting. The front door is wide open for anyone to walk in. That's part of their thing. The welcome of anyone at any time. They swear it keeps the thieves out. Seher appears in the doorway with an apron on, looking oddly domestic.

"Don't mind me. I'm trying something in the kitchen, but it's bound to fail," she says, hugging me.

It's been years since I've seen Seher, but we pick up like this, no big deal. She's skinnier; she's got tufts of white in her woolly hair that she hasn't sought to mask. A beak-like nose, large black eyes, bushy eyebrows, lithe movements—everything protrudes on this woman.

"Come in, come in." She ushers me in. "Did you come with a driver?" She stops abruptly, and I run into her backside.

"Yes, I have," I say.

"Ask him to come inside. It's too hot to be sitting in a car."

I get Jean, the driver. He's new, from a neighboring country, not quite sure of the roads or the people. He looks uncomfortable when I ask him to come in. I'm uncomfortable asking. Seher's equalizing behaviors create uncertainty for all of us who are used to our roles. But that's her, making her own rules, busting class with everything she's got.

Jean enters the house hesitantly behind me.

"Welcome, welcome," Seher says to him in dialect, stretching her face into a toothy smile as though he's the guest of honor. She guides him to a sitting room filled with books, magazines, sofas, a television set.

"Feel free to watch TV. What would you like to drink?" She switches on the TV with one hand and finds a local drama. "There, this should be good," she says.

Jean looks at this skeletal, sprightly woman as though she's mad. He sits uncomfortably on the edge of a flower-printed sofa.

"Water? Lemonade? I have lemonade."

I stand behind Seher.

The driver shakes his head. Apologetic that he's occupying any space or attention at all. He looks like he's in pain from the pampering and questions.

"Water then. I'll get water. The lavatory is down the corridor," says Seher.

She turns to me. "Come, come." We walk down the hall to a massive kitchen, with large windows overlooking what look like orchards of fruit. I see people working in them. Sun hats pop up among trees and branches.

It's as if I've walked into Seher's brain, or what I imagine it's like in there. There's spilt flour on one counter, chopped herbs and stems on another. Brown root vegetables sit soggy in the sink. Greasy bottles, colorful jars of lentils and spices are strewn about. Large tin cans of oil, smeared with fingerprints, sit by the stove. Cooking instruments are everywhere, most of them dirty. I can't tell what on earth she's cooking—or baking? There's something boiling here, something marinating over there. Unfamiliar scents.

"Sit, sit." She gestures for me to sit at the kitchen table upon which the newspaper's spread, splattered with cooking oil.

"Chai?" Seher asks, eyebrows raised.

"Sure, thanks."

She swivels about again, quickly putting a pot on the gas stove, lighting it with an extra-long matchstick, filling a glass with water from an overused plastic bottle, shaking out the matchstick before chucking it behind her.

"One minute," she says, running off with the glass for the driver, spilling droplets on the terra-cotta tile. She won't sit comfortably until she has served the poorest among us. She comes running back into the kitchen, noticing the drips of water on the ground, which she wipes with her red-socked feet. I rarely see women wearing socks here. And never red ones.

Finally, she takes a seat at the table across from me.

"Hello, old friend," Seher says, looking at me with buggy eyes.

"This place is splendid," I say, gesturing around me.

"That's right, you left before we moved. We've been very fortunate. We were able to build exactly what we wanted. I'll give you a tour later. Samosas, do you want samosas? I also have pound cake." She twists to reach for the counter.

"No, please, I'm not hungry. I just came to see you," I say, putting my hand on hers.

"I'm so pleased. Tommy said he'd seen you. How have you been keeping?" That Pakistani accent, the sharp *t*'s, the lilts, the Queen's English. I've missed it.

Before I answer, she says, "Do you want some saalan? You know what saalan is, right? It's what the British call curry. For god's sake, use the proper term already. But they called them Red Indians, so I suppose I can't complain about foodstuffs when they've mistitled entire populations." I've heard this bit about curry before. I shake my head.

"How have you been?" she asks again.

"I've been better," I say. I'm in Seher's crazy, explosive world now. Nothing but the truth.

"Work or personal? But of course, work is personal, it is difficult to separate the two, that's a foolish binary for me to set up." Seher gesticulates as she speaks.

"All of it," I say.

The water boils, bubbles pop. She bounds up, crushes cloves and cardamoms and mixes them with tea leaves, then pours the tea into two dainty teacups, with care. No dribbles here.

"It looks incredible out there," I say, pointing at the orchards.

"There's much more to do, but it's a start."

"How many families are living off these?" I ask.

"About thirty. But one more drought will kill it. We have drip irrigation, but when the water dries up, there's no hope for anything to survive," Seher says. "And then it'll be back to the usual: people will migrate to neighboring towns or cross the border. More conflict, same old, same old."

"Can I ask you something?"

"Anything," she replies, adding copious amounts of sugar to the tea she's poured.

"How do you stay hopeful? How do you stay separate from it? When you see all the shit that happens, how do you stay sane? How can you make tea and samosas?"

Seher laughs. "That's many questions." She carries a heavy tray with cups, biscuits, and samosas to the table. She looks thoughtful. "We get discouraged. But we try to stay clean with our intent," she says, as she passes me a cup.

"What do you mean?"

"We know and we accept. We make more money, we are the foreigners. Tommy's white, he has privilege. I come from a rich family, I have privilege. We've come here and sometimes we will do the right thing and sometimes the wrong, but when we do the wrong, we have to be honest. We have to beg for forgiveness, and we have to improve. That is our moral obligation."

"Hmm."

"You don't look convinced."

"No, it's just—is it enough?"

"It appears small, but it is not. When have you seen one of the mining companies come out and apologize? Or the charities? The militaries? When have they come, sat with the people, and admitted failures? Never. There's never any accountability. Then things can never improve. It is a cycle of mistake. We refuse to perpetuate it."

"Okay, fine, mistakes are one thing, but what about the impossibility of the task at hand? The largeness of all the pain?" I ask.

"No, mistakes are not one thing. If people truly acknowledged their misdeeds, then they would think conscientiously on how to prevent repeating them, the track would change. The largeness, as you call it, would become incrementally smaller," Seher says.

I look down at my tea. Cinnamon floats on the surface.

"It doesn't feel like it's enough. You have Europeans and Saudis buying land to grow food, locking out the local hungry. You have kids shooting people. How can anything be enough?"

"Oh Maya, have you forgotten all the emails I've sent you about protesting land grabs? Or building a rehabilitation center for child soldiers? We're on the front lines!"

"It's just—how can one be happy with this endless suffering?"

"I don't know, maybe we are desensitized. There are devastating moments, you know. I went to purchase milk a few months ago and discovered the farmer and his wife had been slain. Blood everywhere. But you have to honor that loss, then you make something of it." Seher speaks to me in a gentle voice, something she seldom does.

"Make what of it?"

"You can always make something. We started a seed bank during the last hungry season. After the farmer was slain, we set up an early warning signal with neighbors so we can alert one another if the militias come too close."

"You're lucky that you have talents that can be put to use," I say with envy.

"Nonsense," Seher says harshly. "Everyone has basic, common-sense talents. Most are too lazy to make use of them. It takes time and effort to help others, and it is not enjoyable. People always think they want to help, but who wants to bring a smelly homeless person home to bathe? Who wants to deal with unpredictable people on drugs and alcohol? It's hard. But people like you and I, we must."

I imagine bringing a homeless person to sleep on my immaculate white linen couches. "Why must we do anything, Seher?"

"Would you be happy just living for yourself? If you would, go. You obviously aren't because you keep coming back." She leans back in her chair. "Look, any of us idiots that come here, rightly or wrongly, we see things others ignore, and we're arrogant or foolish enough to believe we can contribute something."

"I don't know if I believe that anymore."

"Of course you can—you can start by speaking truthfully. Mind you, it won't be good for your popularity. Look at me, no more friends." Seher waves her hands. "You live surrounded by people who pay no thought to consequences. We all do. You can remind them."

"That's so abstract." I hear myself complaining.

"No. Think of the smallest of actions, say buying chocolate. Do you think people would purchase the chocolate if they knew most of it came from slave labor? Their behaviors would surely change. That would change something else, and the track of action will change," says Seher.

"You're far too optimistic. The only thing people care about is how cheap they can get something, or its brand." I laugh. "Maybe hippies care, but that's it. People care way more about being practical, getting things done. No one ponders how their little choices affect someone else; it's too overwhelming."

"Then teach them," says Seher matter-of-factly. "Life is overwhelming. Making decisions is overwhelming. That can't be an excuse for not thinking about consequences."

"You want me to become a warrior for ethical consumption? In the States? Show up at kids' birthday parties asking parents to figure out where the gifts came from?" I laugh.

"It's a start."

"They'll write me off as a cuckoo social justice warrior."

"Maybe, but you'll be doing something. You ask how we get through things, this is how. We consider every single decision, every act. That way we know every footprint we leave is honest. And if it's not, we acknowledge and apologize. We try to fix it."

"Sounds exhausting." I visualize my Costco grocery cart back home, the multitude of boxes, trying to figure out where my toilet paper was made, under what conditions, while competing with other carts; all of us zealously navigating that air-conditioned terrain, trying to get the most stuff for the lowest price, eyeing the shortest lineups, a whole art form, not made for questioning.

"Less exhausting than contributing to slavery," says Seher nonchalantly. "We're not saints, Maya. Ultimately, this is what gives us meaning and we try. Hopefully not as naively as some of our colleagues who live all the experiences and none of the consequences, but we try."

I take a sip of my tea. The taste of clove spreads on my tongue, as though I'm becoming more of her—her intermixed culture, her way of thinking. It seems so easy when she puts it this way. Why does it seem easier for her, in this nook of the world, looking life and death in the eyes every day? Why do I trust people like her with her seeds and trees to carry the world, when I have stopped doing the same? I've segmented it all, as though Likanni is the only place where truth can happen, where our actions can matter. As though all else is sedated fluff, a cloud through which I can sleepwalk. Maybe being back home requires a different kind of nerve.

"Do you ever get scared?" I ask her.

"Every day. That is why Tommy and I decided not to have children. I can subject myself to the fear, but not children."

"Yes, children," I groan.

"Oh yes, yours must be grown now."

"Chloe's four," I say.

"Can I see pictures?"

I click my phone on and show her the last picture my mother sent.

"Lovely. She's very fair. She doesn't look like your daughter."

I laugh. "That's what people used to tell my mother about me, that I was too dark."

"Oh no, see, I'm applying my own internalized racism. You know I come from a country where people bleach their skin to look white. Her fairness should not matter, I apologize." Seher slaps her forehead.

"That's okay."

"No, no, it isn't, it's wrong. But tell me, what's the problem with the daughter?"

"No problem," I say.

Seher gives me a penetrating look.

I surrender. "I don't know. I don't think I know how to love her properly. I'm too damaged by all this."

"Properly? How does one calculate that? Is this an American thing?" She laughs.

Suddenly she takes my hand in hers, and I realize I've never before held hands with someone the same color as me. I've always been a contrast.

"Jaan," she says, a term of endearment I've heard her call Tommy. "You have to be patient with yourself. Don't forget, you went through hell during the Likanni fire, that must have left deep scars."

My eyes water. I stopped seeing Seher and Tommy after the fire. I had too much guilt. Seher had warned us about the mining companies. I had been so irritated by her anticorporate shtick. She would show up at my office, she would call incessantly, she would invite me for dinners and harangue me for hours about the impacts these companies could have. Instead, I avoided her and befriended those Matts and Todds.

Was that all it took for me to accept people's unintended, foolish violence? For them to be nice? CEOs, politicians, warlords, my husband: they all know how to be nice. When they uncoil, people like me are surprised, rarely connecting the dots, because politeness appears so absolute, so unable to produce harm. We trust the polite ones; we feel like we know them. And yet the Sehers and Tommys forewarned us; they had waved banners before our eyes, thrust petitions in our faces. It's because we see the Sehers and Tommys as hysterical, unrealistic activists trying to stir things up, messing with a pleasant order, not as prophets.

She squeezes my hand.

"You know what is inspiring? The trust humans display for each other every single day. You got in a car and you trusted the driver would bring you here. You trust the food I give you won't make you sick. The people you work with trust that you have their best intentions at heart. Those infinite moments of human trust dwarf the cruelty, the politics, everything, really."

"I'm scared that the pain here will make me lose everyone and everything I love," I say desperately.

"The pain is part of existence. Just feel it. You are not killing anyone by loving your child. If you live honestly, then you know— you haven't hurt anyone. Don't hold love hostage. It's not going to help anyone here."

"It's hard in the States. I'm angry all the time. I'm surrounded by people who have no interest in others."

"People are blind to their hypocrisies everywhere, not just in the U.S. Because it would destroy them to know how much harm they cause. But you can be blind as a bat—at some point, the world will creep up on us all. Maybe as bodies washing upon borders, maybe in diseases that arrive in airplanes. No one is immune. People like us, we need to build the human connectivity now. We need to show how things in one place affect the outcomes in another. We need to bring down the tyrants." She smiles wickedly.

We drive back to the office, my belly full of assorted foods Seher forced me to eat. Yet I feel lighter. People like Seher exist. Annoying, pontificating, but fair and rousing. Even the driver has a smile. He had a rest, which did not involve sweating in a scalding car.

Seher and I, all that garbled talk, it would have made little sense to anyone else. Truth, suffering, samosas. But Seher can always snake things into a human chain. A chain of a million behaviors that bind. She gives me a place on that chain.

Where I have less of a place is with Steven. I remember sensing it eight months after our engagement. I had just returned from Likanni after handing over my keys and responsibilities to Chantal. The villagers had held a goodbye ceremony. Paulsie's young daughter Fetenat had handed me a bagful of little boxes and trays she had woven herself with her eight-year-old fingers. Paulsie told me Fetenat had picked the dried grass herself, selecting the colors she thought I would like. It had been her first time weaving. There had been singing, dancing, embracing. I thought I was happy to be leaving, to be going to my country, to that beautiful man waiting for me, holding our shiny future in his hands. But as each person came to bid me farewell, I felt as if I was being ripped from my family.

When I got back to L.A., Steven was his exuberant self. Ready to spend weekends living the hedonistic lifestyle he was accustomed to sharing with me. His weeks were corporate mergers and acquisition contracts; his weekends were for playing big-boy games, me at his side.

But I was ready to come up for air. To make my life in California something of value. I needed to learn, start anew. Discover who I was going to be in the States. I wanted to keep laughing with Steven, but I wanted the serious too. I wanted to show him the world outside of tourist catalogs. The joys in food stands, unadvertised moments, of finding our causes, not pet projects to receive accolades for, but issues we ached for. I believed we could have that. Steven was smart and curious.

Instead of us falling into each other, or the largeness of the world, Steven entertained himself with pastimes I despised. He played an inordinate amount of golf. That green space, its true verdant nature expunged to create an artificial landscape, that wasted water to keep it fresh, that sport without athleticism, those shapeless men trying to get a small ball in a small hole in the sanitized outdoors, was symbolic of all I rejected. I would watch Steven leave with one of his three sets of clubs and think of Anders. How useful he had made his body. How purposeful he was in every way. Each time Steven left the house, I felt more and more sickened. I blamed it on the memory of the fire, the PTSD, my own displacement. I chalked up my hatred of golf clubs to my own insanities. I would be normal, I told myself, when I could watch him lugging that lugubrious bag to the trunk and feel affection.

In that compressed engagement of ours, I worried about what would bind us; it was hard to know when so much of myself had seemingly slipped underwater. Shapes blurred, sounds opaque, me tired, just moving my body for survival. Not knowing what purpose I served by waking up. Steven tried to be sensitive. Finding me melancholic after my return from Likanni, he tried to entertain me. He lined up concerts, movies, and comedy shows. The sincerity of those attempts was my confirmation: this was love. What's more generous than someone trying to cheer you up? However odd the film choices, the gestures, the affection, they were balm against my coarse skin. And in that I would surely flower. Anybody would.

One day, he told me he had gotten tickets to something that was right up my alley.

Up my alley turned out to be a fashion show and gala called Fashion Feels, a night for the fashion industry to "give back" to charity. It was a sparkling affair with businessmen, philanthropists, and moneyed families.

Steven bought me a stiff red dress; I walked in with him in his tuxedo. There were cello players, performers, thousands of glasses for all types of drinking pleasure placed meticulously at organza-clad tables; the stemware shone. Peonies and lilies filled the room. Gowns slid against floors. And there was me. A woman who had dragged people from a fire, had spent years of her life living in cotton. I was awkward but content, looking at people as if watching a documentary. I was like a Likanni woman sitting on a stoop.

There were speeches about how Fashion Feels for poor kids, how two million dollars would be donated. There were watery eyes and applause, shiny lips and jewels. Everyone looked moved and generous.

Suddenly my dress felt too tight; women's fake eyelashes too long, like spidery legs trawling their lids. Everyone wearing their wealth and brands like furs from stone-age kings. Everything distorted and vulgar, the strange puffed-up lips, the botoxed faces that moved but could not move, the jewels from the earth dangling on ears and necks, desperately announcing status. I felt nauseous, wanting to scream that the need for this charity would disappear if these people simply paid their taxes.

I looked at the man beside me, the corporate lawyer with coiffed hair, the man I had promised to look at every day for the rest of my life. His straight white teeth, his way of nodding ever so slightly to make people feel special. There was something paternalistic in that nod I'd never noticed before. Like Steven knew his importance in the world, that he was nodding to it, getting others to consent to it. I realized then and there. I wanted a life between Anders and Steven; this wasn't it.

On the way back home, we got into a fight, our first fight. I must have started it.

Steven was gushing about the event.

"I wonder how much that whole thing cost," I responded.

"A lot of it was donated. The venue was rented at cost."

I asked why they didn't just donate the money directly and why we all received swag bags.

"Because it's fun. It gets people together for a good cause. Everybody wins," said Steven.

"Except for the people who are actually affected by the fashion industry."

"Excuse me?"

"This thing, Fashion Feels, it's ridiculous. It's great that they are giving money. Programs need it. But they should look at themselves and how they poison rivers, underpay people in sweat-shops, create waste—"

"Do you have any idea how much those tickets cost?"

"I'm not saying—"

"I bought those tickets as a gift for you, to make *you* feel better, to contribute to your world, and you're pissing all over it?"

"I appreciate the gift, I do, but what makes you think that's 'my world'?"

"They're giving money to charity; you work for a charity. How would you feel if people stopped giving to yours? You'd be out of a job."

"I appreciate that people give money to things. It's important, no question. But you have to realize it's always an add-on. It's not a solution. They should start by changing their own practices; they'll have a way bigger impact." Did he really know so little?

"Wow." He whistled. "What a sense of entitlement! Instead of elite-bashing, you should be grateful for their philanthropy. Those folks could have easily spent their money elsewhere. They don't owe you or anyone a damn thing."

"I'm not sure that was philanthropic. It's people at a party, writing off charitable gifts on their taxes," I muttered.

"Are you serious?" Steven laughed. "That's the problem with you social justice warriors. You criticize everyone and don't achieve a thing with your wishy-washy ideas. These are the people who can actually change the world. They raised more in one night than you do in years. Your work wouldn't even exist without people like them."

I should have left him that night, that man who didn't know me or the world. A man who proclaimed knowledge of how things worked but had never spent a night in a mud hut. The man who boxed me in, just as I boxed Seher in. The man who had no clue what a feel-good myth he was living. Instead, I apologized, went to bed, and dreamt of Anders falling in a well.

16

I t's late. Marc ate in his room, avoiding me. Chantal is still working. I sat with her for a couple of hours after my return from Seher's, reviewing sexual assault protocols from different organizations, searching for best practices. Now I sit on the steps, with a couple of flat cigarettes that earlier were snuggled in Chantal's pocket. My jeans creak as I cross my legs. I feel like a teenager, slumped over, smoking on a stoop.

I shouldn't, but I check my phone, hunting for evidence, that it is my mind that's broken, not my marriage. Through the power of legitimized voyeurism, I spy on my home. The entrance, the door that doesn't move. Our foyer is simple: a chair, a white marble console, a mirror. Some keys and envelopes. One thing is different though. A coat rests on my chair. The chair that I bought and placed right there, so Chloe would have a place to sit as she put on her shoes. It's not my coat. It's not my husband's or daughter's.

It's pale blue. A pale-blue coat is frivolous, it's flirty, it wants to be noticed. It's the coat of someone who wants to feign innocence. Funny how things can become lifelike like that. Mute, inanimate, yet truly monstrous.

I'm in a tropical country staring at a Californian doorway, made of blond oak, built by expert contractors who illegally hire Mexicans, erected by a company that writes things off for taxes. I'm sitting on steps crafted by the labor of locals instructed by and for religious colonialists who wanted to save people, make them like them, so much so that they sing hymns in Latin, but not enough to want them back in Paris. But who the fuck does that coat belong to? That coat should know not to be draped so intimately upon my furniture. Are hairs from that coat riding the air in my house, sucked into ducts and spat into all breathable spaces? I want to burn that coat. Maybe I could freeze it, then shatter it like the shards of glass from our Land Cruiser.

Is this what mania feels like? Am I going mad? I look for signs. My legs. They are still. My hands, not shaking. The steps feel solid, anchoring me to this land. It's not mania. It's the truth enabled by the nights here. Of belonging to here and there, to nowhere. Of existing in pieces, in houses visible through screens, in women's embraces at the market, in their loss. Of being Maya and Bigabosse. Maybe more Bigabosse than Maya. I'm sweating. Is this what they call being unhinged? I think calmly of obliterating not only that coat, but its owner, my husband. Myself.

"Bigabosse. It's me, Fanon. I am walking toward you."

I hear the ground being crunched under flip-flops.

"May I sit with you for a few moments?" he asks.

"Hmm," I muster, but just barely. It only seems logical that in this madness, when I'm hungering for violence against a coat, Fanon should creep up, Fanon from a different world, who at night becomes a friend of sorts. A friend who makes sense in the dark. A guy who's called Fanon, for god's sake.

"I thought you may be sitting here at this time," he says.

"I like the nights."

"Like a true Likanni woman. That is when they all come out of our houses."

"What's up?" I ask brusquely. I need to feel angry. He's interrupting me.

"I wish to tell you that I do not know who broke the windows."

"I know that. You don't have to explain."

"The manner in which Miss Chantal spoke . . ."

"She doesn't think you have anything to do with it," I lie. "I'm looking forward to tomorrow."

"Yes, all are. Even Lele. She had her braids done today. She has not let anyone touch her hair in weeks."

"That's wonderful," I exclaim.

"Bigabosse?"

"Yes?"

"What were you looking at? You were making a strange face."

l explain smart alarm systems, surveillance videos, arming and disarming from a distance, through an app; he's incredulous.

"You can see your home from here?"

"Crazy, isn't it?"

"Inside?"

"Yes."

"You can see what is happening this moment?"

"Give or take a few seconds, depending on the internet service, yes."

"May I see?"

I hesitate. Not for privacy, but I am very aware of his thatched roof, the number of people he lives with, the outhouse. I don't want him to see my heavy door, the slate tiles. And I don't want to see the coat again.

"Please? It will be as if I am a guest in your home."

In the spirit of democracy, I flick my phone on. I log into the

171

alarm app. The coat is no longer there. I look closely. Maybe I imagined it. Or someone has slipped through my front door during my pleasantries with Fanon.

I hold the phone out; Fanon peers at it. "What is this?" he asks.

"This is where I enter the house."

He stares for a while. "Is it very cold there?"

"Not really. It's very hot in the spring and summer. We also have shortages of water, like you. In the winter it gets cool, but we don't get snow."

Fanon continues to peer at the screen until my phone turns itself off.

"When are you returning?" he asks.

"I don't know yet. I have a return ticket for three weeks from now, but a lot will depend on how Lele is doing and what I can do to help her. It'll be clearer tomorrow."

"The house is noisy. Mother and the aunts are preparing the feast. It has been a long time since we have celebrated."

"I felt bad when I saw all the preparations at the market."

"You must not. It brings joy," Fanon says.

I'm struck again at his self-confidence; he's one of the educated types who has done a lot of reading and attended the city's university. I'd always assumed that he had been stuck here with a labor job, away from educational opportunities.

"Did you have any trouble after the car?" Fanon asks.

"No, no trouble at all. It was lovely to see everyone. The children have grown, many people have gotten older. It was sad to hear about the deaths and the growing despair. There were so many guns though. And burqas, two of them, and so many abayas."

"They were not there before? The women in abayas?"

"None at all," I say.

"You are surprised."

"I just wonder if Wahhabism has spread here too. Whether this means even less freedom for the women of Likanni."

"Do you think women are more free in America?" is Fanon's amused response.

He's egging me on to debate him. Or maybe he just wants someone different to converse with. I'll oblige. Mostly because I'm sitting here obsessing over a coat, but also because I like hearing his voice. I like being surprised by conversation. With people from my part of the world, conversations take predictable routes, polite forms; they slide down familiar arcs. I can sleep-talk through them, laughing at the right spots, exclaiming at appropriate junctures. With Fanon, I have no idea what we'll be discussing next.

"I don't think women are completely free anywhere. But I think in the West, women have more choices. I'm not saying all our choices are fair, or that everyone has the equal amount of choice. How rich someone is has a lot to do with how many opportunities they get, even where I live. But we have more options."

"Is it not true that girls cannot attend to school if they cover their hair in your countries?"

"In some European countries, but not the United States."

He brushes the difference aside. "It is true then—some girls in the West are not permitted to attend school if they cover their hair."

"Yes," I say, "but only in some countries."

"Is that freedom?"

"Well, no. But in France, for instance, the rationale is that school is a secular space where there should be no religious representation. Although to be honest, I think the French just don't like headscarves. They have a sensual view of femininity, and the headscarf is just not part of their style. There are also those that think the headscarf is a false choice."

"I do not understand?"

"It means that girls may think it's their choice to cover themselves, but it's only because they have been taught to do so by their

173

family. It's not a choice; it's cultural conditioning. One that makes them give up their power to men."

"Why is covering your hair giving power to men? I do not have more power when I see a woman's hair covered. She is deciding what I see and do not see," Fanon says. I hear him crack his knuckles. "Is not everything a false choice? Everything has been taught, handed down through story and what we observe. With your countries, you have the women in your movies and music programs showing their navels because that is what they are to do to entice the men. That is also a false choice, no? Why do your women leaders not say that?"

"There's no band of women ringleaders who decide what is and isn't absurd for women. There are different groups, different views. They often challenge one another."

"Except that there are some who win the argument, because some women cannot attend school, no? Do you agree with them, Bigabosse?"

"It's complicated. I think all our choices are based on men's power. It's hard to say what's more liberating. Whether it's covering yourself or denuding yourself, it's all about men. But I have to say, I do not like the burqa."

"Why is this?"

"It looks extreme. In the West, luckily, very few women do this, and when they do, most people find it unacceptable."

"Why unacceptable?"

"Because it's unacceptable that people want to hide from others in the public realm," I say exasperated.

"What if someone wishes to hide? Here we have Adoni the hermit. He wishes to remain unseen and we permit him."

"That's not the same thing. That's just one person; it's not a system meant to hide all women."

"But you have said very few women wear the burqa. If they wish to keep their faces private, I do not understand the concern?"

I sigh. "In essence, there's nothing wrong with it. But it reflects on the broader oppression of women, that women have to hide from men in order to be safe. It's preposterous. It's not like the West is Afghanistan."

"If one woman, or two, or ten, or one hundred want to not share themselves with the street, why is this a concern? Why can they not wear what they desire? Here there are few. But if a woman wishes to cover, we respect. She has chosen it. In a place where there is violence, it is great assurance to take yourself out of the common market."

"But we don't live in that kind of violence," I contest.

"There are no rapes or killings in your country?" Fanon's accent with his rolling r's makes the word even more dramatic.

"No—of course . . ."

"No, please tell me, are there any abuses in your country?"

"Of course."

"Well, if there is even one crime, then a woman should be as she wishes to remain safe," Fanon says.

"That's absurd. That's essentially saying women in less clothing should expect to be violated," I argue.

"No, it is not that which I am saying. No woman should be violated. What I am saying is every woman can react as she wills in a country where there is any violence."

"A burqa is not a solution," I say.

"Solutions, solutions." Fanon throws his hands up in the air. "You people, always after solutions, forgetting the people and their sentiments. Can we not let the woman be comfortable as she wishes?"

"I don't even know how we got here," I say, annoyed.

"It must be difficult to conceive when your society, your film stars, all they want is to be shown, in pictures, in internet, eating, drinking, exercising. They want to film their most private acts. They wish their faces everywhere, that is what is normal to you people. But some wish to remain unseen. Let them. Maybe some women don't want men looking at them with hunger," says Fanon. He laughs. "Really, you are like the Arabs, but the other way. Arabs, when they come here and see a bare breast, their eyes fall out of their heads. You see a covered woman and you have the same reaction. Bigabosse, you must see the Arabs' face with our women, it is very funny."

"Let's leave dress aside. Think about the lives of women here. They are beholden to husbands and in-laws. It's different where I live: women don't have to get married or have children. Here, and pardon me for saying this, if a woman does not have children, she is seen as barren. People cry at shrines for her. And if she bears no children, the husband takes on other wives. Her life revolves around this forced barrenness."

"You are correct in this. There are smaller choices. But when women become the mothers, they are queen of the household and their children obey. They become the boss, the big boss, Bigabosse. You all care much about our women, sometimes I worry you forget about your own."

"Look at me. I'm far away from my husband and child, with pretty much a stranger. I have the choice to have children and work, and to talk with other men without fear that my husband will overreact. Will you let your future wife or wives do this? Don't you think a woman sitting in the dark talking with a man, who is not family, would be shunned the very next day?" I say with humor.

There are a few seconds of silence, broken by crickets. I hear Fanon opening his mouth to speak. I hear the breath that precedes his words.

"Going to another land or working, that would not be a problem. We did that with Lele. For you, it might not seem far to cross the village, come to the office filled with foreigners, but for her it was, and we sent her happily. Alas, it did not turn well." He pauses. "Sitting with a man in the dark speaking—no, I would not like my wife to do this. I hear every part of your voice. I hear annoyance and the laughing. I am listening with great care. The sound of the voice like this, it is very private. I would not bear anyone I love to give this intimacy to someone. And yes, your husband and your society gives you the freedom, but isn't it sad for you and your husband? You sound different in the night from the day. If you were my wife, I would not want anyone to know the difference." Fanon trails off.

I don't know where to look. My body feels prickly. Fanon has trespassed something. I was enjoying this conversation, his style of speaking, his lens on his world and mine. It's been disrupted. He shouldn't speak of intimacy to me. I can't muse on women's equality when he talks about the sound of my voice. I'm aware that we are only two and that he is a man. And we are in the dark.

I get up, wiping my hands on my jeans.

"I should get to sleep. There is the lunch at your house tomorrow."

Fanon stands as well. "I hope I did not offend. It was not my intention."

"Not at all," I say as cheerily as I can muster. "See you tomorrow."

I disappear into the office quickly. I run up the stairs, two at a time, my flip-flops noisily slapping the stairs. I almost trip.

I should be careful in how I communicate. There are major cultural divides here that I forget because of the easy honesty. It's not that I'm scared; I'm so sad. Steven will never think of the sonorous qualities of my voice or of our nighttime moments as sacred. He's caught up with a blue-coat wearer when we could be listening to each other's tones. The reminder that there are men like Fanon, who want to know the details of a woman, makes me cry.

I keep hearing the sound of the word *intimacy* the way Fanon said it, the way it rolled off his tongue, with a soft *n* and a soft *t* and a familial *m*, right onto me. I want to hear it again.

17

Today I visit Lele.

The roosters bellow. I used to think of them as benign, generously waking the world. Now I see them for what they are: virile attention cravers, competing with one another in a testosterone race, dying to be the first cry of the day, dying to be the last.

I reread the protocol on counseling rape victims The advice is generic: listen, inquire about their needs, validate their stories, provide safety and support. Tell women it's not their fault, believe them, direct them to resources. Put in safeguards, like hiring more women, give them access to mental health resources, to an ombudsman. Ask questions rather than make statements. But there has to be more. The real trauma lies in those white gaps between paragraphs, unaddressed. I look to these guides, to regulations, as solutions, but human behavior can't always be codified.

I go to the kitchen for coffee. Chantal and Marc are already there. He's puttering at the countertop; she's at the table staring into space. We mumble hellos, lost in our respective anxieties.

I pour my coffee in a mug from an alma mater in Ohio. It must have belonged to an intern. I'm tired, unwilling to commence the day, unwilling to articulate thoughts into actual words. I'm very aware of Marc. His body exudes unease. Suddenly I feel for him. He is the indirect subject of today's conversation, which he's unable to participate in. I think of placing my palm on his shoulder, but the urge feels wrong. Besides, he still hasn't apologized for sending that email to headquarters.

"I'm going to go rest some more," I say.

"What time should I meet you down here?" asks Chantal.

"They said lunch, so at two," I answer. Lunches here are long affairs that stretch to dusk.

I crawl back into bed cradling my coffee and distract myself by watching my foyer in California on my phone screen. It's early night there and I stare entranced. It's soothing to look at my home, at the careful calibration of my energy-efficient lighting casting just the right mood in the room.

I watch for over an hour, with droopy eyelids, sedated by the stillness of blurry geometric shapes of my door and floor. Of the familiarity. I listen to a meditation playlist that I downloaded illegally.

The door moves. I jump, having forgotten what I've been watching. The cold coffee mug falls onto my bed, remaining droplets splashing on the sheet. My blurry, pixelated husband appears with a blond-haired woman. It's all haltingly, painfully disconnected because of the poor connection. In only a few broken seconds, they hang their coats and disappear into my house.

Maybe she's a colleague? I tremble. I have cold sweats. I knew. Of course, I knew. But I didn't really. I wasn't certain. I could invent stories and doubt my sanity; that made more sense than him lying to my face. But there he just was, my husband, walking in, ever so casually, with someone else. Like it doesn't matter. Like it's not a betrayal. Like he's not a fraud. Like that's not *my* goddamn home. I think I'm crying. Something pounds ferociously in me, my skin pulsates, I'm about to vomit. I put the bedsheet in my mouth. I bite. I tug as hard as I can, feeling teeth move in their gummy sockets. I scratch my thighs and draw blood. How? How is he doing this?

I'm in a land where guns are used to kill and rape women. That doesn't stun me as deeply as my husband's deception. It's the casualness of it. The smallness of it, the laziness of it. The fact that I have birthed a child, bearing his genes, torn my body in the process, built a human life of hair, nails, and skin, on something hollow. I'm breathed in as a wife, exhaled as an excess that can be shed. I'm hyperventilating. Now I'm pacing. I want to smash something.

I spend the next few hours in a stupor. I kick chairs, feeling ridiculous. I kick the bed. I yank my hair. I indulge in all sorts of strangeness that is both foreign and laughable. I'm inside my body in ravaging pain, and outside it, staring at a pathetic woman kicking a bed. I reek of futility. I can't help it; my body fights to perform this rage, however pathetic it looks. I want to break glass and scratch walls. Everything stings; there is not a single bit of me that doesn't burn.

That pixelated woman. I imagine my husband muttering clichés to her, telling her she's stirred his soul, that he's a desert, that she's the rain. The same shit he gave to me. That he's trapped and lonely, because clearly creating a family isn't enough to satisfy his voracious ego. Because he needs incessant attentions, the way he commands them.

The violence outside is nothing compared to what Steven has made me feel. Because this violence is personal. It's looking at someone you promised a future to, shared a bed with, decided to bring a new existence into life with, and now shoved callously into an unanticipated future. The child soldiers here, they fight for food, for money, for guns that will protect their rogue group. They beat up strangers. They protect their own. The kids here battle for life. Who knows who started the war, and surely no one will finish it, but these are children of war, born into it; they've seen it hundreds of times and they remake it. That's the thing with war. You show it enough times and people become it. They become indignant and righteous, and everyone has justifications, everyone has been wronged.

The personal violence—what the fuck is that? There is no historical grievance here. You were never enslaved, Steven. It's only cold, hard, individual self-satisfaction. You're the real criminal; you're not feeding anyone but yourself. Men like you need women like me to set your fires. We become your experience, your stepladder, and when our bodies become homes, when we truly dedicate our lives, bear children, become practical, cook your bloody dinners, execute your goddamn lives, we're shabbily left and replaced.

But I have Lele waiting. I have people to help, things to feel, and you don't own a goddamn shred of this, Steven. I have a place that you can't even dream up, honey.

18

I meet Chantal in the lobby. We're dressed in long skirts and colorful scarves to honor our hosts. She surprises me by requesting a driver. The Chief's home is near enough, but she's nervous and wants an extra person with us for security.

Jean drives us. He's confused about where to go. The lost guide. He's emblematic of men from neighboring countries who come here to work for international organizations that don't trust the locals and their allegiances to the militias or government.

Like a novice, I roll down the window. Red dust drifts in, sits on our faces and hair. Chantal looks at me as though I'm mad. The dust slaps my face, the physicality of it, feels good. Maybe it can dilute the images in my head. Of that woman and Steven roaming in my home, touching my things, embracing each other against all that is mine. I roll the window back up.

The sun swelters my left cheek through the car window. I have fantasies of burning my house down while those two lie in my bed. I don't want them to burn; I want them to be woken in the middle of the night, forced to run half-naked from my bedroom to the garden, humiliated, while neighbors and firefighters look on. It's things I want to see burn. Blankets. Photographs. That chair. My wedding dress. All those lies. All those perfect white things, at first singed at the edges, then eaten up by flames. If there is no more family, why care about the house or its possessions? We may as well live up to the term *broken home* and demolish the myth of the family along with the trappings of family life.

"Are you ready for this?" Chantal interrupts my thoughts. For a moment, I don't know what she's talking about. Is she talking about the new world order that is about to descend upon my family? I stare at her.

"You okay?" she asks.

"Not really," I confess. "I'm scared." Of so many things. Of so many different futures.

"Me too," she mumbles, looking out the window, biting her lip.

The road to the village is bumpy, our few words jumble in the vehicle, barely audible. White noise of tire against pebble, gravel against rubber. Splintered rocks clang against the metal of the car. The hiss of the air conditioner, on at full blast, is unable to conquer the sweat on our brows. I emit groans and grunts, not laughter this time. The driver leans forward, his hand poised on the gear, changing it meticulously over the rough terrain, as Chantal directs him. We climb up an incline and settlements come into view.

At first we see shacks. Sheets of tin, tarps held down by large rocks. Plastic sheets held up by branches. Then there are homes with thatched rooves, dried grass turned into straw. As we near the Chief's house, the homes improve. There are large circular mud huts, concrete block homes, some with metal doors. There are old men sitting outside chewing on straw. Large cactus-like plants stand as fences between enclaves. Hairdressers have created salons out of wooden planks, spaces narrower than a toilet, with colorfully painted signs of women with fabulous braids. A bosomy woman walks toward the car. Does her man deceive her? Is her future more certain than mine? Kids run, mostly barefoot. As we drive by, everyone turns and stares. It's something we are accustomed to. I wonder if they know that we are going to the Chief's house. I wonder if they think the Chief is selling out by meeting us.

The number of huts, shacks, semi-concrete residences grow. We have reached the Chief's compound. The driver makes a dramatic stop, pulling on the hand brake, hard. Chantal and I lurch forward, then look at each other nervously. We're here.

I carry fruits and sweets. I'm not supposed to in the event they are perceived as bribes, but whoever wrote the rules cannot imagine the lengths to which poor people go to feed the likes of us.

The enclave is in the shape of a semicircle with the Chief's home at the farthest and central point. To the right and left are small mud dwellings. Relatives, nieces, nephews run from home to home.

The Chief has two wives. Nounia is such a force that it's hard to believe a woman came before her. None has come after. The first wife, Lele once told me, left with her older son for France shortly after the Chief chose the younger Nounia. She couldn't accept the humiliation. Since ceding her place, she has been in contact with blurry weekly Skype calls in the internet center, Likanni's power allowing. Calls, which I imagine, she hopes end quickly so she doesn't have to face her indignity for too long. Lele says she has a difficult life now, cleaning houses for French families, living in one room with her son.

Lele recounted the story of her mother and father's union with relish when she started working for us. What broke her mother's predecessor was that the Chief had always advocated for single marriages, though the region had many polygamous families. He had too much to deal with, mediating inheritance disagreements in other families, over which wife would get what, who would live in the ancestral home. He found polygamy impractical. His first wife lived with ease, confident that no one would intrude upon her marriage.

But the Chief forgot his convictions, as well as his Catholicism, when he laid eyes on Nounia, a fearless Muslim girl from a nearby village who was known for arguing with elders at gatherings, unintimidated by men or by their age. She was uninterested in marriage at a time when her sisters and cousins were seeking suitors. She challenged opinions, unafraid for her reputation. The Chief was captivated by this display of female courage. That must have destroyed his former wife, who was dutifully subservient, unaware that what this man wanted was to be battled and toyed with in his homestead.

Nounia burst into the household and the Chief's life with energy and excitement. She told the Chief that if he was ever to marry again, she would kill herself and him. He loved the dramatics; the former wife didn't stand a chance. As a man slipping into late middle age, the Chief felt his blood palpitating again with Nounia. His life, which until then had been an interminable descent into further poverty and dullness, was reignited. There was excitement for the future, joy in unpredictability.

Nounia now is much older. It is hard to imagine her as an impetuous teen. She enjoys the measly ceremonial roles she's been offered as the Chief's wife and has a confident air about her that people respect. One subject that Lele never brought up is who will take on the Chief's role once he dies. Will Nounia and her children be kicked off the property? Will the eldest son return? Will the former wife cast Nounia aside and have her day in the sun?

I think of this as we walk toward the house, made of concrete blocks. It's not very large, with three shabby rooms and a tin roof. The doors are wide open, as they always are, so you can see straight into the living room. There's a latrine in the yard that gets emptied once a day.

Smiling children come to walk with us. I wonder whether these are Lele and Fanon's nieces and nephews. One child holds my hand, as if we take such a walk daily. Something hurts in my chest. I remember Chloe, the sensation of a small hand in my larger one. The way it tucks in. I look down and see beautiful almond eyes. I want to sit her down and explain stranger danger, that she shouldn't befriend any old foreigner. But there is something so trusting about a child putting her hand against mine that I don't have the heart to destroy it.

A crowd gathers in front of the Chief's house. A feast is laid out on wooden tables with people eagerly awaiting for us to cross the property's threshold. The minute we do, the traditional communicators, a group of women, burst onto the scene, singing, dancing, blowing on cheap whistles. They make an on-the-spot song about us and our visit, which we do not understand, and people around us howl with laughter. They grab Chantal and me to dance with them, and we do so in our repressed, awkward manner. I remember a video of Prince Harry doing the same. I find myself laughing, clapping, dancing. I don't understand any of the jokes, but these women are vibrant, full of life, embracing, and for a few minutes I forget where I am and why. I'm lulled.

I remember learning that traditional communicators are women who have suffered great hardship. One named Nina used to show up at every community meeting, singing, wearing sunglasses and toys around her neck, dancing, until people were smiling or clapping. I followed her home one day, for she would never be out of character before the others, to understand why she was putting on such a show and disrupting every meeting I organized. She graciously told me: traditional communicators had experienced deaths of children or were infertile, and to make meaning of their lives, they sing and dance, recite crude jokes and poems to bring laughter in others, performing their grief. They band together, connecting the community, young and old, for they are informers of floods or fires. They share the news, good and bad, bonding story to story, family to family, enlivening every occasion. Nina herself was unable to have children, something she had mourned for years. Then she decided to join the traditional communicators, wear her sadness publicly, and celebrate the joys of her neighbors.

I look at Chantal, awkwardly swinging her slender arms. The traditional communicators change the tone of the song, make it bittersweet, and we stop dancing. They wail soulful melodies. Some observers wipe their eyes; others grip their children tight. Our visit is narrated by them, they must be singing about Lele. They control the tenor of our welcome, freeing us to a range of emotion we release into the air. They end their song with lamentations and a prayer, and the party is kicked off.

Nounia welcomes us warmly, along with her multitude of children, nieces, nephews, and cousins. The tables in front of the house hold innumerable platters overflowing with food. Sheets and mats are stretched on the ground. Four weathered wooden chairs have been pulled aside for us, the Chief, and his wife.

We help ourselves to the food, always a delicate dance. If we take too little, we'll appear impolite. If we take too much, we'll be overwhelmed when they refill our plates, which is cultural practice.

Chantal sits on a chair, talking to the Chief. I take my plate and sit on the ground with the rest of the family. There is a lively din: children speak at once. A girl plays with my hair, calls her cousins to come touch it, while the Chief's brother and his wife tell me about their harvest. Fanon appears from inside the house with a big platter of goat curry. Seeing him in the light of day makes me realize how little I know him, makes me wonder why I answer his questions in the dark. He sees me on the ground surrounded by his family and gives me a wide smile. I smile back without thinking. It's like I have a friend here. The sounds, the foods poured onto my plate over and over by Nounia, her daughters, all these someones calling out to me calm the unsettled pain lodged in my ribs.

I'm chatting with Lele's cousin when Fanon crouches behind me. He puts his palm on my shoulder and says, "Have you eaten well?" The familiarity surprises me but in a pleasant way.

"I'm stuffed. It's very good, but your mother won't stop feeding me," I answer.

"My mother is trying to plump you like our women," Fanon says, as he gets back up. His hand leaves my shoulder, the indelible feeling of his palm stays on me. I look up and Chantal is staring straight at me.

Lunch dwindles into dinner. The food lessens, boys bring drums. The traditional communicators dance, their feet kicking up dirt. I'm lost to my senses, the food and sun make me sleepy, the beat makes me want to dance, the anxiety of seeing Lele gives me shivers. Thoughts of Steven pierce through but are chased away by drumbeats, back into my hollows. I see Fanon from the corner of my eye, nieces and nephews on his shoulders, carrying platters of food. I see him play the drum, his hands skimming its surface. Every beat taking a bite out of my anxieties. Freeing me a little. I wonder what it's like to be a girl here, to aspire to all this. To live in a place where no one seems alone.

Chantal joins me on the ground; we sway together. We're content but on guard. At some point, a young girl puts her hand on my shoulder and tells us that Nounia would like to see us inside the house. Chantal and I look at each other.

"Do you want to do it alone?" she asks.

"No, come," I say. I need the support and confirmation—that she hears what I hear.

We walk inside. A bright-blue pleather sofa sits in the drawing room. There are golden frames with Arabic prayers on the wall, dusty vases with dusty plastic flowers. Nounia stands nervously, clasping and unclasping her hands.

"Lele would like to see you," she says, almost in a whisper. I nod and take her hands. They are cold.

Nounia takes us to the room where the daughters sleep. The floors and walls are made of gray concrete, and the girls have hung colorful posters to render it less bleak. There is a stack of thin mattresses against the concrete wall, which the sisters pull out to sleep on. There are bars on the open windows, raffia baskets in the corner, folded-up clothes and towels. There is a metal closet with broken handles, a cracked foggy mirror with a Bruce Lee sticker on it. Lele lies on her side, on a thin foam mattress, itself laid out on a straw mat. She's awake, rubbing her fingers on the ground as if she's writing something. Nounia goes in first, places a hand on her daughter's shoulder.

"Lele, look who is here."

Lele barely looks up. Her braids have been redone as if she's a little girl. She seems to have shrunk into her prepubescent self. Her eyes are large and fearful.

"Bigabosse," she says in a whisper.

I forget formalities and sit on the side of her mattress and give her an embrace. It's an awkward hug as I'm kneeling, but she folds into me completely. I can feel her bones, her small chest, everything pressed into mine, poking me. I could crack her like chicken bones. I feel maternal, protective, sisterly and hold her tightly. She smells strange. Not like a body. Like something stale. I feel her gentle tremors. Nounia pulls out straw mats for all of us to sit on. As I shift to the mat, my back against the cool wall, Lele shifts with me, keeping her head on my shoulder. The colorful sheet covering her body slides, and she quickly pulls it back over her again.

"It has been this way," Nounia says. "She will not let me take the sheet for the washing, will you, Lele?"

We sit in silence. Lele looks sickly. Her body concaves, her head huge, barely held up by that rod of a neck. A mosquito buzzes near my ear, but I don't dare move to shake it off, with Lele so close, so fragile. It could be carrying malaria or dengue, but I don't want to make any abrupt movement that might startle her. I look at Chantal, her brow furrowed. Pale, taut, she stares at a spot on the ground. Very much a French woman right now. Nounia stretches her legs out in front of her, fixing her own draping fabric. I see the soles of her feet, worn, cracked. I think of the feast outside, the guise of joy; it drains from her face as she stares at her daughter.

I should have prepared a speech for this moment. Some words of comfort. The banal springs to my tongue. "How are you?"

Lele snuggles closer to my neck. Her hair scratches my chin, making me itchy.

"I've missed you, Lele. Chantal tells me that you've been doing amazing work." Chantal nods emphatically.

I've started on the wrong foot, accidentally alluding to work and the site of the crime. An amateur move. The regret burns in my chest.

"Yes, you have been indispensable, and we miss you," says Chantal with forced cheerfulness. It's as if we've never done this before. And we haven't. We are used to victims we don't know. Ones we only meet post-suffering. We should utter the empathetic, open-ended questions, the ones we have memorized as the first line of support before we pass the girls to more specialized expertise. But the questions do not come for Lele. For she has done this too, and she knows the script.

An uncomfortable silence sits in the room, punctuated by joyful music and laughs from outside.

190

Lele leans back and looks at me. "I know you are here to discuss what has happened."

"Yes. We are worried about you."

More silence.

"You don't have to say anything if you don't want to," I say.

Chantal looks expectant, waiting for words to spill out of Lele's mouth. I want to scratch my chin so badly.

"We want to help any way we can," I say. "I know it is difficult to talk about. But if there's anything you want to share, we're here to listen. I want you to know that whatever happened isn't your fault. You have done nothing wrong." The guidelines I've read speak through my mouth. That's why they were written, I suppose, to eat big silences around tragedies.

I pull the sheet tighter around her shoulders, her twiggy arms disappear.

After a long pause, Lele says haltingly, "I'm sorry. I do not mean to be rude."

"You're not being rude," I exclaim. "Take your time, you don't even have to say anything at all."

Lele fidgets. "Bigabosse, may I speak to you alone?"

Chantal and Nounia rise. Chantal leans over and touches Lele on the shoulder. "I'm sorry I haven't been by. I hope you feel better soon. We're here to help you get there."

Lele just looks at her. When they leave, Lele climbs back onto her mattress, lying on her side, covered by the sheet. I stay on the mat and finally scratch my chin. We look like two girls at a slumber party about to share secrets.

"I do not wish to speak in front of my mother," Lele explains. "It is difficult. I do not want to bring pictures to her mind."

"I understand."

"Miss Chantal is very nice. I thought we were friends, but she did not come," Lele says.

"You know how it is, Lele, all the rules at the office."

"Yes, I know rules. They were my rules also. But when one rule is broken so poorly, others should too." Lele's voice is strained in a way I've never heard. "Do you want to know what has occurred?" She stares at me straight in the eyes. She seems to have garnered energy with her mother and Chantal gone, though I don't know how given how gaunt she looks.

"Only if you want to tell me."

"What will you do with this information?"

"I will process it," I say honestly. I can't make any promises. It's just one other thing that doesn't fall under my mandate.

"I spent weeks trying to forget. Then I spent weeks trying to remember, what I should have done, if I said something, when I should have screamed. I should have." Her breath rasps in her throat. "But you don't understand, Bigabosse, I could not move. I could not. I thought it was a joke. I was not even certain it was happening, though this may sound strange." She stares at me, the whites of her eyes huge. But it feels like she's not really looking at me all. "At times, I think my mind made it, but seeing Miss Chantal, smelling her smell, the same smell of the office, brought the memory."

I lean over and squeeze her legs. Bone. I try to erase memories of rough touches with my soft ones.

"I know you want to know who did it. I know you want to get him in punishment."

Her facial expressions change, the forlorn look wanes. She looks angry, and in that anger I see that passionate girl I first met. But it's a different version, as though she has been reprogrammed in ways I don't know.

"He stole everything. He didn't need to. There are many women who would willingly do those things. Miss Chantal would do those things. He stole my honor and that was sacred, Bigabosse. That was for me and my husband, and he took it. Now, now I am

192

in big trouble." She guffaws in disbelief. "He did this without closing the door. What if someone saw? What will they think of me?
That I am that kind? And Miss Chantal? She was my friend—why
she did not come? It is because I will always be an outsider, the
child they showed their charity to, but not one of them." Lele
speaks in fast streams. Words spat out. Abrupt hand motions, fists
clenched, then unclenched.

"It was Monsieur Marc, Bigabosse. I went to his office to for the
weekly input. He made jokes. I laughed. I should not have laughed.
Never laugh with men. They do not understand the laughter." She
slaps the ground with her palm. "I liked it when a European man
like that, a senior of mine, liked me. I should not have liked it. He
said go to his bookshelf, look for the green folder with pictures of
Chakouti visits. I looked and he was behind me. He was breathing at my hair. I thought it was a joke, that he would say boo and
scare me like my brothers. But he pulled my skirt. I should not
have worn a skirt—now I know why you women wear pants, you
know your men—and before I could move, he pushed himself. He
jammed, then he pulled at my skin, down, down, found the place,
then jammed again. I had never known where my monthly blood
came from, but now I know. It is the same place.

"When I could move, he was sitting at the bureau. He said he
would email me a list of activities to put in the newsletter. He was
at the bureau, working. I thought, Was I mad? This had not happened. It had not happened? How could a man do such and then
sit in his chair? How, Bigabosse? But I was hurting. I don't know
what happened. After I left. I didn't wait for Fanon to get me. I
don't know I went where. I disappeared. That's what they tell me.
I don't remember. Coming home, how I walked. I do not know,
Bigabosse, and I always remember everything. He has taken my
mind. I don't remember so many things." Lele has life again. Her
arms have motion, her eyes squint and flash.

I sit, frozen.

"I have a big problem, Bigabosse. I have not told my mother even. I'm carrying a baby. The baby is Monsieur Marc's."

One of Lele's younger sisters comes in with a glass of cola for me. I barely respond. I take the glass with shaky hands, feeling a chill though it's warm.

Lele says to her sister, "Tell Miss Chantal to come in."

Chantal comes in. I'm stiff as a board, unable to utter a sound. Unable to look at Chantal. She sits by me and looks at Lele.

"Thank you for inviting me back. Please tell me how I can help," says Chantal.

"Miss Chantal," says Lele, "it is Monsieur Marc that pushed me against the bookshelf and raped me."

19

"There's been a mistake," whispers Chantal, as we climb back into the car. I don't know where the last few hours have gone, but it is dark. I must have said things; Chantal must have said things. Hopefully we were comforting. Hopefully we thanked our hosts. All I know is I'm freezing and shivering as though I have a fever.

I ask the driver to take us to the bar.

"I don't want to go to the fucking bar, Maya. I have to talk to Marc and deal with this situation."

"We both have to deal with this. But we need to sort our thoughts and figure out how the hell to approach this. We're living with the guy, for god's sake!" I want to rely on her, but I'm in shock and she looks like a mess.

"This is . . . this is just not right, Maya. This doesn't seem right." She is blubbering.

"I know, it's overwhelming. But we have to show some leadership here. I don't want to talk about this at the office while he's there."

Chantal exhales loudly, rubs her temples, and sighs again. "Let's talk here, in the car."

What the hell was Burton thinking, housing us all together? Did he never consider for a moment that Marc could be guilty? That we'd have to go home to him after hearing of his crimes?

We sit in silence until we arrive at our compound. It's not very late, though the sky is black. Lights shine through the windows of the building. Marc must be pacing in circles waiting for us to return. We say goodnight to Jean and ask him for the keys. We remain seated in the back seat, next to each other, without looking at one another. I lean over and open the window, letting the night air in. Chantal crosses her legs on the back seat and puts her face into her hands.

"How? Why?" she says.

"I know."

"What did she say to you exactly? Did she say Marc did it or that he pushed her on the shelf? Did she focus more on pushing? Do you think she hurt her head and it distorted her memories? Was this a consensual thing? Why?" Her mind runs through a million scenarios.

"You heard her."

"But what did she say specifically?"

"The same thing she told you. She said Marc forced himself on her against the bookshelf."

Chantal shakes her head. "This is crazy."

"Chantal," I say, "how did Lele look to you?"

I hear another sigh. Her voice is muffled, from the depths of her palms. "Not good." Chantal raises her head, looks at me with lost eyes. "She doesn't look well. I'm telling you, she was a professional young woman—not this . . ." Then she mumbles, "Do you think that could be it? Maybe she has some sickness? The lack of vitamins is making her delusional? Maya, what do you think? Do you honestly believe that Marc is capable of rape? Could she have been brainwashed by someone, maybe her brother or mother, to accuse Marc? Do you think the militia bribed her to say this, to get us out of their country? Maybe they are threatening her and the family?" Chantal looks at me for hope. "We have to think of all the possibilities. Maybe she got confused because of the trauma. Maybe somebody attacked her in Marc's office and she confused the memory, or maybe she's afraid of revealing the real rapist, and this is her cry for help?" She's a mouse in a maze.

"Look, I'm as overwhelmed as you are. I've worked with Marc for most of my career here, but—"

Someone raps their knuckles on the front window. Chantal and I jump. Marc shines his flashlight into the car. He opens the driver's seat door and pokes his head in.

"You guys scared the shit out of me. The driver's back and you are nowhere to be found. What are you two doing in here? I've been waiting for hours."

Chantal and I exchange a look. She looks guilty. I can't even look at him.

"We're talking," says Chantal coldly.

I can tell he wants to ask us why we aren't talking in the building, but he holds himself back. With the darkness outside, the dim light of the car casts a weak halo on him. He looks creepy.

"Close the door; the battery will die," I say.

"Aren't we going inside?" he asks.

Chantal and I are still. I don't want to walk into that haunted building where Lele's attack took place. Not with him.

Marc gets in the front seat and closes the door. He turns to us. "What did she say? Did she tell you who did it? Have I been cleared?" He expels words in a frenzy, as if they've been held in for hours.

"No," says Chantal. "You have not been cleared."

"Fuck." Marc hits the steering wheel, hard.

The three of us sit in the dark car. I avoid making eye contact, for fear it will establish Marc as a rapist for good. I stare at the back of the passenger's seat. The seams of the fake leather headrest. Where were they sewn, I wonder. Probably in China.

I hear Marc crying. "I didn't do whatever she's accusing me of. Bébé, you know me, you know. You know I couldn't have done this."

Bébé?

Chantal and I remain quiet, while Marc sobs.

"You know me. We were making plans, we were starting our life. You can't believe this. You know my character. Have you ever seen me so much as flirt with a woman here? Have you seen me display any streaks of violence? Maya—you have known me for a decade. Have you ever heard of anyone accusing me of anything like this in all the years I have worked here? Someone else did this, I'm telling you, someone else did this. It's not me. It's not me."

He grows louder, sounding more desperate, making sounds he's never emitted before, confusing me. "Please, both of you, look at me. Please. Don't treat me like someone who could have done this. Please!"

Chantal whimpers. Marc wails louder than I've ever heard a grown man cry, and I've been to Likanni funerals. He wheezes. "How can I prove something I didn't do?" he yelps between sobs and pants. "How?" The word reverberates, a question I have no answer for.

"I would have requested a transfer if I had done this! I would never have called headquarters—I'm the one that told them that I was being accused! Maya, you know I couldn't. I've never, Maya, you know me."

Could it be? Could someone else have done it? Could the trauma have muddled Lele's memories? Could she have confused an earlier meeting with Marc with the attack itself? Could she be confusing the chronology of events? She herself mentioned that she had tried to forget, then tried to remember. Did that process create a gap of memory? This was Lele, with the photographic memory; maybe trauma inflicted greater impact on her than on a regular person. But it's Lele, so certain, always so free of influence.

Marc coughs bark-like. "I can't breathe," he gasps, wheezing loudly, his body convulsing against the steering wheel. He grabs at his chest, panic-stricken.

"He's having a heart attack!" Chantal shrieks.

I rush out of the car to the front seat and pull the door open to give him some air.

Marc gasps, clutching his chest, his eyes lolling. I yank the lever to make the car seat recede.

"It's okay, Marc. It's just a panic attack. Let's try to calm down together. Everything's fine. Focus on my breathing. In. And out. Feel the air coming into your body. In and out. It's a cool night. There's air for you to take in." I do this for what feels like half an hour, while Chantal clutches her face. Marc has a mad look, eyes darting all over the place. His jaw hangs open; drool collects on his chin.

"There's nothing to be afraid of. It's just a panic attack. It will end soon," I repeat.

Marc focuses on me. He sputters, saliva runs down the side of his mouth, his breathing erratic. His palm pressed at his chest, he's able to take some shallow breaths. He hangs his legs over the side of the door and rests his hand on the steering wheel, getting his breath back.

I pat his greasy blond hair unintentionally. "You're fine. Let's go inside and make some tea. Can you walk?" Marc nods and stumbles out of the car. Chantal runs around the car to join us, and he leans his small body against her. Together we walk back into the building.

The lights stun us. I pour water into a kettle. Marc and Chantal sink into the couch in the kitchen, wrapped in a ball. He curls his forehead into her neck. That's when I realize.

"What the hell is going on?" I ask.

Marc raises his head uneasily. Chantal's eyes are bloodshot, a vein pulsates on her forehead. She opens her mouth stammering.

"Come to my office right now," I bark at her without thinking. I have no office. Marc starts to move, but I thunder, "Not you."

Chantal whispers something quickly and follows me. I storm into her office and snap on the lights. She shrinks as I stand large and furious.

"Am I going crazy here? Is there something going on between you two?"

Chantal is pink, trembling. "I can explain everything," she says in a small voice. She leans against a wall for support, her hands shaky. After taking a breath, she regains her composure.

"Marc and I have been in a relationship for eight months, Maya. I'm very sorry I didn't tell you."

I sit on her desk. "What the hell?"

"I know, I know. It sounds crazy, and honestly the only reason I didn't tell you is because I didn't want you to be uncomfortable around us. I wanted you to be able to speak your mind, to criticize Marc as you see fit. I didn't want you to censor yourself."

"Do you see how deceitful this is?" I grip the edge of the desk, wondering if there is a single person I can believe.

"I know, it's awful. I never wanted to lie to you. I promise, this was to make sure we didn't take your attention from the problem," she cries.

"What the fuck are you even saying? Were you involved in this?"

"Maya, no! You can't think I'm involved. Don't you see, it's in my interest to find out whether Marc did anything. I'm planning a future with him. I need to know . . ."

I wave my hands around. "You can't be a part of these conversations. You've got to know that. How did I just let you speak to Lele? What the fuck did I just do?"

Chantal runs to me and grips my shoulders. "Maya, I swear I want justice for Lele. I want to know what happened. I would never cover for Marc if I thought he did it."

I take a few breaths, trying to order the millions of questions I have. "Does Lele know?"

"She was always with me, almost like an assistant. She was the only one who knew. She was so supportive. She teased me, wanted us to get married . . ." Chantal sniffs, rubbing her nose.

"Did you tell headquarters about this?" I ask.

She shakes her head. "It wasn't to protect Marc. I didn't want to take away from the investigation."

I look at her in disbelief. I remember when I first hired her, I was so impressed. She's the kind of woman who has gone shark diving, slept on beaches in Zanzibar. She was unbeholden to a man; she made easy friendships, played with local children. She entered villages comfortably with a respectful smile. She's that type of French girl you meet in the field, so secure in herself and the education she's cultivated. Right now, she looks pathetic.

"Just get away from me. I'll discuss this with you later, but you will no longer be involved with any of this. And tell Marc to stay the fuck away from me right now. And you too, stay the fuck away." I get up. She says something, apologetic, meek, but I don't care.

I walk past her, past the guards who clearly have heard us arguing, and head outside.

20

The stars seem low tonight, stretching infinitely before me. The sky as busy as my eruptive thoughts, one worse than the other. Rape. Pregnancy. Adultery. Deceit. I don't know where to start. I massage my temples, trying to knead down every treacherous feeling.

I can only focus on Lele's safety. She can't be like the others. So many men and boys have entered this region, plucked the rawest nerve of this society. They have broken mothers, young girls, injuring communities at their deepest, for it's the mothers and sisters who march these parts forward, who take people from day to night and to day again. It's the women who make poverty palatable, make it a game for their children to survive. They tell stories, yell and laugh, provide breastmilk, plan marriages, organize funerals, and cook, keeping the adrenaline gushing, the blood running in the young ones, so that they have something to live for. When the women break, entire strands of culture, tradition, and love wither.

I cannot let Lele and all that is to come for her wither away. She is more than the memory of her violation. That curious and daring girl, she needs to return, she needs to be trusted, her words elevated, so she can become who she needs to be. She cannot keep this baby. Ethically, I don't have a right to intervene. But how do I let her live with this? The horror of rape will greet her each day if she bears this child; she'll be ostracized. If Nounia knew, I'm certain she would tell her of the aunties in the village who could help her. Aunties known only to the sisterhood who massage rape babies out of women's bodies.

I hear footsteps. It's Fanon, of course. As if we have set a time and a place. I wish I could lean against him, against that body that labors, the chest that looks like a shield. I feel so weak in my lumpy foreigner's body, the shape of a desk chair, fingertips flattened by keyboards.

"I apologize I am late," Fanon says.

I want to lie and say I haven't been waiting.

Fanon holds two clinking bottles and passes one to me. I can't get the cap off. He reaches over and undoes it with his hands.

"Are you well?" Fanon asks.

"Not really," I admit. "I mean thanks to you and Nounia and the whole family for the feast, but I am very sad after seeing Lele." I don't tell him how fucking furious I am at my lying colleagues.

"Yes."

"She needs help, Fanon."

"She will be helped when Monsieur Marc is punished."

"That's not enough. She needs help now. She needs medical and psychological attention. She needs food and vitamins and assistance with the grief and shock."

"My mother has tried to take her to the Marabout, but she does not want to leave home. The doctor has come, but she did not speak to him."

"There are people, you know. I know organizations that deal with sexual violence survivors. Most of them are in the capital, but I can try and get some resources down here," I say, my mind spinning. There was that Spanish girl, Roberta, I met years ago.

"Sexual violence survivors," repeats Fanon. "You people have nice titles for everything."

I say nothing.

"That is what my sister is now?"

By calling her a sexual violence survivor, I've sent her to join the mass of women who have been brutalized, faceless and nameless in our stories, just victims. I have to bring her back from that anonymity.

"Your sister is your sister. She is and always will be. She's different right now, but she'll be different again in the future," I say gently.

"Will she come out of this?" Fanon asks almost like a boy. One who needs a comforting response, real or not.

"She has all of you. She has a community that supports her. She's bright, she's knowledgeable; her desire for life will emerge once the trauma subsides. Today she was brave and clear and that's the first step to recovery. But we have to help her."

I hear a muffled voice. Fanon's face is against his knees.

"It is as though someone has taken her spirit and left an animal's carcass. The other day as my aunt cut fruit, I saw Lele looking at the knife, without blinking. It made me fearful. What if she harms herself?"

I put my hand on his hunched back.

"This is why we need to make sure that she's okay and has mental health support." I try to convince him. I don't know when to remove my hand. Is it at the end of my sentence? My palm resting there—is it too heavy? Should I make it lighter? I remove it. It's like a betrayal.

The touch must have comforted him, for he sidles toward me. He sits on a lower step, his left arm lightly grazes my right leg in that ethereal sort of way, like on a plane.

"I can call around and find resources, someone she can speak to. I'm worried"—I wince—"about whether she had any lacerations, whether there is any risk for infection."

"Will the doctor people be white?"

I exhale loudly. "Possibly, although it shouldn't matter. In this case, it just means you'll have access to international expertise, to the best there is."

"It matters, Bigabosse," Fanon says with defiance.

I fight my frustration.

"The foreigners do not know our ways. They have given advice in the past that has not been good for my people."

"It's a medical check-up. They have worked here. They know how to respect a young girl's body and local traditions. Nounia can be with her, holding her hand," I say.

"Lele has been attacked by a white man. We are afraid of what white people can do to us."

I know nothing about the local services, only our foreign ones—the good ones.

"I am upset that you do not understand this, Bigabosse," Fanon says.

"What don't I understand? I understand how racially charged everything is. I understand it must be hard when Westerners flood in with money while the local people's situation never seems to get better. But some, and you'd better believe me, some are working hard as hell, living through difficult conditions, which they would never face back home, to make things better in this country."

Damn him. Doesn't he know about people who give up their lives to be here, to right the wrongs of others that they have nothing to do with? Some get threatened, some get sick, yet they stay. People miss Christmases, weddings, and funerals, lose all sense of themselves so they can contribute something to this fucking place.

"Bigabosse, someone gave us a country we did not ask for, gave us a flag of colors that are not our own. Someone gave us a despot and a boundary across which our clans were split. Your people work with these forces. You send your own military to help him, even though he has destroyed us. This is the present, this is today. This is not a history lesson. Farmlands taken by cousins of presidents, chiefs gone. Our people who once spoke the same language cannot communicate, cannot work together because now some of us are francophone and our cousins anglophone. Your people, all these people who come to help, do so after everything has been taken away. What can you give now? Our land? Our language? Our family? If you come to help, why don't you stop the mining companies? What good is your help when everything has been taken?" Fanon's voice echoes.

"What's your magical solution? And if you have one, why haven't your people used it? You want us to leave? Fine, but what happens to those twelve hundred kids in our care? Will you take care of them?"

"Maybe for a start, your people stop raping us."

I groan aloud, frustrated. I put my head on my arms.

"You think it is foolish that I say this."

"Not everyone is here to violate you. I am not here to rape you."

"I do not mean to be rude, Bigabosse," he says gently. "You are a good person. Everybody likes you. But when someone as kind as you does nothing about Monsieur Marc, then we can expect nothing. Even the good ones, they do not help. I do not know why. They see their people making costly mistakes, but they never do anything. They feel sad. They give us vaccines and books. And that is very nice. But the violation goes on. I am not saying my people are better. But when a boy rapes, we stand and yell, we ask for his head, we fight him. Even those in fear, at some point they whisper the truth. I have not heard you say, even once, that Monsieur Marc raped Lele. You have not said it." Fanon sighs with resignation.

A strange, guttural sound is lodged in my throat. It stops there before fermenting into a word.

"It is okay, Bigabosse; that is who you are. You will eat with him and live in the same building and let him live with what has happened. That is what the civilized do. They take our ancestors, sell them across the ocean, but they continue to dine, dance, and be polite. You are only a continuation of a long story."

I can't utter a word.

"But I want to ask, Why? Why can you not say Monsieur Marc raped Lele? Why can you not speak the truth to me? You see us as beggars, not as people like you and Miss Chantal. Why?"

"I believe Lele, I do. I know someone hurt her. But what if there's a small chance there's been some confusion? I cannot destroy his whole life until I'm a hundred percent sure."

"Your concern for his life is greater than what Lele says," Fanon says sadly.

"No, it's not! I will do everything I can to help her. I just need to be certain and not go on emotion. I need to take everything I know about Marc into consideration."

"You spoke to Lele? Yes?"

"Yes."

"What did she say to you?"

"That he did it."

"That who did it?" Fanon presses.

I draw in a long breath. "That Marc did it."

"Then what do you need, Bigabosse?" he asks with desperation.

Sticky tears roll down my face. What do I answer to that? That I need a gut feeling? That I need to erase all those memories of

Marc carrying people away from their death? Of carrying me away from mine? How fucking scientific is that as an answer?

Fanon's voice goes very low. "When it is time to take the decisions, real decisions, you people stay silent. I was wrong: you are just like them. You are protecting your own. But today you can be different, Bigabosse. You can say, say it, say that Monsieur Marc raped my sister." He cries too. "Say it."

My voice cannot be summoned.

Fanon weeps. "You see? You cannot even say that which she told you. How will a lady like you help our Lele? Why do you come here? Why do you ask questions when the responses are to be disregarded?"

My voice takes life, puts the notes together. "Lele says Marc raped her," I say in a cracking voice.

"Again." His voice hiccups.

"He raped her," I whisper.

"Who?"

"Marc."

I hear a soft thud somewhere in the yard. Fanon turns his head to see if there's someone there. There could be—it is too dark to see—but I would have heard the door or footsteps or something. In this dark, every sound is a giant.

"You said it," Fanon says, touched. I can hear him smiling in the dark.

"Yes."

"What will you do now?"

21

I unlock my door and enter my monk's room.

It's all coming undone. I collapse on the bed. I want to go home. Let Burton figure this out. But he can't. He doesn't even remember Lele's name. I curl onto my bed in the fetal position, cupping my phone. I can't get Lele's hands out of my mind. Shaky hands clutching a bedsheet. Nails long and jagged, gray-looking. That body that used to be confident, in motion, now coiled and weak.

My phone pings. It's a text message from Marc.

Thank you for helping me today. I'm sorry that we didn't tell you. We didn't want to make you feel uncomfortable. I am ready to talk about it whenever you want. My relationship with Chantal is very serious and I would never do anything to hurt her or us.

Ugh. I block his number.

I log on to look at my house. I want to remember what it is like to be home, safe from this ugliness. I see my home, but I also see a quarter of a woman's body leaning against the kitchen counter. I see a slice of her side, the coffee cup she's holding, enjoying the intimate art of breakfast. Cups I bought in Paris on Rue de Rennes. Steven had taken pictures of me as I held up teacups and bowls; the owner had been annoyed, maybe fearing that the Brown woman would drop his dishware. The blond now holds the same cup, drifts in and out of the screen, wobbly and broken, her life real and in pixels on a tiny screen. I watch for hours. I can't stop, even when my breath starts making sounds it shouldn't make.

There are minutes of watching blank space, respite, but then she moves back into the frame for a split second, cementing my new reality. I watch this awkward dance, sink my nails into my arms and scratch until they are bleeding. I scratch over and over. Until I have skin residue under my nails. Until it hurts so much I fear it may get infected.

I calmly get up and pull cortisone cream out of my first aid kit. Impressive streaks of red cover my arms. They make me feel strong. They will scar. Especially in the sunlight here. I will carry these scars, gifted by Steven. The physical manifestation of how he's destroyed me, out in the open, for all to see.

It's four in the morning. In a grief-drunk voice I leave a voice-mail for Burton. "She says he did it, Burton. She told me that Marc did it."

I turn off the lights. My eyes have shed so many tears that they are swollen closed. I wish the ceiling wasn't quite so high. It's hard to feel cocooned with it so far away.

22

I wake from an anxious sleep, wondering if the deceptions were big Daliesque dreams. My arms sting. This morning, the streaks of red don't feel heroic. They look stupid. I look mutilated, like a teenage girl who cannot voice her emotions. I'm not sure how I've managed to harm myself to this degree with fingernails. I creep into the infirmary and find long rolls of bandage. This is going to be uncomfortable in the midday heat. What a foolish thing to have done.

I fill out the log book, leave a note that I'm stepping out. It's six in the morning. Too early for Benoit or Cyril to roll their eyes at me. I glance at my emails and see several from head office. I don't read them. I consider writing about Chantal and Marc's relationship but can't be bothered. I'm going rogue. I'm not going to be with any of these people for long. Not them, not my husband. They will soon be meaningless names in my history. I'll have a new beginning, my daughter's name, the only one on my lips. She won't be the shadow to Likanni and its memories. My child. That's what'll matter now.

How soon did Steven start seeing that woman after I gave birth? I think of her drooling on my pillowcase, bathing in my tub, resting her ass where mine sits. Does she touch Chloe's things? Will Steven marry her after we divorce? Does she bear the illusion that she will become a second mother to Chloe? A fucking *bonus mother* as they call them these days, to hide that they're women who step on others' lives. Will they become a matchy-matchy family with their fucking skin tone? Will I be the outsider justifying that Chloe is indeed my daughter? Over my dead body.

I'm not sad. I'm angry as hell. There's something energizing in anger. I hope all the hungry people here are angry too, so rage fills their bellies. Anger feeds, while sadness depletes. I won't let Steven take anything more; I've already given too much of my intelligence in justifying the nonsense I found in my closets. I closed my eyes. I was charmed and distracted by daily rituals, by the complacence of life, by the trust that I thought came from creating life or sharing vows. Not in Likanni. No more lies. I'll bust them with a club. I'll lay out all the lies like colorful fabrics for all to point at, then tear them up. I'll fuck up all the social codes, welcome embarrassment like a garland. This is how criminals must feel: exhilarated and delirious, as if they can transform their situations in an instant. I feel like I could really fuck something up today.

I grab the key to the Cruiser and fire it up. It's been a long time since I have driven manually. As the gear throbs into my palm, I find my familiarity. I'm twenty-six again. I drive toward Anders with a hunger that's almost nauseous in intensity. Driving in that way where every cell is beating, where time is obliterated. Is it taking me hours to get there or mere minutes? I do not know. To be in love and lust is for time to stretch and bend. But there is no Anders, just monsters I have to confront.

I chant to myself: Steven is a liar, Marc is a liar, Chantal is a liar. My voice booms in the car, my empty cathedral, the words sounding holy, hanging on a rosary. The mantra grows, entrancing. I swerve, narrowly missing a rooster, and turn toward the Chief's home. It is early and people on the side of the road look at me with surprise. There's an old man wheeling a cart filled with firewood, a warm bonnet on his head despite the heat. He's lucky to have a cart. Usually women's bodies are the carts. He stops when he sees the car, wipes the sweat from his small mustache. There are teenage girls, walking in clumps, in their long wraparound skirts, escorting little brothers and sisters, with book bags and in uniforms, on their hour-long walk to school. Farmers inspect dry patches of field to see if any miraculous dewdrops appeared overnight.

Steven could have told me he was attracted to someone else, that something felt off. We could have patched things up, gone to a therapist. He would have been great at therapy; he would have loved the introspection, time carved for his stories told in great oratorial style. We could have refashioned ourselves; I could have been better. But he took that opportunity away from us.

I've veered into the rubble and I'm lost. I roll in with my mean machine, interrupting this soft, rooster-filled morning. People come out of their doorways. I disrupt the morning chatter, the yawns, the barks, the pitter-patter, the daily dance of communities rising together. Someone directs me and ends up walking most of the way ahead of the Cruiser, to get me where I'm going.

The Chief sits outside, wearing a long brown garment, peeling some sort of nut. He jumps up and bows in welcome. I give him a long greeting, apologizing for my early and impromptu arrival.

"It is our honor. Let me have Nounia start breakfast for you." He looks around for children to summon their mother.

"No, no, please. I've already eaten. I'm only here to see Lele. Please, Chief."

Nounia walks into the courtyard. She does not look like the glamorous woman she was yesterday. She wears a long, torn dress and pats her hair down when she sees me. She has no lipstick on, and bags swell under her eyes.

"Bigabosse, welcome. Abdi, you should have told me Bigabosse has come."

"I just got here. I apologize for coming unannounced. Thank you for yesterday's feast." I see her mind whizzing at what she will serve me for breakfast and lunch. This is the risk of visiting people: food stress.

"You must have breakfast, Bigabosse," Nounia urges.

"Thank you, but I've already eaten," I lie.

"Coffee?" Nounia asks.

I'll have to give in to something. "Okay, yes, thanks, coffee." A concession. "May I go to Lele?"

"Yes, the girls are sleeping." Nounia ushers me into the room on the left side of the house.

It is a world unto itself this morning. Four bodies lie on four thin cloth mattresses, on straw mats, in various stages of sleep. If I were a photographer, I would click away. All these girls. Arms stretched, legs bent, elbows crooked, wearing colorful patterns. Geometric shapes of human girls, except for Lele, a small lump under a sheet, with just her head poking out. The picture would be in black and white. I'd want it up in a New York gallery. But what if some pervert saw it and had lewd thoughts about these dream-bound girls? The moment would be ruined. All it takes is one lecherous gaze.

One sister stirs, rousing out of sleep. Another lies back, mouth open, snoring. It's cozy in here—all these girls falling asleep and waking together in this space that belongs to all of them, until they get married. I think of myself and Chloe. In separate rooms with our separate monsters goading us at night. At times, she makes a break for it, skids across oak floors, into my arms. But I send her

214

back, lying to her, reassuring her that vagaries of the night don't exist. Here, they breathe each other's scents and odors. They reach for one another's bodies with one stretch. Do imaginary monsters come to visit them? Is there even space for monsters when bodies rest this close? I'll let Chloe sleep with me when I return.

Nounia comes in huffing, yelling in dialect. I hear the words *school* and *Bigabosse*. This makes them look up. I lean against the doorway. They get up, embarrassed, gather their things, smile shyly at me, and run for the water pump outside. One remains sleeping.

"Is it alright if I lie down? Until Lele wakes up."

"Of course, let me find you . . ." Nounia looks around for more comfortable furnishings.

"I can use that mat by her bed. You get the girls ready for school."

She looks relieved that she doesn't have to deal with me, but gives me an odd look.

I stretch myself onto a mattress, so thin I can feel the ground under my body. I pull a sheet from another bed, still warm from an adolescent's sleepy sweat. It's not comfortable, but I'm strangely relaxed. The concrete floors, the covered windows keep the room in a calm, matte state.

Lele is looking at me when I wake up. I give a little start. My left arm is cramped; I'm not used to sleeping on the floor. I have no idea what time it is or how long I've slept. There's a small brown coffee cup and saucer by my mat. I dip my pinkie in it. It's cool by now; I must have slept for a while. I sit up, cross my legs, stretch my arms. Everything creaks.

Nounia pokes her head in with someone's baby on her hip.

"Awake? You must have been very tired Bigabosse. I was worried how long you slept." I ask her if I can stay a while and she beams. I wonder how many hours of the day she's been trying to engage Lele; it must be a relief to let someone else take the task on. Nounia leaves us, her voice a merry echo.

"How are you?" I ask.

Lele doesn't answer. There's no time for meandering conversation. I jump in, telling her I want her to be well and asking whether she'd be open to a medical consultation. "It would be a friend of mine. Someone I trust. Someone gentle."

Lele looks back at me, thoughtfully. But not with that awe she used to have for me, when my words were sacred, when she ate them up. She looks at me clinically, detached.

"You have been so brave. And none of this is your fault. I just don't want there to be a greater injustice against you. Let's make sure you are not at risk of HIV, tetanus, hepatitis, or STIs." Such acronyms don't belong in this room of sisters.

Lele stays quiet.

"Are you really pregnant?"

She stirs. Almost a smile. "Yes," she whispers.

The smile throws me off. "You're happy about it?" I ask, disappointed.

"I have been thinking for many days, Bigabosse. My insides have disgusted me. But this baby has life and will have life bigger than me. Tell Monsieur Marc I am willing to forgive him. But he must take us. He must do the right thing."

"What are you talking about?"

"Bigabosse, he took my honor. He has to give it back. He has to marry me and give this child his name. There is no future for me here. I will be unable to marry. This child will have no rights. I know my parents will love and nurture him, but he will always be a bastard. Once my parents pass, then what? Will I be at the mercy of brothers? Of this village? The only way is to build a new family. I am ready to go with Monsieur Marc, in whichever countries he goes."

"Are you insane?" I blurt out.

She looks visibly hurt. "What is insane, Bigabosse, is that I worked in your office, your colleague did this, and Miss Chantal has done nothing." She hasn't moved, but her words have gained velocity. The feistiness of the childish Lele I knew repackaged in sharp tones.

"What happened to you was horrific, and I'm going to make sure it's addressed. But how could you possibly want to marry someone that did that to you? Come on, Lele, you are a smart and ambitious girl. You want more from your life than this."

"He has taken everything, Bigabosse. Everything. Now he must give me a future." She pauses, then suddenly says, "And why must you decide what I want?"

I'm dumbfounded.

"What exactly do you think is going to happen here? That Marc and you will sail off into the sunset? That will never happen. This whole thing about him restoring your honor, he'd never buy into that, you know him. And Lele, I'm not trying make decisions for you. I want to help you. Just think for a moment: you want to live with the man you say raped you? What kind of future do you think you are setting up for yourself?"

"What future do you think I have?"

"A better one than this charade you are imagining," I say. "You know what I would do? I would get an abortion. I would rid myself of every memory of the man who hurt me, not nurture it, not be owned by it for the rest of my life. If I were you, I would get the organization to pay for your schooling and help you find job opportunities. You can't hold your entire life hostage to one crisis. You're too smart and talented. You could be running this place in a few years."

Lele looks at me, expressionless. It's a Lele I don't know. But I have to stop her before this child becomes a new cross for her to bear.

"I will never be running anything, Bigabosse. Miss Chantal did not even give me the honor of a visit. It is clear how you people see us. The drivers, the gardeners, me, we're all the same to you. We are in your employment, but our sentiments and concerns do not matter."

"You're right. So much has to change with how local staff are treated. But you matter to me. That's why I'm here: I'm your ally, not theirs. You have your whole life ahead of you. Let's force the charity to build a secure future for you. Trust me, marriage is not the solution you think it is." She looks at me for a moment, and I feel I have an in. "Let's prepare a case against Marc; let's expose all the organizational failures. I'll stand by you. You can take owner-ship of the whole thing."

"Ownership? Of the rape? It is mine now?" Lele laughs. "It has always been mine, Bigabosse. You want to help me? Make Monsieur Marc comply, and take me away from here. He will have to give this to us."

A thought I'm fighting pokes its head. What if this whole thing is a ploy to get a passport out of this life of hardship? A headache spreads at my forehead. The cultural chasm suddenly too skewed to bridge. "Try to understand. Marc will not marry you. He won't, and bringing this up will only make you look guilty."

"Guilty?" Lele says, barely audible, the word hardly leaving her dry, heavy lips. Her eyes glued to my face.

"I'm not saying you are guilty of anything. I'm just saying I know how my colleagues operate. If you start saying you want to marry Marc, some might think you made up a story to end up with him—maybe for a foreign passport."

Giant eyes float in her bony face, searing me. But I tell her, with Likanni honesty, that wanting to marry someone who has hurt her seems suspicious in my part of the world, especially when it comes from an educated girl. She shouldn't give the charity more fodder to believe Marc.

"Do you think that? That I've lied to get a passport?" Lele asks.

"No, but I have to protect you. Think of how your family will react if you do this. I know Nounia. She'll want me to put you first. And in this case, I'm sorry but your health, your well-being, your future come first. I haven't told them about the pregnancy, but I know she'd be okay with terminating it."

Lele sits up with such speed that I jump. "You told me I was brave, that it wasn't my fault. Now you say it is my fault. I will never meet your doctor friends, Bigabosse. Tell Monsieur Marc. That is all I ask of you at this time. You should leave." She crosses her arms.

Nounia comes into the room with a platter of food. At the sight of her daughter sitting up, she gives a cry of joy. She places the food on the floor, hugs Lele, swaying her, kissing her head.

"Thank you, Bigabosse," says Nounia.

———

The family talks at me as they serve food and water in dripping glasses. I can't hear them. The alliance I wanted to forge, destroyed. I suddenly remember the story of Marie. The one girl who spoke of rape aloud, whose words Lele translated to me, when she was probably too young to do so.

Many young girls in the orphanage had experienced sexual violence, but they rarely spoke of it. There was never a parent to explain their woes. At best, we would guess; at worst, we would miss the markers. Every orphanage has a counselor who gently probes memories. Those girls were like wells, secrets below ground. Except for Marie.

Marie was brought to me by the World Food Programme team. One of their workers, Micheline, was canvassing a small village, four hours away from Likanni, to scope food aid needs. She walked into a village left in ruins. Most huts had been burned down. The livestock had either been stolen or massacred. Mothers had been violated in front of their daughters. The boys had all been kidnapped. Those who had survived had left, seeking food and shelter elsewhere.

Marie had lived in that village with her mother and brother. Her father and two elder brothers had perished years ago from an illness whose name she did not know. They were living in poverty but survived day to day. From her stories, Marie sounded as if she'd been happy. It was a small village, a community where people shared burdens of their tragedies and grew intertwined through mutual histories and hunger. The area was arid, with little agriculture, and they never saw much interest from warlords, multinational companies, the military, or child soldiers. Without riches, the village survived in its peaceful, languid, at times famished state.

When a gaggle of teenage boys appeared one afternoon, Marie told me, she was excited. Never had she seen so many of them, and with such loud voices. They came with unfamiliar rods, which she later discovered were guns. When she first saw them, she had wanted to play. Finally new children, she had thought. She laughed and slapped her forehead, hard, as she recounted this. "Those were not children. Those were dangerous animals."

Most of the villagers came out of their shacks to take a look at this noisy bunch.

One of the child soldiers bowed dramatically, then grabbed a little boy, and said, "Now, you come with us. You fight for us. But you don't eat until you feed us."

The child's mother, a skeletal woman, came yelling in a motherly way, telling the child soldier to put her son down. Marie remembered the woman's feet, shuffling quickly in the dirt, little dust storms at her ankles, scolding as all the other mothers of the village had always done. But the child soldier said the thing that changed the tenor of their presence.

"I'll put him down, but I take you instead."

Marie, from behind her thatched hut, saw the woman's feet fly up, then down again, as the boys attacked her. They laughed, jostled. They bent her like an elastic. They sounded like school-boys chasing a ball. Other villagers rushed to save her, but the boys shot their weapons at random, asserting their invincibility. They had the magic of gunfire, which the villagers did not.

Marie's brother was plucked next, and when he was grabbed, Marie's mother walked straight to the gang of child soldiers, arms wide and open.

"You do as you like to me. Leave the boy," she said in a calm voice. Marie recounted that that was the last time she heard her mother's normal speaking voice. It had made her proud, that her voice was so calm. But furious that the voice had surrendered so quickly and hadn't put up any protest or battle.

After that, what she told me made me shut my eyes and want to put my hands over my ears. But I had to listen to what she was courageous enough to say. She sat in my office, looking down at a roll of tape on my desk, and calmly described her mother's rape. She told me that as it happened, her mother yelled, "Run!" The voice had gotten hoarser and hoarser, before Marie realized the instruction was directed at her. The boys were spreading among the huts, tossing clay pots, grabbing the odd chicken. So Marie ran for the scant fields. She heard her mother's dry voice for a few more moments until it was stamped out by a foot.

She hid in the tall grasses for three days. When she was afraid, she would lie on her back and look at the sky. When she was sad, she would lie on her belly. She sipped dew off the grass, thankful for the rainy season, and nibbled weeds and the earth. On the first day of lying still, she wet herself and had felt the relief of some hu-manness, some warm touch spreading against her legs. But soon those normal bodily functions disappeared, they too abandoning her to the largest solitude she had ever felt.

After three days, when there were no more sounds, Marie dragged herself to the village. She was hungry, dizzy, her mus-cles weakened. She couldn't see properly, circles of light and dark pulsed wherever she looked. The village was nothing more than bodies; most of them had been covered by grasses and earth by escaping villagers who couldn't bear to leave their neighbors' bodies staring emptily at the sky. Marie squinted as she made it past the obstacle course of bodies, refusing to see her people as corpses, grateful that her vision was distorted. Marie hid near her thrashed home, finding comfort in its straw. When she heard the sound of the WFP vehicle, she thought the child soldiers were returning for her, but she didn't have the strength to run away. Instead, she saw a woman with orange hair, a color she had never seen, and in a terrifying gesture of trust, Marie moaned as loudly as she could. Micheline brought her immediately to me.

"This is a really bad case," Micheline had warned me.

They always were.

I took Marie in and called our closest orphanage to get the process underway. In that time, Marie told me her story with that strange, alien-like wisdom spawned by pain. You see it in these children: they have something quiet about them, even when they speak. They look as though they understand human nature and the haphazard design of the universe, in a way you never could. Like they see atoms and molecules, but that insight can only come from witnessing something truly horrific.

Lele calmly translated all the details of Marie's story for me.

She talked to me about Marie for weeks. Asking details about what had happened and how. By translating, she had taken Marie's memories in her mouth. She had curled her tongue around harrowing words. Did they do something to her?

23

'm about to leave the Chief's home, when Nounia pulls me aside. Her initial excitement at seeing her daughter animated has been replaced by concern, as she noted the tension between me and Lele, who never once looked at me after our exchange.

Nounia takes me to the kitchen and points at my bandages, which have slid downward.

"Let me see," she says and I acquiesce.

I hold out my arms while Nounia undoes the bandages, uncurling each layer. My arms are enflamed purple, hardly look like my own, extending out of my body. Fanon, out of nowhere, comes in and gasps.

"What happened?" he asks.

I try not to answer. "Don't worry, it's nothing . . . it's because I don't have a husband anymore." The words tumble out. Fanon looks perplexed, but nods slowly as if a broken marriage can explain injuries. Like this is a Western tradition that doesn't quite translate.

Nounia waves him away.

"Was it him who did this?" she asks as she gets up, collects some neem leaves out of jar, and crushes them.

"Who? Marc? No, no," I say with shame.

Nounia mixes a few things until she has a yellow paste. She paints it on my wounds, and I feel as though I can finally breathe and release the tightness of the pain. I suggest to her that Lele should see a doctor. The comedy of the moment is not lost on me. I'm being nursed while I suggest her daughter go to someone else.

"Yes, Fanon was mentioning. He is against, but I need to think," Nounia says. She blows on my arms, and the relief is so extreme, I tear up.

"You know, Bigabosse, it is hard for me to decide what is right and wrong at the moment. Lele is the life of the family; no one stops her once she has decided. I have raised them like this—to be strong, to decide on their own."

I nod.

"I like you and we trust you, but your people, they are always so separate. It is hard to come here and live here, I understand, but your people they get much respect from us, but they don't become one of us."

"They can't, Nounia. Even the ones that live here, like Tommy and Seher, they can't. And I can't, and this has been the hardest thing for me to understand. I don't know where that separation is."

"Okay, but then tell your people. They have to come like respectful visitors in someone's home. They have to ask permission. They cannot pretend to have solutions when they are raping our children." She holds my arm up. "Look at you. You cannot help anyone with this. Go heal yourself and then come back." That makes me cry.

She walks me to the front of the home and beckons Fanon to ride with me to the compound. Before she says goodbye, she tells me, "You arrange the affairs at the office so that the man is punished, we will arrange ours."

Fanon seems uncomfortable in the Cruiser, but I'm relieved. The sky is beginning to darken, and as there are no roads, I could miss a turn. I could miss a gang of hoodlums who ignore our foreign logo in the day but can make a mistake at dusk. I can miss a thousand markers that I am no longer used to seeing.

"Are you okay?" He points at my bright-yellow arms. I tell him I'm fine, and repeat that I don't have a husband anymore. He's not dead or anything; he just doesn't exist. Fanon looks confused, like this is a cultural explanation that doesn't quite translate.

"Can you tell me a bit about this thing—about rape victims marrying their rapists?"

"This is what you wish to discuss?" Fanon looks at me quizzically.

"Please. Your perspective makes me see things differently."

He seems pleased with himself. "It does not happen very often. How could it? When a man robs a woman, he tries to destroy her. But some men have great remorse upon their sin and have offered to marry the women. It is symbolic because they are showing that for them these women are with honor, to be valued, to be desired, and that they themselves are dishonorable for the act they have committed," Fanon explains.

"That part I get, but wouldn't boys just go ahead and rape the girls they wish to marry, especially when women reject them?"

"We are not animals."

"No, of course not. But if the end goal is marriage—"

"No, you do not understand. You cannot be loved if you attempt to destroy."

"I don't remember it ever happening here."

"In our ancestral village, a man who had raped a young girl during war came and wept at her feet, promised to give her all his riches and restore the honor he had stolen from her. They were married for many years."

"Sorry to be crude, but that sounds pretty fucked up. How could she not remember every time he approached her?" I ask.

"Perhaps she did, but what were her choices?"

"So, this is not a common practice?"

"No, no. Why are we speaking on this matter?" Fanon is looking at me, the sun setting behind his head framed in the window.

"Well, be calm about this . . . It's Lele, she was asking me about that. She—she wants me to talk to Marc." I expect him to yell and brace myself.

"Will you?"

"What? What are you talking about? Don't you hate the guy?" It's odd to catch Fanon without a response. He holds his tongue, but I don't let him. "You told me you wanted to break Marc's face, now you want me to talk to him about marrying your sister?"

"I hate him. I shall always hate him. I want to kill him. But she's speaking about the future. She has not done this in a long time. She was an ambitious girl . . . I have been afraid she will end her life. This is hopeful."

I dart a look at him as he looks out the window. His reaction does not make sense. Did he know? If Lele leaves for Europe, the door opens for everybody in her family. Passports can make people do crazy things.

I don't really know anyone.

"You want to go somewhere to eat?" Fanon asks suddenly, as though he is appeasing me.

"Not today."

"Tomorrow then?" He peers expectantly. "I want to take you to a place you have not been. There is music and food. It will be different for you, another Likanni." The adventuress in me is not quite dead. She raises her sleepy head, she imagines this place, somewhere with strangers, with music, other bodies and faces, sitting and laughing with Fanon, like a carefree youngin, like a non-wife, not thinking about all the shit. A place with sticky tables, unpredictable conversation.

"Tomorrow," I say, regretting the commitment as soon as it's made.

He taps a beat on the glove compartment. "Biga—"

"You know, my name is Maya. You can call me that."

He looks surprised that I have another name. I almost feel surprised to hear the two syllables aloud. I like being Bigabosse, like I'm theirs, appropriated into a new person. But Fanon and I are friends now. It's time to be honest.

Fanon guides, I drive. I like the simple obedience of it. I open the windows, and the breeze rushes in with twigs and leaves. I could do this forever. Grinding against uneven grounds, hearing the night air, feeling the proximity of Fanon's strong frame, listening for *right* and *left*. The drive is cryptic in its blackness, so much so that I'm up against the steering wheel, enchanted by the light show of headlights in leaves and dirt. The mystery of moving shapes gives me a rush. Nothing is clear or known; anything could lie before me, inspiring a different kind of adrenaline.

Once I am on the straight road, Fanon speaks. "You said you have no husband?"

"I don't want to talk about it."

"But how did you get hurt?" he asks. The confusion must have been sitting with him. I bite back a smile.

"My husband is with another woman. You probably think I deserve it, leaving him like this. But it has been going on for a while, even though I wasn't sure. I finally saw it. And when I go back, I have to end my marriage, because now that I've seen the truth, I can't live with it." I speak matter-of-factly, my voice strong, surprising myself.

"You saw him? In the phone?"

"In that exact thing. A miracle of modern technology."

"What will happen to the child? Will he take it away?" Fanon asks, thinking about steps I haven't considered.

"No. He won't want to do that. It's too much work. We'll probably figure out some arrangement and share her," I say.

Bile-like dread appears on my tongue. Can there be anything worse than logistics around the death of something? With the severing of our family, there will be practical and administrative tasks. We'll have to slice up our daughter's life. We'll have to get lawyers. We'll have to agree to schedules. I'll have to worry about who he introduces Chloe to. The mundanity of it disgusts me and I haven't even waded in.

"Share her? The child?" Fanon asks, as if I'm speaking of a houseplant.

"Yes, she will spend some time with me and some weekends with him. I don't know."

"That sounds very strange. Good but very strange."

"It is good, but strange, probably. Maybe she'll get more attention from both of us. She deserves better." I speak to myself, as if he's a shadow asking the primal questions that I should have answered in my mind already.

"You will find a father for her?"

I laugh. "No way. She doesn't need another father and I don't want to be married again. I'm done with that bullshit. The house will be for me and my girl," I say, as I think it up. I imagine a happy, bustling home, where the two of us live and grow without a man. It's a pleasant fantasy in which children don't cry and I'm not exhausted or worried about money, where Chloe and I are friends, comrades, like a funny but sentimental sitcom. "Maybe I'll get a companion someday, but no husbands." I turn red as the words surface. What I've said is shocking in these parts. It's shameless and a little shameful. Sometimes we really are the women they see in film.

Fanon continues, posing question after question, each one a small prick. He's very much his sister's brother. We turn into the compound. I see four lights illuminating the windows of the building. Marc and Chantal must be waiting for the sound of gravel.

"Thank you for riding back with me. I would have gotten lost for sure. We can meet at eight tomorrow?" He nods as we climb out of the vehicle.

I stare up at the invisible building with its lit windows floating in the darkness, when I feel Fanon's hands land softly on my waist. I gasp. He's standing right behind me, his lips close to my earlobe.

"Please do not hurt yourself."

I shouldn't, but I back up and am in his arms. I hear him draw a sharp breath as my bum touches his pelvis. I lean my head back, his sticky face against my cheek. There are security cameras aimed at the car park, I know there are security guards, I know that Chantal and Marc can see shadows moving, but for a few moments I don't care. I want to selfishly lean into real human mettle that breathes and moves. I want to be in the velvet of his voice, cocooned in its layers. I want to erase any gaps between our flesh.

"I cannot do anything with you. I'm still married," I say, while leaning back further, grinding my frame deeper into his, betraying the words coming out of my mouth.

"I understand," Fanon whispers.

He spreads his hands from my waist to my stomach. They travel on my clothing, and yet it's the most arousing of touches, like he's coaxing the most private realm of my body into life. My abdomen, the place no one has touched in years. This is the skin that housed my daughter, the skin that hangs, the ugliest of me. His hands flit over my belly, first with soft caresses, then with big sweeps, like he's washing a smooth window clean. I moan un-sexily. The sweeps get larger and larger, over my shirt, over my breasts, over my pants, over my thighs. I no longer hear the crick-ets; I hear his panting, my own loud moans as if I'm breaking. I'm ecstatic but sad. My head back, I open my eyes and see the stars that never come out to play back home, all witnessing whatever the hell I'm doing right now. A tear rolls down my cheek. I let it. Every part of this country is intoxicating. Me getting rubbed, over my clothing, against this strong man. In this night air thick with insect chants, far away from my husband, my home. It must be like this for all those old white men with young girls too, who come here to forget their failing lives.

"Stop," I say.

Fanon stops moving his hands. I'm still leaning against him, and he folds me in. I'm held. Supported. And thankful we can't look at each other. I wouldn't know how to look. I would be reminded of who he is. Right now he's just a body. He wraps his arms around my waist. I feel every part of him throbbing, but he's stopped. It's such an unfair playing field I've led him to. I can never bring him into my life, yet I travel to his.

Pillowy lips kiss my cheek. I reach back and put my hand on his face. He kisses my palm.

"I can't really do this, okay?" I say.

I don't know what *this* is; I'm still pressed against him, still being held. Still feeling his sharp edges.

"Okay," Fanon says. He takes a step back, lifts my hair, and kisses me where it meets my neck, at its sweatiest.

"Goodnight, Ma-ya. I will see you tomorrow." He disappears. The air around me left vast and empty. I touch my waist, trying to apply the same pressure as his hands. With him gone, everything feels cold. Drunkenly, I wobble to the back door, searching for keys, which I had been holding at some point. I'm sure Fanon's here, somewhere in the dark, ensuring I get in safely. But I don't look around.

I disappear into my room. I'm lucid. I know what to do about Marc. I know what to do about Lele. I know what to report back to my boss. And Fanon, that was just delicious. I'm reeling from that pleasure. It was a gift when all else had been taken away. I take off my shirt and sniff. I smell him. I lay the shirt on my bed and snuggle my face against it. He'll never forgive me for taking Marc away. But I can make amends. We can't jeopardize all the work that has been done here. Everyone can emerge from this. I know we can. Even Lele—she's on her way, envisaging the future. I just need to alter her vision and show her something that is better for her. I gave her a path once before; I can do it again. I need to get Marc out of here before our reputation suffers. He can be dealt with at headquarters.

I can only do that which I can do.

I jump up and snap open my laptop. So many unread messages from work; people must be in a panic. I ignore them all.

Dear Burton,

It's time to execute Marc's evacuation. Please arrange for a transition team to run the office. Chantal wants to leave, so please initiate recruiting processes. I suggest we move Marc on next Monday's flight. I can travel with him to the capital on Friday morning.

I will stay on for a few more days after that to manage the transition with Chantal. I can present the new team to the community. The villagers should be told Marc has been removed for their safety. We can throw a community welcome from the new staff and provide food on our grounds. Our show of generosity will be appreciated.

On the subject of Lele, the victim, please note that she is pregnant. She was a contract worker for us. Please consider what kind of package we can offer her as a staff member who got harmed on the job. She has to think of our organization as one that provided in her time of need. I want her to have educational training abroad, with a guarantee of work with us once she is done, as she is highly skilled. Our brand, our work, and all the other foreign workers in this country are at stake; please be generous.

As for Marc, the victim has clearly stated that he com-
mitted the crime. I trust you and the executive to follow
the appropriate process. We'll have to figure out what
geographic jurisdiction this falls under. I know I've been
difficult to contact, but let's convene tomorrow. I will be
available as of seven a.m. your time.

Maya

There. Black on white, the words have been sent. Now they
can take a life of their own.

24

I sit at the kitchen table, sipping tea. I'm relaxed, still stirred by Fanon. I smile into my mug, replaying moments in my mind. My body's been asleep for so long it doesn't know what to do with itself. I try to be still, but everything wants to quiver.

Marc and Chantal walk into the kitchen in T-shirts and shorts, cautiously. I ask if I can talk to Marc alone.

Chantal does not move.

"I think Maya is right," Marc says.

She glares at him and shuts the kitchen door with a bang. A lizard goes scuttling.

Marc looks at me curiously as he sits across from me. I don't bother discussing their relationship. I honor Lele's request and blurt out her demand without any preamble. "Here's the thing: I spent the day with Lele. She's pregnant. She says you raped her and are the father. She's open to you marrying her and raising the child with her." The absurd words pile on top of each other. There is nothing to sugarcoat them with.

Marc stares at me blankly, then laughs. "This is a joke, right?"

"It isn't. This is what she wants."

"You see how crazy this is?" He laughs again, shaking his head with incredulity. "You see what this is all about, don't you?" He leans forward.

"Let's focus on your evacuation right now. I know you don't want to leave, but for everyone's sanity and security, we need to change the strategy," I say, avoiding his question.

"Come on, even you see the setup. They trashed my reputation and now I have to flee like a criminal. My only other option is to marry her and take care of someone else's baby?"

"For someone who is being accused so directly, you should be glad that you are being sent back. Can you imagine if this were dealt with by local authorities? If you were incarcerated here?"

"You still don't believe me! Fucking unbelievable. Don't you see what is going on, Maya? Are you so blind to everything around you?" he asks with disbelief.

I feel a wave of panic. I was blind to my husband, to Marc and Chantal's relationship.

"What does this evacuation mean for my reputation? For my future with the organization? I'm getting closer to becoming regional manager. Lele's completely screwed this up." Marc's face is scarlet, his eyebrows almost vertical.

"You've been here long enough; you've done what you've needed to do. Yes, it's not ending the way you want it to, but not all missions end well. These are conflict zones we work in. Things are messy. Sometimes people end up dead, for Christ's sake," I say.

"But I'm being sent away for a crime I didn't commit. That's not the same as dying for a cause."

"Well, when the baby comes, the truth will come out," I say plainly.

"Do you hear yourself? She knew about Chantal and me, and she wants to marry me? This is what all of them are about. They take anything they can get, then they want more. I don't blame them, but that's the truth. It's the handout culture we've created. They blame outsiders for everything. They don't take any responsibility. They're the ones killing and raping each other, not us, and they look at us like we're the criminals." Marc is full of venom.

"I'm going to invite Chantal in now," I say. She can deal with his antics.

"They've made their country a shithole; they have no respect for human life. They can celebrate their stupid independence days. We all know they were better off when we were running things. And people like you worsen things. You're in so deep you can't even see the truth anymore. You never should have hired her. She had no credentials. She was too young. There are a hundred more qualified women who needed that internship more than her."

"I'm going to bring Chantal in," I repeat, my face hot.

"You know, I saw you earlier. With that boy," Marc says, eyebrows raised, still looking at his hands.

I freeze, my tan skin likely a flamingo pink.

"Not exactly Mother Teresa, are you?"

"There's not much to report. I stopped things before they got out of hand," I say with a false note of confidence, as if rubbing up against one of our beneficiaries is a perfectly normal thing to do.

"That was an abuse of power, especially when his sister is so vulnerable. This could put our female staff at great risk."

I wince at how cheap I've made it look. How he suddenly sounds like the thoughtful authority, and I, the exploiter. Why does he go sit in the security booth? I never did that when I worked here. What faces did he see me make? How ridiculous did it look? What will he tell our superiors? Will I face legal repercussions?

"I'm going to bring Chantal in now."

Chantal is in the hallway smoking, against policy. She comes in and sits next to Marc. He puts his arm on her shoulder, and she brushes it off.

She stares straight at me. "When are we getting out of here?"

25

The next morning is all business. I receive a call from Burton at ten, eight his time. He has assembled all the board members to my surprise. These include ex–European ministers, former executive directors of NGOs, a journalist, along with the director of the organization, the chief information officer, and two high-level managers. I don't have time to be intimidated; I'm thrown right in. I should have read their emails.

Burton's assistant posts an agenda on the screen, which I jot down on the back of the closest piece of paper I can find. It reads as follows:

1. Exit strategy
2. Transition team
3. Long-term recruitment

4. Benefits package
5. Marc Briois: trajectory

Lele's and Marc's fates are concealed under headings four and five, which we discuss after a four-hour session on issues one through three, which are presented purely as logistics. No one breathes a word about the accusation, about Lele. All of us, hiding behind bureaucratic language, our agendas and protocols. By the end of the first discussion, it is determined that I am to stay with Chantal and not accompany Marc; transition staff will descend upon us by next Friday and Chantal will be deployed out six weeks later.

After a long, drawn-out discussion and meticulous planning, we have a half-hour recess to eat. I text Burton frantically, trying to gauge how we will present things, but he doesn't respond.

I grab the agenda, my pen, and phone and go to the kitchen, where Marc and Chantal are lunching. As I peer into the fridge to find a quick lunch, Marc grabs the agenda, which I've left on the table.

"Why is my name on this? What's this about a benefits package? Am I getting fired?"

I poke my head out of the fridge. "This is the agenda from the meeting I'm having with the executive. The benefits package is about new staff. Your trajectory, so to speak, is their way of captioning your return home," I say.

"Wouldn't my return be covered under exit strategy? Why am I a separate agenda item?" Marc asks.

I find a guava that will soon meet its demise and slice it open. "We haven't gotten to the last two agenda items."

Marc looks at me with doubt. "I'm not comfortable with you discussing my future without me being in the room."

I savor his discomfort.

"When do I give my point of view? Defend myself?" asks Marc.

"This isn't that kind of a meeting. We're not discussing HR grievances. We're trying to put in a transition plan. You can have as many meetings as you want back in Geneva. Right now, the priority is getting you out of here safely." I look at my watch. My stomach growls. I grab the guava, crackers, leftover sweet potatoes. "I'll inform you after the call." I take the agenda from him.

Chantal nods. Marc stares at me sullenly.

I race upstairs and switch my screen back on. The camera is still on in the meeting room; mine is off because of the poor connection. I see people milling about in nice clothes with coffees. It looks like a world away. I imagine them having taken a tram or walked to work. Heels clicking on clean sidewalks.

Everything looks tight; there's no other way to explain it. The suits look tight, the dresses look tight, the shoes look tight, the way people move around—with their arms at their sides or crossed at their chests—looks tight. Their facial expressions look restrained, as do their slender bodies, held in with diets, with clothing, with appropriate behaviors.

I spread further. I think of the Likanni air, the physical freedoms it allows. I open my legs a bit more. I relax my shoulders, shedding the stiffness that comes from being surrounded by Europeans or Americans, a stiffness that disappears only when people drink. I try to forget the performance that is the public space back home. Here, if a woman wants to run her hands on tall grass, kick a pebble, or spit, she can. If she wants to lovingly touch the cheek of a child that isn't hers, she can. Movements back home are relegated to workouts, stretches, yoga, permissible only in the realm of sport or specified leisure, with the appropriate tight clothing. We've forgotten what our bodies can do outside of manicured games.

They are taking long. I clear my throat at the mic, reminding them I'm on this invisible end. People slowly head back to their swivel chairs. A student intern rushes through the door with baguette sandwiches for all. I would kill for one of those right now.

"Maya, are you still there?" Burton asks.

"Yes."

"Wonderful. Let's get started. Thank you everyone for your timely return, and for the fruitful discussion in the first session. Let us resume our agenda." Burton clears his throat. "Maya, can you present the following agenda item?"

I thought he would speak and I would pipe in; I'm caught off guard. Instead, he's unwrapping his baguette. It is retribution for my lack of emails. I stickily swallow the spoonful of sweet potatoes in my mouth. After a few *uhs*, I launch into an unwieldy description of why I think we should provide for Lele and her baby, what some of our options are, like giving her a staff position at headquarters, childcare subsidies, a training subsidy to upgrade her skills at a European university. I wish he'd told me that I would be presenting; I would have done a better job justifying why this is necessary.

People exchange looks, fidget. They have forgotten that I can see them. After I finish, there's silence.

Marijke, an imposing woman who once headed a health NGO, takes off her glasses and puts them on the table. "Pardon me, Maya, but is there any evidence that a crime has been committed?"

"What do you mean? Lele told me she was raped by Marc. I have met with her; she's a mess. As you know, the police have little to no capacity in these parts. There are no DNA kits . . . The only evidence is her word." I hear sharp inhalations. I said it without dressing it all up.

"Has a doctor treated her?" Marijke asks clinically. I tell her he has.

"Is he a local doctor?" pushes Marijke.

"Yes, very respected in the community," I say.

"Were there any witnesses who saw or heard something? Who saw the victim alone with the accused?"

"No, but we know that Lele went to interview Marc in his office alone. He confirms this."

"Interesting. Well, I'm just going to say what others might be thinking and are too polite to ask. Do we know if this really happened on our property? Aren't there child soldiers running around molesting women all over the place?"

"Well," I say, "for one, she tells us, and second, in case her word has no value, there is video footage of the entrance in which she's rushing out of the building."

Another woman pipes in. It's Olivia, a Brit who has never really liked me. "Rushing hardly constitutes assault. You should have seen me after our meeting this morning. I rushed out of here to get some coffee."

The colleagues murmur uncomfortably. Polite coffee-scented laughter. Civilizing the ugly through humor.

"Look, it's your choice how you want to position the organization. We could forget it; this can be another rape in this part of the world that no one addresses. Except for a few things. This is the Chief's daughter we are talking about. People are upset. If she sees us as failing her, the community will see us as failing them all. This can create serious risks to future staff."

They look surprised by my outburst, my lack of respect for hierarchy, my lack of thoughtful words such as *risk management* and *mitigation, gender-based violence* and *outreach*. Those words that house trauma in easily digestible terms.

I continue, "You also have to consider that Lele was working for us and did a damn good job. She's as much a part of our team as Marc is. With all due respect, a communications fiasco involving our local staff, someone we didn't look after, could tank this work and have donors hand the money over to UNICEF or UNDP. I know none of you want to lose the funding. The Danes, the foundations, the EU, they have drooled over this work. Losing our role in this country, which is of vital geopolitical interest right now, would be a huge loss."

They exchange alarmed looks as though I'm threatening them.

I march on. "Things are volatile. There's a strong antiforeign sentiment since the American military came in. It's not just our programming that is at risk, but everyone else's as well. It's your choice. If we delay, we may end up with a crisis threatening other foreigners working in the region. If we get ahead of it, we'll look like a fair organization that protects its workers and respects local community rights."

Burton looks around nervously, embarrassed by me. I'm strident, undiplomatic; I'm committing professional suicide. I feel fantastic.

Marijke jumps in again. "Supporting this claim without due process, in my opinion, is premature. It is an admission of guilt without having undergone the appropriate procedures and investigation. It sets a dangerous precedent: that anyone blackmailing our staff will be handsomely compensated."

"No one wants to flaunt that they have been raped," I say. "Women kill themselves after having been raped here. It's not like she'll jump on social media and announce her prize money. And what procedures are you talking about? A victim, a contract worker no less, tells us she's been raped. That's it, that's what we go on, that's the procedure."

"You may have forgotten that I spent a decade working in Darfur where I dealt with rapes on a daily basis. You wanting to bring her here is absurd. She isn't permanent staff; she's a contract worker. You brought her into the organization without going through the proper channels. She was never selected by the Geneva office, as is protocol, but let's ignore that for a moment, even though you increased risk both to her and the organization. You know how hard it is to get the Swiss to give a working permit to someone from the developing world. Frankly, this request is neither feasible nor practical." Marijke crosses her arms and sits back in her chair.

242

"We're always talking about how to attract talent from the global south—well, here it is," I say. "Lele's smart. We can finally have staff in Geneva that understand the needs of the people we're supposedly serving." I use their buzzwords against them, the very ones they use to attract healthy donations. "This is hard for me too. I've worked with Marc for over a decade; it's something I never could have imagined. But Lele has told me twice that Marc has raped her, so we have to treat this accusation seriously, like we would if one of our Western staff members was making such a claim." I've used the inappropriate words. I've said *Lele*, instead of *victim*; *Marc*, instead of *personnel*. I've said *rape*, instead of *assault*. And I've questioned whose claims have more worth.

"This is a very serious accusation against a long-term senior staff member," Burton says carefully. Now he's screwed. No one can hide behind anything. I've stripped us all.

"Yes, it is. But I can't just cover it up because of my history or Marc's otherwise clean record."

"No one's asking you to cover anything," Burton says uneasily, looking like I've lost my mind. "There will, of course, be a full investigation."

"We have to get a safeguards expert in," Olivia says quickly. To be on the right side of history, I suppose.

"I'll start by collecting testimonials," I offer.

Burton jumps in. "That's not a good idea; you are too close to the victim, and there may be a conflict of interest."

"What conflict of interest?"

Burton responds in a firm tone he's never had to employ with me, because I used to be tactful, I knew my place. "There are several problematic aspects to your involvement, Maya. First, you hired the girl without consultation. Second, it appears there is an unnatural closeness between you and some of the victim's family members. If we investigate Marc, we need to be above board on everything. No compromised staff, no allegiances or intimate relationships, nothing for a labor lawyer to critique. We must be exemplary. Safeguards and HR experts who are removed and have no affiliations are the only ones that should be engaged."

"You do know that they won't talk to strangers about something so personal, right?" I scoff.

"Well, Maya, this is something you should have considered earlier," Burton says sharply.

"And," says Marijke, "you are effectively Marc's boss. There is very much a power dynamic here. You've also complained about him in the past. It could be perceived as you having something against him."

"I tried to improve relations between him and Chantal, who he, by the way, is sleeping with."

"Alright, alright, let's avoid mudslinging," interjects Burton. "Thank you, Maya, for bringing this to our attention. Rest assured there will be due diligence on the matter. Given your history and relations, I request you do not liaise with the community any further. I would ask you to merely execute the evacuation plan. The board will discuss this matter further during the closed session. We appreciate your input. The beneficiaries are, of course, of utmost importance to us and we will take into account any undue hardships and mental-health impacts the posting could have had on our personnel, including on you."

With that, I'm politely let out, with deliverables and dates. I'm the one who came across as emotional, making poor decisions and violating our polite spaces.

I sit Chantal and Marc down and give them the plan: when they are leaving, when the next folks are coming, what needs to be wrapped up, and how.

"I'll stay on for another week after Marc leaves to ensure everything goes smoothly," I say.

"Thanks." Chantal smiles. A real smile from a woman I recognize. They are finally getting out of their hamster wheel.

"What did they decide about me?" Marc asks.

"I don't know."

"What does that mean?" he demands.

"They've been told I'm too close to the victim, so now I'm cut off. I have no information or decision-making power."

Chantal looks embarrassed for me. Marc, defiant. I wonder which one informed headquarters about Fanon.

"You should start packing," I tell Marc, without looking at him. I can't look at him. "You don't have that much time and there's a lot to sort out in your home and office. Chantal, can you arrange an escort for Marc to gather his belongings? You should schedule one for yourself as well. I would prefer if you guys pack in the daytime. Let's avoid bright lights and movement at night."

Chantal gets up while Marc stares at the table. She leans to him and says, "Bébé, we're free. Let's go." There is life in her face, her wheels whirring about all that needs to be done, all that she needs to bid farewell to. Chantal has been here for the last five years, poring over emails, driving to sites, making plans, hugging children, managing staff holidays, executing everything from vaccination programs to drawing lessons. And now she will simply walk away. All of these things which felt essential for so many years will be shelved. Goodbyes are strange that way.

"Oh yes, and both of you should know, I'm going to have dinner with Fanon tonight. See, Marc, no need for secrets." I get up from my chair, swinging my keys, and head up to my room.

26

It's early evening, a few hours before I am to meet Fanon. I'm buzzing. To busy myself, I repack my whole suitcase. Rolling shirts into tubes, trousers into squares gives a semblance of order, the hope for a future goodbye.

But the guilt doesn't fade. I'm in a transitional space, here but already gone. Fanon is a mere shadow of this time and place, not even fully real. I won't be able to uphold any pretensions; I'm not going to be a great love. I'm not even going to be a mediocre one. He'll see that on my face. I'm fumbling. With myself it's okay, but with another it's a sin. He'll say he can play along, but he can't. I'm playing with myself; he's just a bystander. This is some obscene masturbation I'll indulge in. There is nothing for him to consent to. I'm drawing unfair rules.

I think of Chloe and send messages through the ether: *I'll be home soon. Mommy loves you.* In the meantime, she's about to meet a guy. Who knows what will happen, because Mommy is very, very hurt. And she should know better, but she doesn't. She just needs this one last thing.

The evening is doing its trick. I follow its snake-charming. I have lipstick on. Already a bad decision. I hear scampering, doors being shut. They have retreated to their private realm, away from my prospective drama.

I meet Fanon outside by the carpark. I switch on an external light. He stands looking uncomfortable in a stiff, purple polyester button-up shirt. Shit, he dressed up. Nothing good can come of this.

Then again, I'm in a long, spaghetti-strapped cotton dress; it swirls around my legs as I walk. My arms are bare, but for the yellow-stained scratches that look like they may scab soon, skin stretching across wounds to reconnect, reseal me.

His face breaks into the widest grin I've ever seen. I won't be able to steer this ship. It's too late. How to greet him? The good-bye the night before was so intimate, so unruly.

"Fanon, I don't think we should go out tonight."

His smile falters. "Why?"

"Maybe we can eat here?" I gesture toward the building.

"Maya." He rolls my name uncertainly in his mouth. "Please. Come."

"I'm sorry, I don't think it's a good idea with everything going on."

He looks around, helplessly. "I promised you something special. I will get it. You wait here. Yago works at the restaurant; I will call him. He will start the cooking. I will be back in an hour." He tears off into the darkness, before I can say another word or offer to drive.

As Fanon covers kilometers with his feet, I fuss in the kitchen, place mismatched plates and cutlery on the table. Does he use cutlery? This is everything that is frowned upon. There is no future here. What will happen to this man whose sweat I'll wear, what do I leave him with? I'll use him for magic, be a Stella-Got-Her-Groove-Back, what does he get?

I hear him before I see him, almost two hours later, on our stoop. I hear Styrofoam boxes, squeaking against one another in plastic bags. There's deep panting, like he's out of breath from running. I hear shoes, not flip-flops, on the gravel.

"I am here," Fanon says.

"I can't believe you did that. How far did you have to go?"

"Not far," he lies. I know he's lying because I've eaten every damn thing in the vicinity, and the smells coming from the boxes are new to me. He looks around. "The only challenge is we shall require a flat surface. You will need light."

"We can eat inside," I say.

Fanon shifts uncomfortably, one foot to the other. I hear his stiff shirt crinkling. "I don't think I can go inside."

"Marc's not there," I lie.

"It is . . . it is the site of the crime. It is where my sister suffered her aggression. I do not know if I can control my anger. I wish to be happy tonight," Fanon says.

I should heed his wisdom, but I've made my decision: I will take the lead. It is my foray into not waiting to be desired, but of desiring. Of breaking the rules and the false permissions they profess.

"Remember, it's also the place where Lele worked for many happy years. I promise I won't take you anywhere near where it happened. We'll stay on a different floor. It will be just us. Alone."

That does the trick.

Fanon picks up the bags he set on the steps. "Okay," he says, with resignation.

I open the front door and sign Fanon in with security. Cyril requests his identity papers. Fanon is flustered, pats all his pockets. They won't let anyone in without ID, but Cyril and Benoit exchange a look and let him pass. They are not allowed to do that,

248

but I hold my head high, nod professionally at them. They smirk at each other. They probably think the old boss needs a shag. I can't even reprimand them.

Fanon looks at everything. Every poster, every door. He pokes his head into dark offices. The corridor is still, our footsteps reverberate. I am far ahead of him.

"Are you coming?" I'm impatient. The hunger for what's to come balloons.

"Yes." He picks up his pace. "I've wondered what is inside. Lele spoke of it. It is a different world."

I try to look at it through his eyes. He asks me about blinking printers, about our generator; he asks me about fluorescent highlighters and air-conditioning. He asks me about power cords and every sound he hears, which I realize are all linked to machines. I barely notice them, but to him they are loud, incessant, worthy of attention.

We walk into the kitchen and Fanon places the bags uncertainly on the table. He is drenched in sweat after having run god knows how far; his tight purple shirt looks black. He dabs the dribbles at his neck self-consciously.

"I have a special meal for you. I hope it is not dry." Fanon takes out the boxes, pops them open. There's one filled with meat and brown sauce glinting in the light. There's cassava, yellow yams, a box with boiled eggs sitting in ground meat covered with spices. He must have spent so much money.

I gesture toward a chair. "Please sit," I say.

He's awkward in this space, in the overbearing noise of machines that only he can hear, on this chair, in this building. The bright lights do nothing to ease his discomfort.

I stick my fingers in the food, let the sauces dribble in my mouth. I grab mouthfuls, trying to feel the fullness.

"This is delicious," I say to fill the silence. "You didn't have to do this."

249

"I want to. I want to do something for you. You do so much for us."

This makes me feel terribly sad. Because of how untrue it is. "I'm sorry about yesterday. I acted badly."

"No, no. Maya, you did not do anything wrong," he protests, my name still foreign in his mouth.

"I did. I have to be truthful. I cannot give you anything."

"I think you give many things."

He pulls his chair over with a loud screech, then drags mine over to his, until we are facing each other, our knees touching. "Please do not apologize. I desire you very much."

That honesty. I shuffle my knees against his. I smile, he smiles back, the awkwardness abates. I take his hands in mine. Palms against palms.

"I'm still married, I'm not quite ready to be with other men."

"Hold my hands, that is all. You do not have to sin. Let me look. You are very beautiful. Tell me you will stay here, like before."

That startles me. I can't stay here. I live in a land of highways. I see them in my mind: broad stretches of black and white, with trailers, convertibles, minivans. I see my red SUV, Chloe in her booster seat, sippy cups, ridiculous songs about farm animals playing, me catching her big eyes in the rearview mirror.

He holds my hands tighter. Then moves forward and ever so gently kisses my eyelids. It feels restful. Like he'll give me sleep again. He's widened his legs so mine are between his. There is a strange dance happening between our limbs; it is most unpredictable. It's not the amorous travels of bodies back home, the typical opening of blouses and zippers. No, we are taking backroads, touching wrists against knees, elbows, and index fingers. Touches unseen in movies. We smile shamelessly. I like this freedom. No posturing with sexy faces. He puts his fingers through my hair, combing it with his hands. I cup his knees with my sticky hands.

"It is like silk," Fanon whispers.

I laugh. My hair is a humid nest. His fingers trigger spots on my scalp linked to nerves I didn't know existed. I go into this sensation, in its very nucleus, to feel it reverberate. To forget all else. To use this touch to blur Steven out.

"I can be the companion. I can also help with children," he whispers.

I've led him too far. Words spoken without care have become his stories.

"This right now is for right now, okay? I can't draw this into the future. Do you understand?" I ask.

How do you ask another to be temporary?

Ever so slowly he draws me in, kisses me gently under my ear, on my neck. I know he hasn't understood, but this feels too good. I've told the truth; if we venture now, I am innocent.

Fanon rubs the tip of his nose against my hairline. His breaths nuzzle every inch of skin framing my face. Suddenly, he stops. I peek and he is alert, his head cocked to the side. Voices from upstairs, through the plaster and tile. Indistinct, but there. I try to distract him and hold his head boldly between my palms, forcing his gaze upon me. Look here. Look at me, what a thing we are doing. But it is too late.

"It is them?" he asks.

Why are they so loud?

"Ignore them," I say uselessly.

Fanon hugs me, as if to distract but keeps listening over my shoulder. His body is vigilant, on guard. The tenderness turns to angles. The voices have loud starts, abrupt silences; they feel wide, as though there are more than the two of them. Marc sounds furious. I hear the bass of his voice amplify and boom from the conference room upstairs, its cadence unfamiliar.

I let my fingers slide to the back of Fanon's neck. Trying to coax him back into our interrupted moment. He looks at me,

251

distracted. What pleasures can this man give or receive when threat looms near? The voices sputter through the walls.

"Lele," Fanon says. He jerks back so suddenly that I stumble forward, nearly falling out of my chair. He tears out of the room. I follow awkwardly, tripping on my own feet. We hear a scream and a loud thud.

27

Lele lies gnarled, blood pooling by her head, at the foot of the stone staircase. She blinks. Fanon races to her, leans over her, panting, yelping, his hands careful on her forehead. Benoit and Cyril run in from the entrance, looking at me, then at Lele. Chantal crouches on the landing, hugging the handrail, howling, while Marc runs frantically down the stairs. "It was an accident," he yells at me, too loudly.

I can't move, frozen outside this tableau. Everyone else seems to know their part. Marc is saying something.

"She was pulling at me, I tried to get her off!"

Cyril and Benoit look as perplexed as I feel.

Fanon whispers softly to his sister, holds up her head, blood colors his palm, spills on the tile. He looks at me with desperation. Something clicks.

"We have to get her to a doctor. Quick." I look at the guards. "Go get the car to the front." They exchange a few mumbled words and one of them runs off in long strides.

Marc grabs my shoulder. "She fell, Maya. I did not push her."

I don't understand what he's saying or why, but Fanon hears him. He rests his sister's head gently on the ground and lunges for Marc. Before I can react, he punches Marc with fists covered in Lele's blood. I hear the crunch of bone, teeth, again and again. Chantal screams. I hyperventilate, reaching too slowly.

The remaining guard grabs Fanon from the back and restrains him; Fanon jerks in his arms, a large wet fish.

"Get out of here!" I yell at Marc's botched face. "Just go!" He scampers down the hallway, holding the left side of his face, strings of blood trickling as he ducks into an office. His and Lele's spatter now mixed, indistinguishable.

I hear loud honks. The car is in the front. The guard lets go of Fanon and holds Lele's ankles. Fanon follows and gently lifts his sister's shoulders, resting her head against his shirt. I see her eyes open and close; she looks more surprised than in pain. I hold the doors open and we rush outside.

What is this? The guard has brought round the old pickup truck we use for transporting furniture to the orphanages. I don't ask why we are not using the regular Land Cruiser. They place her gently in the back, her head in Fanon's lap, soaking his tight jeans. I grab the side of the truck to climb in the back, when Cyril pulls me aside.

"Madame, no," he says in a low voice.

I look at him confused. I have to go with Lele and Fanon.

"Madame, please. You have to stay. Let them go," he says nervously.

I look over at Fanon who does not notice or need me anymore; his eyes locked to his sister's, he whispers to her.

I listen to Cyril, my staff, who needs me. I let go of the side of the pickup, and it drives away, the truck rattling down the driveway, Lele and Fanon becoming smaller behind clouds of blowing dust lighting up the dark. Fanon does not look back at me, our moment over.

We race back into the office. Chantal stands there, staring blankly at the splatter of blood. Marc hobbles out from the office he had hidden in. I can't tell if it is his nose, eyes, or teeth that seep blood into the brown paper towel he holds against his face.

"Madame, you all need to leave. If something should happen to the girl, we cannot protect you," says Cyril. The three of us just stand there, trying to stomach what has happened. Marc groans.

"Madame, the girl has been hurt twice. This time her brother saw it. You have to leave now. Come in a few days when things are safer. We kept the car for your travel. Please, Madame."

"He's right," says Marc, sounding as though his mouth is full of sand. I should check whether his face is alright, but I can't move, can't comprehend.

Thankfully Cyril is here to take charge, a prophet in this moment. He is insistent. "Madame, this can become a dangerous security situation, please."

I keel over, hands on my knees, trying to get my bearings. Lele and Fanon are being taken care of. We have not abandoned them. They have a guard and a car. I do not think I'm at risk by staying, given my relationship with everyone, but who knows what could happen. Fanon did not even look at me. I have to treat this like any other threatening situation: avoid risk, minimize the chance for conflict. In fight or flight, there can only be one option; I have to get out of here and protect the staff. We can deal with the rest later.

"Chantal, you okay with this? Let's go to the office in the capital. Maybe we come back in a couple of days, depending on what happens?"

She looks at me blankly.

Marc starts up the stairs and tugs Chantal's limp arm. He tells her he will get his stuff from the other room. The room they kept to hide their relationship.

I walk past the splotches of blood to climb the stairs. How quickly they become a thing on the ground to avoid. The urgency of the moment sudses within me, my brain, my insides warning my body—move quickly. Move, move! The same feeling as during the fire. One has to move but can't fast enough. That the brain and body have unclasped, as if in a bog of thick mud. The stairs are monumental. Muscles refusing the climb, the same place Lele tumbled down. The stairs become a mountain.

I wade through invisible currents to my room. Will villagers break down the door when they hear? Does Lele have a head injury? What happened? What the hell was she doing here? The suitcase just needs to be zipped. My dirty clothes on the chair, my books, the toiletries can stay. I stuff my laptop in a shoulder bag. Passport. That's all I need. Passport. Phone. I don't know if I'm taking seconds or hours. Can't forget the passport. Move faster. Faster.

Chantal appears in the doorway, pale, clutching a laptop and a wallet and nothing else. "He's in the bathroom cleaning his face. He thinks I'm packing."

"Okay," I say slowly.

"He pushed her, Maya. I saw him," Chantal whispers hoarsely. She sucks in her breath and closes her eyes for a moment. "Yes, she shoved him, but it was nothing big, but then he pushed her down the stairs!" She grips me by the shoulder. "I saw him. And when I tried to run down and help her, he held me back."

I grab my suitcase and shoulder bag and use my elbow to nudge Chantal out of the room and down the side stairs. My body performing what my mind must accept.

"We can't take him," I say, my head back in my body.

She hears me and balks, but I know she agrees. I see it in her too, the battle to control her body, the labor to put one foot in front of the other, quickly enough, efficiently enough so we can mimic walking.

We exit the back door to the car park where Cyril has the trunk open for our things. He is talking to Jean, who toys with a set of keys, trying to understand what is going on. Jean argues that he doesn't know the roads toward the capital, that he can't do it in the dark. The outdoor lights are ablaze, sending the night bugs into a frenzy.

I look back at the large building, the lights are all on upstairs. If Marc sees us, he'll think we're just packing up the car.

"Okay. Let's go." I say, barely breathing.

I throw my suitcase in. I loosen Chantal's caseless laptop from her grip and toss it in the trunk. Ever so gently, I nudge the trunk closed, avoiding any suspicious clangs.

"We're doing this, okay?" I ask her as I open the passenger door. She nods shakily.

"Jean, hand her the keys," I say. There is no time to indulge a lost driver and I don't know the roads anymore. I'll have to make her do it.

"Madame?"

"Get in the back, Jean," I order him. He settles awkwardly in the middle of the back seat.

Chantal gets behind the wheel, her muscle memory turns the key. Cyril pokes his head through the open driver's window.

"Will Monsieur Marc be getting in from the front door? Shall I tell him you are ready and to bring his things?"

"No," I say in as calm a voice as I can muster. "Cyril, you do what you have to do to be safe. Don't resist anything; feel free to go to the village. Tell Benoit to stay with Lele's family."

"I'm Benoit," he says.

"Tell Cyril to stay with the family, and keep the car at their disposal for wherever they need to take Lele, for as long as they need. We'll call you tomorrow."

"And Monsieur?" Benoit looks genuinely befuddled.

"Monsieur Marc will not be coming with us," I say.

The car throttles into life, and in a matter of seconds we tear off the property, leaving Marc behind.

Thank you

My ammi, Roohi Hasan, from whom all my stories begin. For holding books over my head as we snuggled against your chest, for teaching that every life has a story that should be valued. My abba, Abrar-Ul-Hasan, for seeking beauty, toying with words, and teaching me to play devil's advocate in perpetuity. For populating my life with literature, poetry, and sculpture.

My editor, Pia Singhal. This book was always meant to be yours. Thank you for giving it a home and making it what it needed to be. My agent, Jackie Kaiser, for taking on a newbie and supporting a novel that went out in the world in the strangest of times. To Crissy Calhoun for diligently finding needles in haystacks, then using said needles to thread the novel tightly. To the whole team at ECW for making this a reality.

C.S. Richardson, friend, guide, and mentor. Because of you, I tell my children to speak to strangers. Thank you for your generosity, for your time and care. I would not be here if it weren't for your red markings, critique, and encouragement.

To my first readers: Pheona Wright (and Brady who is around you), Teresa Pavlinek, and Ingrid Johansen for giving honest feedback and the confidence to continue. To Adam Segal, for sharing his art and becoming an indelible part of my story.

Audrey Macklin, Richard Moon, Adina Macklin, and Holly McDaniel for being my community and moral compass. To Dr. Michael Lynch of ASP fame, for telling an eighteen-year-old to hurry up and write a novel. I'm a few decades late and you are no longer in the world, but you were the kind of teacher inspirational movies are made of.

The friends who were there before and will remain after the hubbub: Ingrid Johansen, Sarah Noble, Nicola Sarn, Nicola Gillis, Anna Pellicioli, Anne-Christine Chapman, Flavia Thome, Émilie Milroy, Tania Haas, Mona Zaidi. You make this real. Marianna Kapala, for touching my breasts. Joana Talafré, for showing me the world.

Nayyar Javed and Hamid Javed for making me their daughter and modeling what it is to be good. To Rais Shaikh, Mukhtar Shaikh, Raisa Shaikh, Rashida Masood, Khadija Aijaz, and Samina Amjad for filling my childhood with laughter and love. Your histories are part of me.

Abbas Hasan for being my constant through ebbs and flows. For your critical eye, your creativity, and the endless laughter you bring to anyone who really knows you.

To my wonders. I'm so proud, awed—slightly scared—of how just and empathetic you are. Aiza Javed, I want to be like you when I grow up. Never lose your spunk, courage, or intuition. This love you have for life and its people, let it be forever. Xavyan Javed, your serenity, existential questions, and desire to heal people of prejudice and anger, let it be your guide. I love you both as you are. In your slender hands, there will be a better tomorrow.

To Safwan Javed for giving me this life. For urging me to create. For this partnership of a lifetime. It's good to be home.

Thank you to all those within or outside of the aid industry who try to better people's lives in precarious situations while questioning themselves and respecting the humanity of others.

Erum Shazia Hasan was born in Canada, raised in France, and is of South Asian heritage. She works with marginalized communities to strengthen livelihoods, protect biodiversity, and create empowerment opportunities for women in the face of climate change. A Sustainable Development Consultant for various international organizations, she lives in Toronto with her husband and their two children.

This book is also available as a Global Certified Accessible™ (GCA) ebook. ECW Press's ebooks are screen reader friendly and are built to meet the needs of those who are unable to read standard print due to blindness, low vision, dyslexia, or a physical disability.

At ECW Press, we want you to enjoy our books in whatever format you like. If you've bought a print copy just send an email to ebook@ecwpress.com and include:

- the book title
- the name of the store where you purchased it
- a screenshot or picture of your order/receipt number and your name
- your preference of file type: PDF (for desktop reading), ePub (for a phone/tablet, Kobo, or Nook), mobi (for Kindle)

A real person will respond to your email with your ebook attached. Please note this offer is only for copies bought for personal use and does not apply to school or library copies.

Thank you for supporting an independently owned Canadian publisher with your purchase!

This book is made of paper from well-managed FSC® - certified forests, recycled materials, and other controlled sources.

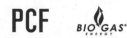